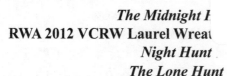
"Raand has built a complex world inhabited by werewolves, vampires, and other paranormal beings...Raand has given her readers a complex plot filled with wonderful characters as well as insight into the hierarchy of Sylvan's pack and vampire clans. There are many plot twists and turns, as well as erotic sex scenes in this riveting novel that keep the pages flying until its satisfying conclusion."—*Just About Write*

"Once again, I am amazed at the storytelling ability of L.L. Raand aka Radclyffe. In *Blood Hunt*, she mixes high levels of sheer eroticism that will leave you squirming in your seat with an impeccable multi-character storyline all streaming together to form one great read."
—*Queer Magazine Online*

"*The Midnight Hunt* has a gripping story to tell, and while there are also some truly erotic sex scenes, the story always takes precedence. This is a great read which is not easily put down nor easily forgotten."—*Just About Write*

"Are you sick of the same old hetero vampire/werewolf story plastered in every bookstore and at every movie theater? Well, I've got the cure to your werewolf fever. *The Midnight Hunt* is first in, what I hope is, a long-running series of fantasy erotica for L.L. Raand (aka Radclyffe)."—*Queer Magazine Online*

"Any reader familiar with Radclyffe's writing will recognize the author's style within *The Midnight Hunt*, yet at the same time it is most definitely a new direction. The author delivers an excellent story here, one that is engrossing from the very beginning. Raand has pieced together an intricate world, and provided just enough details for the reader to become enmeshed in the new world. The action moves quickly throughout the book and it's hard to put down."—*Three Dollar Bill Reviews*

Acclaim for Radclyffe's Fiction

In **2012 RWA/FTHRW Lories and RWA HODRW Aspen Gold award winner** *Firestorm* "Radclyffe brings another hot lesbian romance for her readers."—*The Lesbrary*

Foreword Review Book of the Year finalist and IPPY silver medalist *Trauma Alert* "is hard to put down and it will sizzle in the reader's hands. The characters are hot, the sex scenes explicit and explosive, and the book is moved along by an interesting plot with well drawn secondary characters. The real star of this show is the attraction between the two characters, both of whom resist and then fall head over heels."
—*Lambda Literary Reviews*

Lambda Literary Finalist *Best Lesbian Romance 2010* features "stories [that] are diverse in tone, style, and subject, making for more variety than in many, similar anthologies… well written, each containing a satisfying, surprising twist. Best Lesbian Romance series editor Radclyffe has assembled a respectable crop of 17 authors for this year's offering."
—*Curve Magazine*

2010 Prism award winner and ForeWord Review Book of the Year Award finalist *Secrets in the Stone* is "so powerfully [written] that the worlds of these three women shimmer between reality and dreams…A strong, must read novel that will linger in the minds of readers long after the last page is turned."—*Just About Write*

In **Benjamin Franklin Award finalist** *Desire by Starlight* "Radclyffe writes romance with such heart and her down-to-earth characters not only come to life but leap off the page until you feel like you know them. What Jenna and Gard feel for each other is not only a spark but an inferno and, as a reader, you will be washed away in this tumultuous romance until you can do nothing but succumb to it."—*Queer Magazine Online*

Lambda Literary Award winner *Stolen Moments* "is a collection of steamy stories about women who just couldn't wait. It's sex when desire overrides reason, and it's incredibly hot!"—*On Our Backs*

Lambda Literary Award winner *Distant Shores, Silent Thunder* "weaves an intricate tapestry about passion and commitment between lovers. The story explores the fragile nature of trust and the sanctuary provided by loving relationships."—*Sapphic Reader*

Lambda Literary Award Finalist *Justice Served* delivers a "crisply written, fast-paced story with twists and turns and keeps us guessing until the final explosive ending." —*Independent Gay Writer*

Lambda Literary Award finalist *Turn Back Time* "is filled with wonderful love scenes, which are both tender and hot." —*MegaScene*

By Radclyffe

Romances

Innocent Hearts
Promising Hearts
Love's Melody Lost
Love's Tender Warriors
Tomorrow's Promise
Love's Masquerade
shadowland
Passion's Bright Fury
Fated Love

Turn Back Time
When Dreams Tremble
The Lonely Hearts Club
Night Call
Secrets in the Stone
Desire by Starlight
Crossroads
Homestead

Honor Series

Above All, Honor
Honor Bound
Love & Honor
Honor Guards
Honor Reclaimed
Honor Under Siege
Word of Honor
Code of Honor

Justice Series

A Matter of Trust (prequel)
Shield of Justice
In Pursuit of Justice
Justice in the Shadows
Justice Served
Justice for All

The Provincetown Tales

Safe Harbor
Beyond the Breakwater
Distant Shores, Silent Thunder
Storms of Change

Winds of Fortune
Returning Tides
Sheltering Dunes

First Responders Novels
Trauma Alert
Firestorm
Oath of Honor

Short Fiction

Collected Stories by Radclyffe
Erotic Interludes: *Change Of Pace*
Radical Encounters

Edited by Radclyffe:
Best Lesbian Romance 2009–2014

Stacia Seaman and Radclyffe, eds.:
Erotic Interludes 2: *Stolen Moments*
Erotic Interludes 3: *Lessons in Love*
Erotic Interludes 4: *Extreme Passions*
Erotic Interludes 5: *Road Games*
Romantic Interludes 1: *Discovery*
Romantic Interludes 2: *Secrets*
Breathless: *Tales of Celebration*
Women of the Dark Streets
Amor and More: Love Everafter

By L.L. Raand

Midnight Hunters
The Midnight Hunt
Blood Hunt
Night Hunt
The Lone Hunt
The Magic Hunt

Visit us at www.boldstrokesbooks.com

THE MAGIC HUNT

by

L.L. Raand

2014

THE MAGIC HUNT

ISBN 13: 978-1-62639-045-4

THIS TRADE PAPERBACK ORIGINAL IS PUBLISHED BY
BOLD STROKES BOOKS, INC.
P.O. BOX 249
VALLEY FALLS, NY 12185

FIRST EDITION: MARCH 2014

CREDITS
EDITORS: RUTH STERNGLANTZ AND STACIA SEAMAN
PRODUCTION DESIGN: STACIA SEAMAN
COVER DESIGN BY SHERI (GRAPHICARTIST2020@HOTMAIL.COM)

Acknowledgments

Five books and almost as many years later, what began as an experiment has become a challenging, ongoing adventure. I have always let the characters lead, and never more than in this series. My original plan had been to write standalone paranormal romances connected primarily by the universe in which the characters lived, but as in the Ptown Tales and the Honor series, no matter which new romance predominates in a particular book, the original pair claims a major role as well. Reese and Tory, Cam and Blair, and now Sylvan and Drake are at the epicenter of the world in which other characters claim the stage for a time. The challenges for them and me continue, and I am very grateful to all the readers who have embraced this series and given me a reason to keep writing it. With this book I have expanded the borders of "their world," and I hope you all enjoy the newest members of the Hunt.

Thanks go to Sandy Lowe, who somehow makes work fun; to Ruth Sternglantz for always finding the words beneath the words; to Stacia Seaman for making me feel fresh book after book; and to my first readers Connie, Eva, and Paula for constant encouragement.

Sheri, irreplaceable and eminently talented, my deepest appreciation.

And to Lee, adventurer extraordinaire—*Amo te*.

Radclyffe, 2014

For Lee, for believing in possibility

CHAPTER ONE

COALITION LEADER TARGETED IN BOMBING
PRAETERN RIGHTS NEGOTIATIONS DERAILED

Over a month has passed since Sylvan Mir, the head of the Praetern Coalition negotiating for state and federal recognition of Praetern governing bodies along with civil protections for their members, was the target of an assassination attempt at the governor's gala in Albany, New York. Mir, the wolf Were Alpha, her mate and several members of her party were injured, one fatally, when a car bomb exploded as they were leaving the gathering of the state's elite. No one has come forth to claim responsibility and the local police investigation has generated no suspects.

This most recent attack follows only weeks after Mir Industries was bombed, resulting in extensive damage and multiple injuries. Reports of attacks on Praeterns and their establishments throughout the nation point to the growing resistance to Praetern sovereignty and legal recognition. HUFSI (Humans United for Species Integrity) and other radical opposition groups have advocated internment or population control, including chemical neutralization.

Senator Daniel Weston, chairman of the House Committee on Praetern Affairs, was unavailable for comment, as was Alpha Mir. In the face of these attacks, the future effectiveness of the Coalition is in question, while these events underscore the increasingly vocal and violent disapproval among humans to Praetern equality. Confidential sources have revealed some private groups with close government ties have begun experimenting with biological and chemical means of controlling Praetern species, in some cases with unwilling participants as test subjects. To date, human law enforcement agencies have devoted few if any resources to the investigation of these allegations, despite the mounting evidence.

For updates on these and other developing stories, follow the Land Report at the Albany Star.

—Becca Land, investigative reporter

Francesca hissed and tossed aside the newspaper her servants had brought to her bedroom at sunfall along with the usual silver tea service and tray of assorted canapés. She insisted on the formality even though she awakened with only one need—for the blood that coursed in the veins of her blood slaves, the blood she needed to survive, the blood that gave her strength and filled her with power and desire. She swept her hand down the length of Michel's naked back as Michel, who reclined beside her on the large bed that dominated her boudoir, fed indolently from the breast of a dazed young wolf Were. "Jody Gates's consort is becoming a problem."

The Were convulsed as Michel withdrew her incisors from the soft underside of the female's breast, breaking their blood connection and abruptly terminating the sexual thrall. Michel murmured an apology and licked the punctures closed, injecting a pulse of feeding hormone before closing the wounds, inciting yet another orgasm in her pliant host. She rolled onto her back, her Mediterranean-blue eyes bright with bloodlust and renewed power. "Becca Land? What has she done?"

Francesca leaned down and kissed her, tasting the lingering essence of the Were host, briefly wondering if Michel found satisfaction from the countless male and female Weres she fed from night after night. No matter how often Michel fed, her eyes always gleamed with a hunger that never seemed to abate. Even the orgasms she experienced when feeding appeared to go unnoticed, a reflex and nothing more. Ever since the fiasco at the fundraiser, Michel had been absent from her bed with increasing frequency, a situation Francesca would need to address soon. Right now, she had other concerns. "The human has written a newspaper article that unwisely draws public attention to Praetern matters better left private."

Michel pushed up on one arm, her midnight hair framing a sharp, ascetically handsome face. "Has she mentioned us?"

"Not yet." Francesca grimaced. Ever since Sylvan Mir's father had forced the Praetern species out of hiding and into the awareness of humans, she—along with many other powerful Praetern leaders—had been bracing for the backlash while trying to fortify her own position in a shifting political landscape. After centuries of relative peace, the Vampires had grown complacent. The wolf Weres, who had once been their subjects and the heart of their armies, had rebelled and won their struggle for independence generations ago. Since then, the Weres had carved out their own territories, and their Packs had grown in size and strength. Now the Vampires were vastly outnumbered and militarily weak. Even though Francesca commanded all Vampire seethes east of the Mississippi River, without an army she could not afford to be drawn into a war. "But Becca Land doesn't understand what she's dealing with—if she exposes the Shadow Lords and our attempt to destroy the Coalition becomes known, we'll have a Praetern war—and we're not prepared."

"To say nothing of what Mir will do if she knows one of the members was part of a plan to assassinate her." Michel moved the Were aside and slipped her arm around Francesca. The blood host moaned in protest and tried weakly to drag Michel's hand between her thighs. Michel gently brushed the hand away and cradled Francesca's full breast in her palm. Satisfied when Francesca arched in pleasure, Michel murmured, "Let me see the article."

"We don't need a reporter keeping the story alive when the humans, at least, seem more than happy to forget all about it." Francesca handed Michel the newspaper and stroked Michel's taut abdomen as she read. They'd both fed, and their sexual power and needs were at the pinnacle. Her blood slave had been a more than adequate fuck, but no one ever satisfied the way Michel could. After a millennium together, Michel intuited her needs almost before she did. Francesca motioned to Daniela, a handmaiden who waited in the shadows by the ornately carved wooden doors, to approach the bed. "Dispose of this host and leave us."

"Yes, Mistress." Daniela's eyes shone a deep scarlet and her thighs glistened with arousal. Newly risen, she could not yet master her hunger when inundated by the sexual force of two Vampires as powerful as Francesca and Michel.

Smiling, Francesca skimmed her fingertips along the inside of Daniela's thigh, lingering when she reached the swollen apex to idly finger her clitoris. Daniela swayed, her incisors gleaming. Francesca never let her servants feed until she and Michel were finished. Daniela was starving for blood and sex, but her control was improving. "You may avail yourself of my prisoner once you've seen to this one."

"Thank you, Mistress," Daniela gasped.

"Go now." Francesca closed her eyes as Michel squeezed her nipple to attention.

Michel returned the paper to the serving tray and waited until Daniela lifted the somnolent Were from the bed and carried her out. She debated how much to say—Francesca was a master at laying traps for friend and foe alike, and never tired of playing complex games. After centuries of existence, very little else was of interest. Until recently, Michel hadn't given much thought to what might happen if she and Francesca were ever at odds. She knew without doubt if Francesca deemed her a threat, she would order her execution. Francesca might do so regretfully, for a moment or two, but she would not hesitate to do whatever necessary to secure her power. Michel had always known her true death hinged on Francesca's whim, and for centuries she hadn't really cared. Immortal existence had outstripped all pleasure except for the fleeting power and oblivion of bloodlust. Sadly, indulging in that kind of oblivion was a perfect way to lose one's head.

She couldn't recall experiencing true pleasure until Katya. Michel forced the image of the young Were from her mind. Francesca was too close, in body and mind, for her to shield her thoughts. Bending her head, she mouthed Francesca's breast, feeding the sexual tide surging in Francesca's blood. "Becca Land seems to be focusing on the Weres. She is after all a Vampire's consort. She wouldn't want to cast suspicion on us."

"Mmm. Perhaps. But Jody Gates is heir to the Night Hunter clan, and Zachary would not mind taking my place. Perhaps Jody and her human have a plan to sway opinion to Jody's father. That could lead to rebellion."

Michel laughed. "It will take more than rumor and suspicion to dethrone you, Viceregal."

"Wars have been fought over far less." Francesca ran her fingers through Michel's hair, drawing her crimson-painted nails down the back of Michel's neck and over her shoulders. She let the sharp edges break skin, inhaling the lush scent of ferrous-rich blood. She didn't take sustenance from other Vampires—none of them did. They were predators, and part of the thrill of feeding was enthralling prey—but she did enjoy the taste of domination in another's blood. "Sylvan already suspects us of involvement. If the human uncovers proof of Nicholas's experiments and our involvement, Sylvan will break her pledge to support us. We will be defenseless against her greater strength."

"Nicholas is the weak link," Michel murmured, caressing Francesca's abdomen, teasing the heat from her depths, drawing blood and power to her sex. Her own blood fired, caught in the undertow of Francesca's supreme allure. "His repeated attempts to eliminate Sylvan only draw attention to all of us. He needs to be controlled."

"In time." Francesca straddled her, rubbing her clitoris over Michel's stomach. She arched, her lids slitted, her full red lips curved into a self-satisfied smile. "Nicholas has not yet outlived his uses, but Becca Land is expendable."

Francesca's fingers closed around Michel's clitoris and Michel groaned. Her hips bucked as Francesca rode her, bringing herself to orgasm while she tugged and twisted Michel's turgid length.

"That's right, darling," Francesca crooned, her orgasm spilling out onto Michel's rigid torso. "Isn't this so much better than those undisciplined Weres? They can never give you this, can they?"

"No." Michel choked as the backlash from Francesca's release flooded her with lust and power. Her body spasmed and she came again, unable to hold her shields, unable to stop the images of Katya raging through her mind.

Francesca scored the pristine flesh of Michel's small, perfect breasts with her nails, leaned over, and licked the red streaks away, joining them by blood and sex. Vestiges of lust and longing and fleeting glimpses of golden eyes and tawny hair flitted through her awareness. Michel was strong, but she was stronger, and she did not allow anyone to keep secrets.

❖

Drake McKennan, Prima of the Adirondack Timberwolf Weres and mate to Sylvan Mir, stood alone by the wide-open window on the second floor of the headquarters building, scenting the evening air. With the ending of summer, nightfall came early to the mountains, and twilight shrouded the dense forest just outside the protective stockade that circled the Were Compound. A hazy glow to the east foretold the rise of the nearly full moon. In a few days the moon would be full, and Sylvan would call the wolves to hunt. Drake breathed deeply, letting the sounds and scents of the land and Pack flow through her. The heartbeats of a hundred wolves moving about in the Compound resonated in her chest, each series of strong, steady beats distinctive, each adding to the whole, creating something greater than any of them alone. She was learning to identify each Were by their subtle but unique rhythm, picking out the *sentries* on the perimeter ramparts, the *centuri* standing guard on the long porch just below her, and the soldiers in the barracks. In the very heart of the Compound the beta wolves and maternals tended the young, defended by ever-widening circles of armed Weres who would die to protect them. The young were the most precious members of the Pack, and any Were would sacrifice themselves without hesitation to keep them safe.

Even knowing that, Drake's wolf fretted, clawing at her insides, demanding Drake seek out her young in the nursery where they slept under the watchful eye of Roger, a beta wolf and their designated trainer. She and Sylvan were parents to the twins and would be responsible for teaching them to hunt and eventually lead, but Roger would play a large role in supervising their socialization with littermates and, eventually, Pack. He would be their teacher and guide until they reached adolescence and began training to join Sylvan's guard. They were only a few weeks old and had already begun their journey toward leading the Pack one day.

Drake appreciated the need to socialize them with others their age, the need for them to understand and for others to recognize their place in the Pack. But even a few hours' separation from them was like missing a part of herself. And in recent days, the loneliness had become more acute. She was missing more than her young. She was missing her mate. She scented the air again, seeking the wave of power that would signal Sylvan's return. Her heart sank when she caught no trace of her. Sylvan had only been gone a few hours this time, but after all that had happened, even a few minutes' absence was almost more than Drake could tolerate. Physically, she craved her mate's presence at all times. They were bonded, their chemistries attuned, biologically changed and interconnected at the moment of their mating. But her soul, her spirit, was bound to Sylvan too. And since the attack—the latest attack—Sylvan had changed. Her wolf was nearly always in ascendance, barely restrained, hungry for battle, raging for retribution. And at the heart of her, such sorrow.

Drake was at a loss to help her. She was Sylvan's mate, her strength, just as Sylvan was hers, and every day she felt her failure more keenly. A ripple of heat rolled over her and she tensed. Sylvan was close. Drake pushed her worry and sadness aside. The Pack needed Sylvan now more than ever, and even if she didn't know how to heal her, she knew what Sylvan needed. Sylvan needed her, and she would give whatever Sylvan asked. Twisting to one side, she barely missed being struck by the huge silver wolf that bounded through the window and landed in the center of the floor, wolf-gold eyes bright with fury and lust. Drake went still, watching the air around the great beast shimmer.

Sylvan rose, naked and glorious, her sun-kissed hair longer than usual, wilding around her sculpted shoulders. The gold of her irises faded to a ring around the glacial blue center, the wolf band never completely receding these days. Sylvan's mouth twisted into an ironic smile. "Prima. You await me?"

"Yes," Drake murmured, liquid heat stirring at her core.

Sylvan stalked her, striding slowly, methodically closer, the muscles in her shoulders bunched, her skin gleaming with the sheen of sex and power. Drake gave way as Sylvan bore down on her, backing up until her butt hit the edge of Sylvan's wide wooden desk. She braced her hands on either side of her hips as Sylvan closed in. They'd played this game of hunt and trap many times, and each time Sylvan claimed her, her soul knew with certainty where she belonged.

When Sylvan was a foot away, Drake lifted her chin, turned her head, and exposed her neck. Not submitting, inviting. The low rumble in Sylvan's chest struck Drake's belly low and deep, and she quivered, need and desire rising through her like flames in dry tinder. Sylvan tore Drake's shirt down the center, sliced her pants open along her thighs, and shoved the remnants of clothing away. Drake's pelt rolled beneath her shimmering skin, and she readied. Her breath escaped in harsh pants, and the mate bite in the curve of her shoulder pulsed in time with her heart, awaiting her mate's joining.

"Sylvan," she murmured, arching in welcome.

"Mate," Sylvan growled and pressed Drake to the desk with the weight of her body.

As Sylvan's power spread over Drake's skin and into her cells, the scent of forest, crushed pine and vibrant life, enclosed her. She opened, took Sylvan between her thighs, and jolted as the hot, heavy length of Sylvan's engorged clitoris notched below her own, joining them. Igniting her.

Sylvan unleashed the power of her wolf, in a fury to join, to taste and take and fill the dark empty places with the essence of her mate. Drake was all she clung to in the midst of her tormented rage. She fit herself tighter, felt Drake enfold her, anoint her, and she buried her canines in the warm, welcoming flesh of Drake's shoulder. Distantly, lancets of pain raked down her back, Drake's claws pulling her in, urging her on. Her hips thrust, the heavy glands filling with the *victus* that rose only for Drake, called from her depths by her mate's unique chemistry.

"I must have you," Sylvan gasped. "Always."

"I know, I know." Drake dug her claws into Sylvan's back, calling Sylvan's wolf with her own. "I'm here."

Sylvan rumbled, the fire in her belly driving her hard, beyond control, demanding she bury herself, flesh and spirit, in her mate. She gripped the desk, her claws gouging the wood, and gave herself over to the storm. Gave herself to Drake. When Drake's canines found her breast, Sylvan threw back her head, roaring in primal victory as she came.

"I'm here," Drake whispered, holding Sylvan tightly as she sagged, momentarily at rest—a vulnerability Sylvan only ever allowed herself when they were alone. Drake stroked Sylvan's damp hair, kissed the corner of her mouth and the hard angle of her jaw. She'd lost weight, become only muscle and bone, a warrior honed to a killing edge. Drake's heartbeat slowed in time with Sylvan's as she caressed her. "I missed you."

Sylvan shuddered, rubbed her cheek against the bite on Drake's shoulder. "Where are the young?"

"With Roger." Drake nuzzled Sylvan's neck. Bit lightly. "I love you."

Sylvan pushed herself up on extended arms, shadows darkening her eyes. "I'm dangerous."

"No, you're not."

"My wolf is too much in charge. I'm afraid I can't—"

"You can control her. You already have. You are our strength, but we are yours too." She caressed Sylvan's cheek. "Take from us. Let the Pack help you."

Sylvan pushed away, strode to the window, her back to Drake. "I can't. If I do, if I lose more of you—"

Drake went to her, threaded her arms around Sylvan's waist, pressed her cheek to Sylvan's back. "We are yours, and you are ours. We will fight as one. You cannot do this alone."

Sylvan growled, her wolf angry and hurt and, for the first time in her memory, uncertain. What kind of leader could she be when she did not trust herself?

Drake caressed her breasts, her belly, pressing tightly to her back. "I love you. *We* love you."

Sylvan gripped the windowsill, stared down into the Compound where her wolves moved in the flickering light of fires burning beneath food cauldrons and on torches along the walls. How could she keep them safe when she could not name her enemies, when she was helpless to stop even those she suspected? When she had failed? Her wolf rose, pressing her to shift, to run, to lead her Pack into the wild.

"We cannot run," Drake whispered. "We cannot go back." Sylvan did not answer, and the silence tore at Drake's heart. She sensed Sylvan's wolf drawing away. "Stay."

Sylvan shuddered, struggling to hold on to the connection with her mate. "I want to see the young, but not like this."

"It will be all right. I'll go with—"

A knock came at the door, and silently, Drake cursed.

Sylvan tilted her head, appraising the Were who had once been one of her *centuri*. The scent of this Were had altered since she'd been turned, since she'd become Vampire, since she'd left the Pack. But this Vampire was still part wolf, still hers, and she recognized her. "Lara."

Drake broke away, opened an armoire in the corner, and tossed Sylvan a pair of black fatigue pants. She pulled on a pair herself. As much as Sylvan was hers, she also belonged to the Pack. Her wants, even Sylvan's, must wait when the Pack needed them. "See to Lara, Alpha, and then we will see to our young."

CHAPTER TWO

"Come," Sylvan snarled, standing in the center of the room, legs spread wide, arms folded, muscles bunched and ready to spring. Lara, a dominant wolf, broadcast power that was very nearly a challenge, and Sylvan ached to fight. She struggled to keep her wolf from taking control. From forcing a shift. Her skin prickled with the pressure of pelt ready to burst free. The bones in her face ached as the heavy planes of her jaw shifted. A warning rumble churned in her chest. Everywhere she turned, danger. Everywhere she looked, enemies.

A warm hand pressed to the center of her back, and her wolf stopped pacing, cocked her head, shuddered. Drake stroked her, calming them both. "Lara is not here to challenge. This is your territory, your Pack. You do not need to fight here."

Sylvan jerked her head, refusing to be absolved. "I failed to keep Andrew safe. Placed my mate in danger. We could have lost the young. I deserve to be challenged."

"No. You are the only one strong enough to guide us through the battles to come. We know that."

"Am I?" Sylvan slid her arm around Drake's shoulders. Her mate was solid, steady, strong. "Maybe you should lead them."

"We already have a leader." Drake pressed close to Sylvan's side as the tall heavy doors swung open and Lara strode in. A wave of heat and power streamed over her skin as Lara approached.

Lara, nearly as tall as Sylvan, glided forward with the effortless grace of a Vampire and the sinuous strength of a Were. Her eyes, wolf-amber, burned with an undercurrent of crimson. Her chestnut hair framed bones carved from stone and tempered by a Vampire's ethereal beauty. She was far too elegant to be a Were and too much of an animal to be a Vampire. She was both and neither, and what she might become was still unknown.

Sylvan growled softly, a dominant Were warning another to be cautious in the presence of her mate.

Lara tipped her head ever so slightly but did not drop her eyes. She stopped a few feet away, not close enough to challenge Sylvan's space or to be a threat to Drake, but far closer than even Sylvan's most trusted guards would approach without explicit permission. Lara smiled with a hint of Vampire arrogance. "Alpha."

"*Centuri*," Sylvan said, intentionally using Lara's previous rank even though technically Lara was no longer part of Sylvan's guard. Lara was blood-bonded to her, as were all the *centuri*, and would be for as long as she lived, but she no longer answered to Sylvan. Lara served as Jody Gates's Vampire warlord by Sylvan's leave because Lara needed to be among the Vampires to learn how to live as one. No matter who she served, however, Lara was still wolf, still less dominant than Sylvan, and still subject to Sylvan's rule. Lara had been a frequent guest in the Compound since the time of the attack at the governor's gala, serving as liaison to the Vampires and also looking after her new cat mate and cubs. "What do you need?"

"Raina is healed and the cubs are healthy. I have come to seek your permission to take them into the northlands. Raina will be close enough to Catamount territory to organize her cats, and I can secure her stronghold in Timberwolf territory."

Sylvan smiled fleetingly, the muscles along her back rippling as her wolf tensed. "Until a month ago, the cats were our sworn enemies. Now you ask that I give their Alpha free rein in my territory? How do I know she will not gather an army to march against me from within my own borders?"

"Raina nearly died saving your life." Lara's eyes flashed and her canines lengthened. "She is a sworn ally, and still you do not trust her?"

Sylvan half-shifted so fast even Lara's Vampire speed could not intercept her. Her face and hands morphed, her jaws lengthened, her clawed digits grew to twice the size of a human hand. She gripped Lara's throat and squeezed, forcing Lara's knees to bend. "Be careful where you show your teeth, Wolf."

"I meant no challenge, Alpha," Lara gasped, finally ducking her head, and leaned her forehead against Sylvan's thigh. "Raina cannot regain control of her Pride if she remains here, and the cubs need to learn the mountains soon."

"And what about you?" Sylvan asked, releasing her hold. Lara rose but kept her gaze averted. "Where will you be in all of this?"

Lara's head snapped up. "My first allegiance is to my mate. But I am still wolf, and you will ever and always be my Alpha."

"And the Vampire in you?" Sylvan asked softly. "Does she not want you to rule your own Dominion one day? Or failing that, your own Pack?"

"I am slave to neither my Vampire nor my wolf." Muscles knotted along the carved elegance of Lara's jaw. "I am more than either, and I know where my loyalties belong. I will not challenge you or Liege Gates. I do not want to lead unless it is at Raina's side."

"Being separated from Raina will be difficult," Sylvan said. "Especially for a newly mated Were."

"But I am not Were." Lara's mouth twisted into a cool line and her torment was clear. Even Raina's love had not been able to banish her self-loathing. Not yet.

"Not Were *only*, but Raina is. She will suffer without you near her, especially when she comes into her heat."

"I know what you say is true." Lara's rigid stance broke and she paced, her wolf too agitated to be subjugated by the glacial control of her Vampire will. "It is…difficult for me to be away from her, but I have no choice. I have given my oath."

Sylvan glanced at Drake, smiled wryly. "The difficulty you experience when you're away from her will not lessen in time. Just the opposite. You will both suffer when parted. Are you sure Raina wants to rule again? I'm sure Gates would welcome a cat Were among her security forces. And she would protect your cubs."

Lara's eyes shone, the fury gone, replaced by pride. "Raina is an Alpha. She was born to rule. And *we* will protect our cubs."

"Spoken like a true mate."

"If it comes to war, Raina's cats will be needed," Lara said. "She needs time to reunite them. Her Pride is fragmented after the attempt by the mercenaries to kill her and the cubs."

"You will be needed as well." Sylvan gripped Lara's shoulder. "I value Raina's loyalty and skill, as I do yours. I can speak to Jody about altering your service—"

"No," Lara said. "I would not have you in her debt because of me. Raina and I understand what we must do, and we are prepared for it. We will be all right."

"I will send wolves north with you. You have two cubs, and if you cannot be there to protect them at all times, then Raina should have guards."

Lara bristled. "Wolf guards? I don't want my mate surrounded by dominant wolves."

Drake laughed and Sylvan said, "You don't think Raina would be tempted."

Lara snarled. "No, but some young pup might be."

"I think an Alpha cat can handle one of our randy young," Drake said reasonably. "Take the offer, Lara. You can't afford to have Raina unprotected."

"And," Sylvan added, "as you said, she is our ally. She can use her cats to protect our northern borders and help us find the mercenaries who worked in the human labs. We need whatever information they may have."

"All right," Lara said, her reluctance evident. "But I would like to choose the guards."

Sylvan nodded. Lara was a powerful Were with near-Alpha powers who had sworn her loyalty and forgone her right to challenge. She deserved this show of respect. "As you will."

Lara inclined her head. "Thank you, Alpha."

"You are welcome." Sylvan looped an arm around Lara's neck and drew her close. Lara's skin glowed against hers, her bonded scent rich and strong. "Be careful, Lara. I would not want to lose you."

"You cannot." Lara rubbed her cheek over Sylvan's bare shoulder, a sign of submission and trust. "No matter what else I am, I will always be your wolf."

"Go find your mate," Sylvan said softly and let her go.

When the doors closed behind Lara, Drake encircled Sylvan's waist. "Replacing any lost Were is impossible, but naming Dasha in Andrew's place on your guard has helped the Pack see we are healing and returning to strength. They are your wolves, but without faith that you will protect them, they will falter."

"I need to name at least one other." Sylvan listened to the fading sounds of Lara's footsteps. "Whoever I choose will be in danger."

"The *centuri* share your blood—they are the strongest of the strong. And every wolf envies them the honor."

"You are a wise and clever mate."

Grinning, Drake kissed her. "And you are a wise Alpha to recognize that."

❖

Daniela hurried down the hallway with the Were host curled in her arms. The Were breathed shallowly, muscles faintly trembling, a low moan emanating from her chest. Daniela barely noticed the young female's weight as she glided through the semidarkness. She had only one goal: to feed, to fill the dark chasm that consumed her, slowly driving her mad. The smell of fresh blood on the Were's throat and breasts and belly ripped at the threads of her tenuous control. Her incisors throbbed, her mouth filled with feeding hormones, and her mind hazed with crimson fog. Bloodlust beat at the fiber of her being. If she took her, she could ease the terrible pain that pulsed through every cell. If she took her now the pain would abate, the emptiness would be filled—

She couldn't. The mistress had not given her permission to feed. She would be punished. Locked away. Starved. Worse, she would be banished from her mistress's presence, cut off from the sensual bliss of her mistress's power. She would rather walk into the sun than be exiled from her mistress's chambers. She had begged to be turned, begged to be bound. If only the hunger would relent. Blindly, she found the door handle to one of rooms reserved for hosts, pushed it open, and hurriedly laid the somnolent Were on the single bed against the wall.

"Please." The naked female arched, her breasts and belly glistening with sex-sheen. A fine line of golden pelt scored her lower abdomen. She was still covered with blood and her own sexual emissions. Her scent was intoxicating. "Take more. Please. I need…"

Daniela's lips drew back, and she hissed. Lust clouded her senses—the form on the bed was featureless, nothing more than heat and blood and pulsing life. Food. Release. Pleasure.

Almost unconsciously she checked that the container holding the restorative compound on the small nearby nightstand was full. The Were would wake in the morning and consume the supplement and leave no worse for the experience. But if Daniela took her—

Daniela forced herself to back away. One trembling step at a time. Finally she reached the door, stumbled out into the hall, and closed it.

I give you permission to avail yourself of my prisoner.

Daniela ghosted down the hall to the heavy metal door at the far end. A human servant stood guard, nodding deferentially as she approached. She was the mistress's handmaiden, and she had free rein of the lair. She ignored him, already tasting the sweet tang of her prey's blood. She pressed her hand to the plate on the wall that recognized those with access to the prison chambers. The door slid soundlessly open and she passed inside.

Another long hallway stretched in front of her, dim ceiling lights illuminating closed doors, some with foot-square glass view plates, others with thick metal bars. Not all the cells were occupied, and of those that were, not all held prisoners. Some held Vampires being punished for all manner of indiscretions with solitary confinement—completely solitary. The Vampire inmates were not allowed to feed while serving their sentences. The other cells were occupied by humans or Weres who had violated the club rules or had displeased Francesca in some other way.

Daniela rushed along the narrow corridor to the last cell, keyed in the combination on a lock pad, and slipped inside. Deep underground, the windowless cell was dark except for the faint glow from a row of small lights along the floor, but she didn't need light to sense her prey.

The sweet aroma of the blood rushing through the prisoner's veins was a siren's call, and Daniela could see her clearly enough. A female reclined on the bed in dark tights and a gauzy white shirt with flowing sleeves, the collar open wide to expose her neck and the tops of her small, round breasts. She was barefoot, her collar-length, chestnut hair shaggy, her eerily beautiful otherworldly face calm. Below the cuffs of the white shirt, iron bands encircled her wrists, connected by a short length of chain to a ring in the wall. Iron, the one material that rendered Fae magic powerless.

The prisoner turned her head, studied Daniela. "I wondered if you would come to visit. Did you just come to talk?"

Daniela hissed, beyond conversation, beyond thought, beyond

restraint. She didn't bother to cast her thrall. The Fae were immune. She launched herself across the room, her mouth at the female's neck a heartbeat later, her incisors slicing into flesh.

Torren arched, the force of Daniela's feeding hormones exploding through her body. The burning wound in her neck dulled beneath the orgasm that exploded an instant later. Daniela writhed on top of her, her hips spasming with each desperate swallow. Daniela had taken her before, but never so violently, so mindlessly. Tonight the Vampire was deep in bloodlust, and Torren imagined Francesca had tormented her for a long time, starving her just to the edge of control. Vampire games. Not so different from the games the Queen of Thorns played, and Torren was used to playing games. Her body might respond to Daniela's enforced sexual stimulation, but she was not susceptible to bloodlust or thrall. She could think, and while she could think, she could plan. She'd been planning for this moment since the night the Vampire Regent had taken her as a blood slave.

"Let me give you more than my blood," Torren whispered in Daniela's ear, infusing each word with the Fae power of persuasion. "Let me give you everything you need."

Daniela whimpered, lost in lust, her body wild with need.

"Let me fill you," Torren urged. "Free my hands."

With Daniela's incisors still deep in her flesh, Torren twisted, turning their bodies so Daniela was beneath her. Her blood ran in warm rivulets down her throat. Daniela's need drenched the air. Torren edged her thigh between Daniela's, felt the hot, slick evidence of her need. She pushed her cuffed hands low, just barely able to brush the Vampire's clitoris with a teasing stroke. She pushed her power against Daniela's shields.

"Daniela, let me inside you. Let me fuck you."

Blindly, Daniela fumbled at the locks in the cuffs, the ones she released to allow Torren to eat and bathe. She whimpered, "Please. Now."

"Yes, now," Torren whispered as her hands came free, and she wrapped Daniela's mind in the mist of forgetting.

CHAPTER THREE

Drake and Sylvan crossed the Compound on their way to the nursery, stopping frequently so Sylvan could connect with the Weres passing by, all of whom wanted to greet her. All of whom needed the sense of safety and community she provided. Finally they reached the two-story building that housed both the infirmary and the nursery. The two *sentries* guarding the door saluted as Sylvan approached, and she paused to let her power enfold them before continuing inside. The hallway running the length of the building through the treatment area was empty except for another *sentrie* standing guard at the fortified entrance to the nursery wing. He snapped to attention, an assault rifle slanted across his chest.

"Any unauthorized visitors?" Sylvan asked.

"No, Alpha," Alex said. "Only those on the list you approved."

Sylvan merely nodded, slapped her hand to the sensor on the wall, and moved on as the steel-reinforced doors slid open.

"You've added extra security." Drake kept stride beside her, resting one hand lightly on her back. Sylvan's wolf seemed calmest when they had physical contact. "Do you think we have a threat to our young inside our walls?"

Sylvan halted abruptly, gold shards glinting in the blue depths of her eyes. "A month ago I never would have believed one of my wolves would betray me, but Andrew is dead because I was not vigilant. That will never happen again."

"I'm not complaining about the security," Drake said, only too aware of how vulnerable their young would be until they could shift at will. Theirs were not the only young in the nursery to be protected, either—Raina's cubs and several other Were young were also in the communal training area. Drake sighed. "They'll be glad to see you."

"I know you don't like their being here."

"I won't pretend differently, but I understand the need for it." Drake stroked Sylvan's back. "I'd be lying if I said I didn't wish we could take them somewhere, just the four of us—alone, and forget everything else."

Stopping again, Sylvan grasped her shoulders and kissed her hard. She rubbed her cheek over Drake's. "I'm sorry. If I were anyone else—"

Drake gripped her shirt, kissed her back. "If you were anyone else, I wouldn't love you. And I wouldn't be worrying about offspring because I wouldn't have any. I'm here, and so are they, because we are yours. I wouldn't change that or anything about you."

"You honor me."

"No, I love you, even though you have a hard time accepting it."

Sylvan laughed shortly. "You know me too well."

"Not well enough, but I've got a lifetime to learn." Drake took her hand. "Come, Alpha. Your daughters sense you, and they're growing impatient."

"They take after their Prima that way." Sylvan grinned for the first time in a long time.

The newborn annex was a large room with open cubicles along one wall that held cribs and a central open-air courtyard, accessible through a set of double glass doors, where the young could play. Another pair of armed Weres stood watch outside. The annex doors opened, and Niki Kroff, Sylvan's second-in-command, strode out. She halted when she saw them.

"Alpha. Prima. I didn't expect you."

"Problem?" Sylvan asked.

"No, Alpha. Everything is quiet. I was just visiting Sophia." She looked from Sylvan to Drake. Nearly as attuned to Sylvan as Drake, she would sense Sylvan's agitation. "I can stay if—"

"No, we won't be long. Convene the *centuri* along with the captain of the guard, Alpha Carras, and the Vampire warlord in my office. One hour."

"Yes, Alpha." Niki hesitated. "If we're convening a Were war council, the Vampire shouldn't—"

"The *warlord* needs to be there. See to it."

Niki stiffened. "Yes, Alpha."

Sylvan smiled thinly. Niki and Lara had once been inseparable: littermates, sometimes bedmates, and lifelong friends. Their relationship had always been complex and was now even more so. Lara was a Vampire, and Niki had always held the species in low regard. Now Niki was blood addicted, and she had hosted for Lara more than once. The effort it took Niki to repel the mindless desire to exchange her blood for the sexual pleasure of a Vampire bite, and her pain at losing her connection with Lara, only added to her anger that Lara had been turned. The greater her frustration and pain, the more she took it out on her old friend.

"Lara is our ally," Sylvan said softly, "and your friend. Try to remember that."

"As my Alpha commands," Niki said, her face stony.

Niki strode past them and the door shut behind her, silently enclosing them in the innermost section of the nursery, the true heart of the Compound. Above them, a huge skylight opened to the evening sky. The air was thick with forest scents—evergreens, fallen leaves, mushrooms and moss, the tantalizing whispers of prey. Sophia sat with Roger on the far side of the room, each of them holding a madly wriggling pup—one silver with wild blue eyes, the other midnight with eyes of deepest black. Kira and Kendra. Drake caressed Sylvan's arm.

"We have an hour until you convene the war council," Drake said. "For one hour, I don't want you to think of anything except your family."

Sylvan slid her hand around the back of Drake's neck and squeezed. "As you will, Prima."

"Go then," Drake said, laughing, "before they hurt themselves."

Sylvan rumbled, and the silver and black wolf pups suddenly stilled, their glinting eyes tracking the room and fixing on Sylvan. Their ears came forward, their tails straightened, and they yipped in unison, sharp and demanding. Sylvan laughed, and power, pure and bright, rolled through the room.

Sophia, her golden hair so pale it was nearly white, laughed an instant later, her joy free and unfettered. Roger's baritone joined hers, and the simmering rage reverberating from Sylvan's heart calmed. Her grip on Drake's neck gentled, and heat flooded Drake's chest. Desire rose within her and Sylvan's grumble deepened. She looked at Drake through wolf's eyes and her message was clear. *Mine. Now.*

"Soon," Drake whispered. "I promise."

"I'll hold you to that," Sylvan said and strode toward the young. She brushed a hand over Sophia's cheek, slung an arm around Roger's shoulder. "These two are a noisy pair."

Sophia smiled. "They felt you coming. They shifted just a minute ago."

"The first time all week," Roger said, his pride apparent.

"They can smell the hunt on me," Sylvan murmured, holding out her arms. Roger and Sylvia passed the pups to her and she cradled them both in the crook of her arm, drawing Drake closer with the other. "They want to run."

"When?" Drake asked.

"Very soon." Sylvan hefted them, rubbed her face over theirs, lifted her head so they could lick her throat and jaws. She kept her chin just above theirs, a reminder of her dominance. "They're getting bigger every day."

Sylvan was right. Their coats were thick and sleek, their limbs longer, their round, furry bodies beginning to elongate. Sylvan's young, bearing the blood of generations of Alpha Weres, were stronger than any of the other young in the nursery, even those much older. Their early shift to pelt was a sign of the dominant wolf Weres they would become. Callan and Fala's son, born only a few days after Kira and Kendra, had yet to shift. He might not shift for months, possibly not even then.

Drake hadn't known what to expect as her young grew, but when she'd agreed to move them to the communal nursery, she'd talked to the maternals who had attended Timberwolf young for generations. None could remember any pups who had shifted so soon after birth, not even Sylvan herself. Drake wondered if part of their unusual early maturity was because she was not a born Were, but *mutia*, turned as a result of clandestine research that had been undertaken by humans to destroy them. As the primary mitochondrial donor, whatever she was, so were her young.

"They're healthy and strong." Sylvan nuzzled Drake's neck. "You worry needlessly."

"I can see how strong they are." Drake shook off the melancholy.

She was a doctor, a scientist. What she needed was answers, and she knew how to get them. She'd asked Sylvan to put her worries aside for an hour. She could do the same. She took Kira from Sylvan, cradled her on her shoulder, murmured to her softly. "You want to run with your Alpha, precious one?"

Kira licked her ear, nipped playfully, and Drake laughed, burying her face in the soft silver fur.

After a few minutes, she and Sylvan took the pups to the play area and settled on the ground with them, letting them tumble and crawl all over them. When Sylvan was absorbed in a mock game of dominance with her two daughters, Drake slipped away to rejoin Sylvia and Roger. "Is everything all right?"

Roger nodded. "They're very bright and learning quickly. Their instincts are true."

Drake glanced at Sophia, a medic who would understand her unspoken concerns.

"They're perfect, Prima. Mentally and physically healthy and strong."

"Roger, would you give us a minute," Drake asked.

"Of course." He moved away.

"I plan to meet with your parents soon," Drake said. "I want them to sequence my DNA and that of the mutated Were virus in my blood. Yours as well. We need to know as much as we can about the induced Were trait. We still have two infected humans in the infirmary in a coma who need our help."

Sophia sighed. "I know."

Drake took her hand. Sophia had resisted testing for years, fearing she was still a carrier of the Were fever virus. That same fear had kept her from giving Niki a mate bite and sealing their bond. All the same, since Niki had declared herself mated to Sophia, Niki had resisted any sexual contact with others. "There's nothing we'll find out that will change how Niki feels about you. But she needs the mate bond. So do you."

"I don't hold her to her vows. I know how hard it is for her to resist others without a bond."

"Her vows to you are what make her strong. But she needs the bond to be at full power."

Sophia nodded. "Yes, Prima." Her eyes shone liquid with fierce possession. "So do I. She's mine."

Drake glanced at Sylvan, who growled and shook Kendra by the ruff. Their mate bond was the foundation of her world. She had feared the effect of the mutation in her blood on Sylvan too, but Sylvan had shown no signs of a problem. The mutation in Sophia might be— probably was—biologically different, and only testing could determine that. She brushed her fingers over Sophia's cheek. "Then we'll do the tests, and you will make it so."

❖

Daniela nodded perfunctorily to the human servant as she left the prison wing and glided down the long corridor to the staircase at the end of the hall that led to the club above. Nocturne was already crowded with Vampires and the humans and Weres who hoped to exchange their blood for sex before the night was out. Moving quickly, while not seeming to hurry, the pale Vampire crossed the wide space and slipped out the door into the night. The vast parking lot—an overgrown concrete expanse punctuated by scrub brush struggling up through cracks in the decades-old surface—was nearly full. Daniela slid between a row of cars and disappeared. A moment later a wolf bounded across the concrete and into the undergrowth along the riverbank.

Torren trotted stealthily along the narrow path toward the nearest Otherworld Gate, following the river, staying in the shadows and avoiding the highway with its slashing headlights and traffic noises. She kept her head down, scenting the air, using the heightened senses of the Were form she had assumed after leaving Nocturne as Daniela. Transforming diminished her power, and she'd done so twice in rapid succession, but now that she was out under the moon, drawing strength from the earth beneath her and the heavens above, she could feel her magic resurging. Her glamour went beyond illusion, her mutable DNA allowing her to change physical form into whatever template she had stored in her cellular receptors. The chimeric trait was ancient and rare, and even those in Faerie, save for Queen Cecilia, didn't know the extent of her magic.

She neared a group of vagrants crouched over a fire sputtering in a metal can under a few scraggly trees by the river. She smelled the humans first, then heard the low murmur of their voices. She skirted wide around them, snarling at a few stray dogs who cautiously approached as she loped along. The gate was not far, hidden under an arch of the great bridge stretching across the Hudson River. As she drew closer, she sought the faint shimmer in the air that only the Fae could discern, the tear in the fabric of adjacent universes marking the contours of the Gate connecting the human world and Faerie. She slowed, unease pricking at her senses. The Gate felt wrong, and as she drew closer, probing the shimmering portal, her magic recoiled as if reflected from an impenetrable surface. The Gate was locked. She was a tracker, and she'd been to the human realm dozens of times. She knew of other Gates.

Traveling fast, she checked first one and then another, and then another, traveling north away from the city. All the Gates were barred, preventing anyone from entering Faerie from the human world. Why, she didn't know. Perhaps the Queen expected an attack—perhaps there had already been one. Or perhaps the Fae had finally withdrawn from the Coalition and severed all connection to the human realm. Whatever was happening in Faerie, Torren was exiled for now. Still in Were form, she crouched in a forest clearing and thought about her options.

Cecilia, the Queen of Thorns, had charged her with finding her runaway niece and returning her to Faerie, and Torren had fulfilled her mission. However, in doing so, she had violated the Vampire Code and been taken as a blood slave for a century. The Queen had not protested her sentence, not that Torren had expected her to. Cecilia would not risk a rift with the Vampire Regent, even for a highborn member of her court, and having one such as Torren inside the Vampire court, even as a prisoner, could have its advantages. Now that Torren was free, her choices were limited. She could not return to Faerie, and Francesca would undoubtedly send a search party after her. Fortunately, they would not be tracking a Were. Still, she would still not be safe in the city, where the Vampire population was concentrated. She would need sanctuary.

Torren heaved herself up, put her muzzle to the air, and continued running north into the forest.

CHAPTER FOUR

D rake stood at Sylvan's right side as those summoned to the war council filed into the gathering room. Flames leapt in the huge stone fireplace, its mantel a slab of granite a foot thick, the hearth bordered by boulders as tall as her. The vast ceiling soared upward, supported by rafters as big around as tree trunks. The floor was river rock, the color of earth, worn smooth by aeons of flowing mountain water and generations of wolf Weres striding through the halls.

The space might dwarf an ordinary being, but Sylvan fit perfectly, claiming the center, radiating power as tangible as the structure itself. Drake's skin vibrated with her mate's call. Sylvan wasn't as tall as Jonathan, the young blond *centuri* with the slender grace, or as muscular as Max, the bearish male who stood with massive arms like elm saplings folded across his broad chest, but Sylvan radiated such primal strength she appeared larger than any in the Pack. Her eyes pierced distances far beyond where the rest could see, her Alpha-enhanced senses able to detect her wolves miles away by their scent and heartbeat. She could shift in a fraction of a second, or change partially into her half-form, an ability only the strongest of the strong demonstrated. Her speed on four legs was unparalleled.

Drake stroked Sylvan's bare back and edged her hand under the waistband of Sylvan's leather pants. Sylvan's wolf controlled the emotional, physical, and sexual tenor of the whole Pack. Every wolf Were was energized by her presence. When her wolf was on full alert, the entire Pack hummed with vitality, quivering on the edge of shifting, ready to be called to run or hunt or fight by their Alpha's side. When Sylvan and Drake coupled, the lash of Sylvan's sexual force whipped through the Pack and bore down on all her wolves, capable of pulling all the females into heat and the dominants, male and female, into breeding frenzy. But she wasn't their Alpha just because she was the most dominant or her power unmatched. She ruled because she lived to protect her Pack and preserve their future.

Sylvan glanced at her, a cocky smile angled across her face. "This won't take long, and then I'll take care of your needs."

"This will take as long as it needs to take," Drake said, "and then *you* are *mine*."

"I am always yours," Sylvan growled, gold leaping in her eyes. Her skin shimmered with a pulse of sex and power, and around the room, the other wolves grew restless.

"They won't be able to concentrate if you keep them on edge," Drake said.

"Not my doing. You always keep *me* on edge."

Laughing, Drake kissed her. "And I am always ready for you. It's only fair. But have pity on them for now."

Sylvan smiled again for a brief instant, and the effect was as if the heavens parted on a winter day to allow a brilliant shaft of sunlight to pierce the darkest glade in the forest. Drake's heart leapt, and her wolf sighed with the contentment of peace and home. "I love you."

Softly, almost as if she still didn't believe what Drake had said, Sylvan said, "I love you too."

And then Sylvan's face lost its soft edges and she was all wolf, fierce and fearless. Drake put aside thoughts of having Sylvan naked above her. They had a war to plan. She surveyed those standing in a loose semicircle around them, their strongest and truest warriors.

A year ago she'd known nothing of this wild, perilous life. As an ER doctor, she'd seen death and trauma and tragedy. Working as a doctor was all she'd ever wanted to do and all she'd ever thought she'd need to be satisfied. Her life had been defined by her work, and she had never imagined a love so consuming that all else became secondary. And then Sylvan strode through the hospital halls to claim one of her injured adolescents, and Drake's world had changed forever. Now she was mated, a Were herself—turned by the bite of an infected young girl just before she died. She was responsible for the lives of hundreds of wolf Weres, just as was Sylvan. Here in this room were her most trusted friends and loved ones.

She took them in by turn. Sylvan's elite guard: Niki, the *imperator*, Sylvan's general and second-in-command; Max, a genius at communications; the twins, Jace and Jonathan, fierce and fast fighters; and the newest *centuri*, Dasha Baran, security expert and master strategist.

And a newcomer amidst the inner circle. Katya, a young dominant barely past adolescence, was attending the council for the first time. She was not unseasoned, however. She had fought for her life, for all their lives, by surviving captivity in a human laboratory where she'd been the victim of sexual experimentation, physical abuse, and psychological degradation. Just thinking about what she had endured stirred rage in Drake's heart, a rage she knew Sylvan, driven by her primal need to protect her wolves, lived with every second.

"You will see them safe," Drake murmured.

"We will see them safe." Sylvan slipped her hand around Drake's neck, caressed her, and cast her call to those who waited. "We have much work to do. Our enemies have brought the war to us. They've captured our young, violated them, destroyed our property, and taken our lives. We have cause to retaliate, and the longer we wait, the weaker we will appear and the stronger our enemies will grow. The human factions will consolidate and their organizations will spread and strengthen. The smaller, weaker Were groups will become targets. We cannot allow that to happen."

"We must strike back," Niki said sharply, cloaked in fury as thick as her winter pelt.

"Who, *Imperator*?" Sylvan asked flatly. "Who shall we attack?"

Niki growled, her features feral, eyes slanted, lips drawn back from her canines. Claws broke through the tips of her digits, streaking them with blood. "All of them, starting with the politicians who treat us like mindless prey."

"An open show of aggression will bring all the human forces down us. We would not survive an all-out assault from the human military. Even if we retreat deeper into the mountains, we would have to live in hiding forever. Our young would never have the chance to live outside the forest. Our Pack has evolved beyond that. Many of us have already integrated into human society. They would have to choose between Pack and the lives they've built. Unless we face annihilation, I cannot ask them to make that choice."

"How many of us must die before we choose," Niki snarled.

Drake rumbled, "Be careful, *Imperator*, not to try the Alpha's patience. Or mine."

Niki grumbled softly but backed down under Drake's warning tone.

"Not all humans are our enemies." Sylvan looked to Max. "Andrea and her brother first informed us of the experiments and led us to the labs. Have they made any progress in locating the other labs?"

Max growled, a grating sound like rocks careening down a mountainside. "Andrea is in contact with Praetern supporters who have infiltrated hate groups like HUFSI, but she has to work through a complicated network of informants, and even then, the intel she receives is fragmented. The group members never meet in large numbers, keep their identities secret, and usually don't know anyone other than their own cell members."

"Do you think she'll be able to get us hard intelligence?"

Max nodded, and pride glinted in his eyes. "She will, but it might take some time."

"You work with her, assist in any way you can, and protect her. She is a valuable ally."

"I will, Alpha." Max's smile was predatory and possessive. He was unmated and Andrea was a human, but apparently his wolf didn't see that as an obstacle.

"Lara," Sylvan said next. "Your Liege is our ally, but there are powerful Vampires opposed to Praetern integration, including Francesca. If Francesca supports those who attack us, Gates will be forced to choose between our alliance and civil war with the Vampires."

"Liege Gates has given her oath," Lara said, "and she knows of the consequences."

Sylvan nodded. "Her consort is one of our best sources. Becca has many contacts in the human world. I think the plan to destroy us reaches high into the human government. We need to know how high."

"My Liege will not allow her consort to be put at risk, not for any reason."

"As it should be," Sylvan said. "So I am tasking you to see that Becca Land is never in danger."

"Yes, Alpha," Lara replied.

"Katya," Sylvan said gently.

Katya had come dressed in the usual Were garb of T-shirt and jeans. She was barefoot, her golden hair loose around her shoulders, the shadows in her blue eyes belying her age. She was young, but she had endured as much pain as anyone in the room. She was a soldier, battle tested. She faced Sylvan with a mixture of uncertainty and excitement in her face.

Drake tensed. Even knowing Katya had been summoned to fight didn't prevent her wolf from wanting to protect and shield her. Only her trust in Sylvan prevented her from growling a warning.

"Yes, Alpha," Katya said, her musical alto steady and strong.

"You were the first to warn Niki of the impending attack on us at the gala. Can you remember any more of the details? Can you tell us how you knew?"

"I...I've tried, Alpha. All I remember is a sensation, a..." She shook her head, frustrated and angry.

"A premonition?" Drake asked. "As if you had a feeling of what was about to happen?"

"Yes, but more than that." Katya's eyes glazed, as if she was looking inward, or back in time. "I...I saw fire. I *heard* an explosion inside my head."

"And did you know who was targeted?"

Katya shook her head. "No. The blast seemed to take in everything, everywhere. It was massive, but I knew—" Her eyes glistened as if they had filled with tears, but her voice never wavered. She stared at Sylvan. "I knew you and the Prima were in danger."

Sylvan snarled at the threat to her mate, as real now as it had been then. Her wolf exploded past her frayed restraints before she could stop her. Sylvan managed not to shift, but power flooded the room. Jace, a volatile dominant still evolving, instantly shifted. Belly low, uncertain of her welcome, Jace inched forward to Sylvan's side and rubbed her shoulder against Sylvan's leg.

"It's all right, Jace." Sylvan buried her fingers in Jace's salt-and-pepper ruff, soothing her. "Katya, has that ever happened to you before?"

"Not...not like that, Alpha."

Gently, Drake asked, "Anything similar?"

"Sometimes," Katya said after a long pause, "sometimes I feel as if someone is reaching out to me. Reaching inside me, calling to me."

Niki snarled and glared at Lara, the Vampire among them. Lara's expression remained impassive, her stance relaxed, although that casual demeanor was a ruse. With her Vampire speed, she could disappear, or attack, before anyone with the exception of Sylvan could react.

"Who?" Drake asked. "Who calls you?"

Katya squared her shoulders, lifted her chin. She had been degraded, abused, and violated, but she was a dominant wolf, strong and proud, and that was something no captor could take from her. "I am almost certain...No, I'm sure. Michel."

"She has been enthralled," Niki spat, pelt streaking down the center of her torso.

Katya swung to face her, gold exploding in her eyes. "No! I am not enthralled. I know who she is and what she wants, and I know what I want."

"You can't know when a Vampire distorts your mind."

"She doesn't."

Niki took a step toward her, shimmering on the verge of shifting. "You can't tell the difference between desire and force when a Vampire enthralls you."

"I'm not you, Niki." Katya's voice held no challenge, only the pride of a wolf, but she stood her ground with a low growl of warning. "I know where I go when I go to her, and why. She has never taken me against my will. Even when I was in chains."

"You—"

"Niki," Sylvan snarled, "enough. Katya deserves your respect."

Niki dropped her head under the force of Sylvan's dominance. "I do respect her, Alpha. It's the Vampire I don't trust."

"Katya," Sylvan said, "if Michel warned you, then she knew of the plan. We don't know what that means. She could have warned you because she's on our side. If she went against Francesca's desires, she is in danger. Or her part in this could be an elaborate plot we do not yet understand."

Katya's skin flushed and a dusting of light brown pelt emerged in a fine line on her lower abdomen. "I will not endanger her."

Sylvan sighed. The Exodus had brought the Praeterns together in a way they hadn't interacted in centuries, and now her wolves were forming problematic attachments everywhere she looked. She loved her father, but she wondered if he'd had any idea how complicated his dream of freedom would make life for all of them. But what was done could not be undone, even had she wanted to. "Michel is a powerful Vampire who has survived for centuries through strength, cunning, and skill. She can take care of herself."

"I will not lie to her."

"I would not ask you to. Talk to her. Find out as much as you can of what the Vampires knew of this attack against us. She may be the key."

Katya's eyes glinted with anticipation. "As my Alpha commands."

Chapter Five

R unning hard in Were form, Torren passed the outermost perimeter into Timberwolf territory just as the moon reached its zenith. Silver shafts of moonlight sliced through the dense foliage and flooded the forest floor. The grating rumble of engines and cacophony of human sound had long since dissipated, and all she heard was the crackling of animals moving stealthily through the brush and the occasional hoot of an owl. No Vampire would follow her out here unless they came by armored and UV-shielded vehicle, and she'd have plenty of warning if they did. She'd outrun some dangers, even as she raced toward others.

She scented the first patrol a minute later. The fierce aroma of Were pierced the feathery odors of pine and loam. She lifted her muzzle. Sniffed deeply. Two, three, four Weres—moving away. She angled downwind and moved on, slowing to a trot to avoid drawing their attention. The deeper she penetrated Were territory, the more her skin tingled with the heavy press of Were power. Her magic rose, unblunted even in changeling form, and surged back against the foreign force. The glow of her magic burned off the last taint of imprisonment, banishing the bone-deep ache in her wrists from the iron shackles and erasing the lassitude that had left her weak and confused.

She would not soon forget the Vampire Regent's pleasure in torturing her. Torren, like most Fae, had no great love for Vampires, whose only claim to power was their graceless ability to enthrall hosts who were most often willing to be taken to begin with. Now she had even less. In service to her Queen, she had agreed to the sentence imposed on her by the Vampire Regent despite the humiliation of being made a blood slave, of having her body and blood available to any

Vampire the Regent willed. She would not have dishonored her Queen by trying to escape. But she was also a Fae royal, and Francesca had disregarded her status and her word, enjoying her power too much to allow Torren to serve without degrading her. Francesca had kept Torren in chains for no other reason than to flaunt her dominance, and she had created a formidable enemy.

Torren picked up the concentrated scent of many Weres having traveled north over a well-worn trail through dense forest. The signs were clear—this was one of the main pathways leading to the Were Compound. She bounded along at an effortless pace, enjoying her lithe muscular form, covering large patches of ground in loping strides. The occasional deer and possum skittered out of her way, close enough to catch her attention, but she was not interested in prey. Her Were form allowed her to assume the physical abilities of a Were but did not alter her basic drives and urges, any more than it diluted her powers. She didn't have the primal predatory urge of a Were to take her prey to ground and consume what she killed. Her prey, when she hunted, was of a different nature. Her biology remained her own, and she was driven by more subtle desires—the excitement of seduction, the thrill of absorbing another's energies, and the sexual satisfaction of enchantment. Unlike the Were and Vampire predators, she controlled the power of the senses, not of the flesh.

She'd traveled close to an hour before the scent of Weres grew into a palpable force enshrouding her, and she knew the Were base was very close. She'd make contact soon. She slowed, listened, and—a minute later—sensed the first Were shadowing her, moving parallel at the same pace. A moment later, a second joined the first, and she slowed even more. If she ran, they would give chase, and she suspected when they caught her she would not have time to explain her presence before they tore out her throat. Up ahead, the black sky lightened unexpectedly, and an instant later she recognized the glow of firelight painting the undersurface of the clouds a pale yellow. A break in the heavy forest—a clearing. A big one. She was almost there. If she could reach the gates and—

A wolf leapt onto her back, massive jaws snapping closed on the muscle at the junction of her neck and shoulder. Pain exploded down her leg and she stumbled. The weight on her back and the agonizing pain threw her off stride and she went down, rolling, writhing, twisting—

struggling to unseat the snarling wolf that dug claws into her side and bit down harder into her flesh. She tumbled onto her back, and a second fur-covered missile drove into her chest. A bone snapped, fire exploding in her chest. Claws tore at her belly and the sky overhead dimmed. She didn't fight back—she was no match while in Were form for two wolves, and she hadn't come to fight. She'd come to negotiate.

She went limp, lifted her muzzle, and exposed her throat. The jaws clamped into her shoulder eased only a fraction. Warmth trickled into her fur. Blood. Not the first she'd shed in service to her Queen.

Torren shed her wolf form and gasped, "Sanctuary."

The last thing she saw were the burning coal-black eyes of an enraged wolf.

❖

"I can come in with you," Sasha said hesitantly. "You ought to have backup."

"I do—that's why you're here. If I need you, you'll know." Katya stared out the windshield at the blank face of Nocturne, a windowless, nondescript one-story building bordering a huge parking lot filled with every type of vehicle from battered pickup trucks to sleek stretch limos. Everyone, rich and poor, human and Praetern, frequented the Vampire club in search of excitement and adventure. And pleasure. She imagined she could hear the ecstatic cries of human and Were hosts as they were catapulted into blinding orgasm, Vampires feeding at their necks and breasts and groins, injecting feeding hormones into their blood to force their release and made them forget the violence and pain of possession. She remembered the waves of heat and the cataclysmic release that punched through her whenever Michel took her. Her canines lengthened and pelt flared low on her belly. Her clitoris tightened, her sex pounded, and frenzy churned in her gut. "I'll be fine."

"I could wait a few minutes, come in later." Sasha drummed the wheel and whined uneasily. She was a young soldier just finished *sentrie* training, dominant, but not nearly as dominant as Katya, which was why Katya had chosen her as a driver. The Alpha had ruled no one was to leave the Compound alone, and she had not wanted a more dominant wolf whose protective instincts would interfere with her plans. Sasha's instinct was to obey her.

Katya let her wolf show in her eyes. "Wait for me here. I'll be out by dawn. You don't want to go inside."

"I…I think I do. The things I've heard." Sasha shuddered, and in the dim moonlight illuminating the inside of the Rover, her skin shimmered. "You want it. I can tell you do. Your call is strong."

"Yes, I want it." Katya's lips drew back and her canines gleamed. She had been forced to do many things that haunted her, shamed her still, but she was not ashamed of this. "But I know what I'm asking for."

"I want to go with you." Sasha's scent grew darker, richer.

Katya narrowed her eyes, recognizing the signs. Sasha wanted to tangle. "It's not like tangling with another Were. You won't be in control, you won't even be able to *give up* control on your own. They take what they want, and they make you glad that they do."

Sasha's grip on the wheel tightened and her back arched abruptly. "I understand." She turned her head, her gaze fixed just below Katya's. "Please."

"There's no Pack law against you hosting a Vampire. Just be careful. Only one at a time. You're not ready for more." Katya snarled when Sasha's eyes glowed amber. Her face gleamed with sex-sheen. She would go inside no matter what Katya said—she was already half-frenzied. "Come on. I'm not going to leave you alone in there."

"I can handle myself," Sasha snapped, her wolf's pride affronted.

"Yeah, that's what you think." Katya jumped out of the Rover, loped around the front, and yanked open the other door. She grabbed the younger Were by the scruff and pulled her out. "You'll do as I say for the rest of the night. Understood?"

The female ducked her head. "Yes, Katya."

As soon as Katya stepped into the club, the scent of blood and sex rolled over her, and she growled softly. Next to her, Sasha gasped and her wolf rose sharply. Sasha's control was not nearly strong enough to stand against the clouds of Were pheromones and blood thickening the air. She'd fall prey to the first Vampire who cast their thrall in her direction.

"Hold your wolf."

"I'm trying," Sasha gasped. "I need…"

"I know what you need." Katya dragged her deeper into the room, away from the throngs of Vampires near the bar. Sasha was a young, strong, dominant female, and if her call wasn't blunted soon, she would attract a group of Vampires who would bleed her dry. Katya looked around, saw a svelte, dark-haired Vampire leaning against a post, his red-ringed midnight irises pulsating beacons that tugged at Katya's core. He watched them draw closer, his incisors slowly appearing over his lower lip. His thrall flowed over her, sweet and languorous. Her pelt flared and she readied. Still in her grip, Sasha shivered, deep in the mindless chaos of sex frenzy.

"Your friend seems eager." The Vampire, beautiful as they all were, spoke to Katya, but his heavy-lidded gaze swept over Sasha.

"Sasha?" Katya murmured. Sasha radiated sex and need. "Him?"

"Yes." Sasha's eyes glowed, and her muscles rippled with the effort to contain her frenzy. "Hurry, help me."

"She wants to host," Katya said.

"And you, pretty young wolf?" He drew one finger along the edge of Katya's jaw. "Perhaps you too?"

Pleasure lanced through her, her clitoris tingled, and she pulled her head back quickly. "Just her."

"That's not what your blood whispers to me."

Katya snarled. "No."

He smiled, crimson spreading through his gaze as he lowered his thick dark lashes. He pointed to the shadowy hallway behind them. "Come."

"No. Out here." Katya motioned to an empty sofa nearby. She had no idea how many Vampires were waiting to feed in the dark recesses of the club, but she couldn't protect Sasha if she had to fight off Vampires who wanted her. She drew Sasha to the sofa and settled against the arm with Sasha reclining between her legs. She cradled Sasha against her chest, Sasha's head on her shoulder, and glanced at the Vampire who stood over them. She pulled a long knife from a leather sheath on her thigh and let the blade catch the light. "I'm not leaving her, and if you try to drain her, I'll take your head."

He grinned wryly. "How is it you come here armed? You don't trust us, my sweet wolf?"

"I'm not your wolf, and I'll never trust you. Take her, but be careful with her."

He looked intrigued. "And may I touch her?"

Sasha moaned, her thighs parting as she pushed up her T-shirt and fumbled to open her leather pants. Her cinnamon pelt line cut a stark swath down the center of her taut belly, and she writhed between Katya's legs. "Please. Please. Now."

The Vampire hissed and opened his pants. His pale, slender cock lay against his abdomen as if carved from ivory. Sasha's sex hormones spilled over Katya, driving Katya's need higher.

"Remember," Katya said, fighting her own rising frenzy, "endanger her and you will not see another sunfall."

She never saw him move. He was between Sasha's legs, his arms braced on either side of their bodies, his smile predatory and so beautiful. He could just as easily have taken Katya's throat as Sasha's, but he dipped his head and buried himself in Sasha in one swift strike. Sasha jerked and released with a feral growl.

The Vampire fed, his hips thrusting slowly as he came with each swallow. Katya stared at the ceiling, one hand clenched, the other pressed to the side of Sasha's neck, feeling her pulse. Sasha writhed, her *victus* coating them both as she released over and over. Katya's clitoris strained for contact, her pelt rippled beneath her skin. The muscles in her abdomen cramped from the strain of holding back.

Finally Sasha's frenzy eased, and Katya growled, "That's enough."

He seemed not to hear her, his body shuddering. Were blood was so potent, the pleasure so much more than that obtained from a human host, that often young Vampires, and sometimes even the most controlled Risen, succumbed to bloodlust. Katya gripped his shoulder, let her claws dig into his flesh. "Release her."

When he didn't, she pressed her blade to his neck. "Last warning."

"Patience, Wolf," a cool voice from above murmured. "Richard, enough."

Instantly, the male disengaged, closing the wound in Sasha's neck with a swipe of his tongue. He sat up between Sasha's legs, adjusted his trousers, closed his fly. Appearing dazed, he smiled at the Vampire standing over them. "My apologies, *Senechal*. I'd forgotten how sweet these females can be."

Michel's eyes were blue flames. Her sculpted cheekbones stood out sharp as the blade in Katya's fist. Her power and fury washed over Katya with such force Katya's sex convulsed and she nearly released.

The male glanced at Katya and reached for her neck. "And I still have one to go."

Michel's strike was swifter than Katya could follow. She jerked Richard off the sofa with a hand around his throat and held him suspended as if he were a feather. "She said she did not want to host for you. You know the rules."

His eyes widened in terror.

Michel pulled him closer until her mouth was against his ear. Katya heard Michel's whisper deep inside her mind.

And she belongs to me. Touch her, and you will spend a hundred years in a cell. I will put you there myself.

His eyes pleaded, and she let him go.

"My apologies, *Senechal*," he whispered, backing away. He didn't look in Katya's direction. "I didn't know. Thank you for your mercy."

"Go." Restraining her urge to take Katya instantly, Michel knelt beside the sofa and stroked Katya's face. She'd known Katya was coming before Katya walked through the front door. She'd sensed her presence growing stronger for close to an hour, and she'd used that hour to feed from several hosts. If she hadn't, she wouldn't have been able to wait to take her. Her hunger still lashed through her, a flame that gutted her endlessly, a hollow pain she couldn't assuage no matter how many times she fed, no matter how many female Weres she held under her, no matter how many times they spread their essence over her. She'd waited in the shadows at the back of the bar, knowing Francesca would be watching. Francesca would know before the night was out that Katya was here and that Michel had not been able to stay away. But Francesca didn't have to know that Michel had been waiting day after day, night after night, for her.

"What game are you playing, my little one?" Michel murmured.

Katya kissed her, her canines scraping Michel's lip. "No game. I came for you."

Michel smiled. "Not yet, but you will."

Chapter Six

Misha crouched over the naked female lying in a pool of moonlight, her skin glowing as if she were the source of the silvery illumination herself. Her tousled dark hair framed a narrow face with bold arching cheekbones, an angular jaw ended in a firm, triangular chin, and almond-shaped blue eyes glinted like stones in a clear mountain pool. Her body was willowy and long-limbed, her hands delicate but strong looking. Her breasts were small, her hips narrow, and for an instant, Misha had the image of slender blades of grass shimmering in sunlight.

Shaking her head to dispel the potent sights and sounds and scents that left her reeling, Misha rasped, "Guard her while I get my weapon."

From behind her, Gray, still in pelt, whined uneasily and Misha rose, staring down at the stranger. Something wasn't right. The female had appeared out of the dark—a lone wolf, unannounced and uninvited in Pack territory—and the law was clear. Without free passage, she was the enemy. She had looked like a Were, but she didn't smell like one. Even now, Misha couldn't scent the tangy sweet odor of another wolf. Instead, her senses tingled with the aroma of spice and nectar, as if she had fallen into a field of wildflowers kissed with rain. A rush of pheromones misted her skin and she shivered. She realized she was still staring when she should be getting her weapon and, feeling slightly light-headed, glanced around the clearing. Mist clouded the forest, obscuring the familiar trees and brush. Dark shadows, elongated and vaguely menacing, flickered at the edges of her vision. Misha's wolf growled and paced. Misha backed away from the stranger and checked on Gray. "Are you all right? Did you see—"

Gray's lips pulled back in a snarl, and her sable ruff stood on end. Eyes glinting and belly low to the ground, she stalked the naked female, one measured pace at a time. Her shoulders and haunches tightened. Her gaze fixed on the female's throat and her jaws parted. She was ready to spring. Ready to kill.

Misha jolted alert with an intense and unexplained need to protect the unknown female. Growling softly, she slid between the helpless prisoner and Gray's nearly wild wolf. "She submitted. She is our prisoner. If she resists, subdue her. Don't kill her."

Gray flicked an ear but didn't look away from her prey.

"*Gray.*"

The charcoal wolf reluctantly halted and took up a guard position.

"I'll be right back." Misha loped through the underbrush to the last outpost where she and Gray had both shifted in order to pursue the interloper on four legs. She grabbed her rifle from the hidden cache and yanked on a pair of pants, a heavy long-sleeved T-shirt, and boots. Tucking a spare rifle and clothes under one arm, she raced back to find Gray crouched low over the prisoner, growling steadily. The female's eyes were open and startlingly blue, captivating even in the subdued moonlight. Or maybe...for a heartbeat, Misha could have sworn the moon danced in the female's eyes, and she was there with her under a brilliant night sky, her wolf darting and daring and inviting. Misha gasped, a hot streak of pelt exploding down her midsection, and she quickly shouldered her rifle and pointed it at the stranger on the ground. "I have her, Gray. Your weapon is at the edge of the woods behind me. Get it."

Gray continued to growl, vibrating with rage so potent Misha's wolf surged to attention, sensing challenge. She and Gray were nearly the same age, but she had been promoted faster than Gray, and she outranked her in dominance by a slim margin. Any other wolf in Gray's position would have obeyed her instantly, but Gray was as close to an outlaw as she could get without being declared a lone wolf. Since Gray and Katya had been liberated by the Alpha from captivity, Gray had been angry and unstable, almost feral. She constantly tested everyone in the Pack, and the Alpha had charged Misha to partner with her in the field and to help her find her balance again. Misha would have assisted her without the order—they were friends—but she was never really sure how to help her. Mostly she followed her instincts, and that seemed to be enough to keep Gray's shaky control intact. This was the first time they'd faced an aggressive challenge, and Gray's hold on her wolf was fragile. Or maybe she just didn't want to control her. Misha couldn't worry about Gray's motivation—she didn't care. Her wolf demanded obedience from a less dominant Pack member. That was the law of their world.

"Gray," Misha barked, letting her wolf's power flare. "Back away, get your weapon."

The charcoal wolf quivered and finally slowly retreated. In a flash, Gray turned and disappeared into the underbrush.

"Thank you," the prisoner said, her voice as deep and melodious as a hawk's call on the wind.

Misha stalked forward and leveled her rifle at the female's head. "Who are you?"

Torren looked up into the onyx eyes of the white-and-gray wolf that had taken her down by the throat. Only now, the wolf was a young female, radiating strength, and quite beautiful. Mahogany hair fell to her shoulders in loose waves. Even in the moonlight, her eyes shone black as the River Ribl in Faerie, glinting with diamonds and putting the night sky to shame. She was average height, average build, her beauty even more in the way she held herself than in her smooth full breasts and tight muscular body. The force of her power was surprisingly clear and strong for someone so young, and Torren's magic rose to her call. She'd tried to enchant her, to draw the Were into the mists of *aerous* and compel her to her will, but the Were's shields were too strong. She had not been able to completely enchant or persuade her as she had Daniela. And, unlike her immunity to Vampire thrall, she was not immune to the Were's power. Her magic glowed hot from the stroke of this wolf's tongue along her senses.

The Were growled softly. "I will not bother to ask again."

"I am Torren de Brinna," Torren said softly, "and I seek an audience with your Alpha."

"I don't recognize your Pack," Misha said suspiciously.

Torren smiled. "I don't have one."

"You're a lone wolf? You know the penalty for trespassing in Pack land without permission. I could kill you now."

"I am not a wolf."

Misha scoffed. "I took you down, remember? I tasted your blood." Misha hesitated, frowned. She *had* tasted her blood and hadn't registered in the heat of battle that she had not tasted Were. The stranger's blood was not the thick, dark richness of Were blood, but light and teasing, spring sap shot through with the essence of mountain air. She narrowed her eyes. "What are you?"

"I would prefer to tell your Alpha that."

Misha had two choices. She could escort the stranger back to the Compound, or she could kill her. The decision wasn't as simple as it seemed. If she brought her to the Compound, she would be exposing the location of their sanctuary to this female who was something she could not identify. A spy, possibly. An enemy, probably. Dangerous, certainly. She was within her rights to kill her, but everything in her resisted. The brilliant eyes held hers, and her wolf stirred, pelt prickling beneath her skin.

"Why?" Misha asked. "Why are you on Pack land?"

"I have been a prisoner," Torren said, reading the indecision in the young Were's eyes. Seeing something else too. Something that spoke to her blood in a way she couldn't explain. Her hawk's song soared, filling her with light and heat. Magic danced along her skin. "I am alone. I am friend."

"Who took you prisoner?" Misha snarled, furious for no reason that made sense.

"The Viceregal."

"From where did you escape?"

"From the dungeons beneath Nocturne."

"How long? What did she—"

"That is unimportant." Torren's pride would not allow this female to view her as a victim. "All that matters is that she failed to keep me captive."

Misha growled. She didn't agree, but the stranger was not hers to avenge. "Get up."

Torren flowed to her feet. She stood naked in the moonlight, blood drying on her neck, side, and belly from the bites and gouges sustained in the fight. They would heal soon enough. She watched the wolf scan her body, saw the brief spark of gold. Were power washed over her and her nipples tightened. "I am not going to resist."

Misha met her eyes, held the rifle on her. "I have no reason to trust you."

"Not yet," Torren murmured.

Gray stepped into the glade. "We should kill her."

"She is not a Were." Misha motioned with the rifle for Torren to start walking ahead of her. "So she is technically not a lone wolf."

"Even more reason not to take her any farther."

Misha kept a tight hold on her wolf. Gray's threat to Torren made her bristle. She glared into Gray's eyes until Gray grumbled and looked away. Satisfied Gray would follow her orders, her wolf relaxed and settled back to watch warily. "If she runs, shoot her. If she doesn't, do not touch her."

The silver cry of a hawk floated through Misha's mind.

Thank you.

❖

"I can't leave her," Katya said to Michel, nodding to Sasha, who still lay in her arms, somnolent after her torrential release. She would be prey for any Vampire who wanted to feed from her.

"I'll have someone guard her," Michel said. "She will be safe."

"Your word."

"My word," Michel murmured, smiling inwardly at the request. Any other Were, any other Vampire, would doubt her, would expect treachery or duplicity. Vampires were masters of deception and rarely trusted anyone, even those closest to them. But this Were trusted her, and her faith stirred Michel in a way nothing had for centuries. She caressed Katya's cheek, watched the blood pump faster in the great vessels in her throat. Her hunger exploded, robbing her of caution and control. She had waited too long, and her need ruled her. "Will you come with me?"

"Yes." Katya believed her. Michel had never lied to her. "Call your guard."

Nodding, Michel signaled telepathically to the nearest Vampire guard, who appeared instantly. "See that no one touches this Were."

The blond Vampire nodded calmly. "Yes, *Senechal.*"

"You will be rewarded at dawn."

"Thank you, *Senechal.* I will stay with her until you say otherwise."
The blond hesitated. "If she requests to host, *Senechal?*"

Michel raised a brow in Katya's direction.

"She is a dominant Were, and if she chooses to host, she is within
her rights." Katya stared hard at the blond. "But she should not be
harmed."

"Of course."

"You can trust Louis to protect her."

"I trust *you*," Katya said, settling Sasha on the sofa and slipping
out from behind her. Rising until she and Michel were face-to-face, she
slid her arms around Michel's shoulders and kissed her. Her clitoris
was distended, the shaft swollen and full. Her glands throbbed, tense
and primed to explode. "I am ready for you. I want you to take me and
I am tired of waiting."

Michel slid a slender arm, strong as a steel band, around Katya's
waist and dragged her close, bloodlust suffusing her so quickly her
awareness of anything except Katya disappeared. Her mind hazed to
red. "I've waited for you, hungered for you. Tell me you want my bite,
my bond." She slid her incisors down the hot ridge of Katya's jugular.
"Tell me."

"Yes, yes." Katya grabbed Michel's hand, pulled her away from
the sofa where Sasha stirred and toward the dark recesses of the club.
She would not risk another Vampire trying to join them. Michel would
kill anyone who came close. "Not here. Take me somewhere where we
are alone."

Michel lifted Katya into her arms and cut through the crowd until
they emerged in one of the myriad hallways in the depths of Nocturne.
She set Katya down in a narrow alcove and pressed her to the wall.
Michel's eyes were pure crimson, burning torches boring through
Katya to her core, reigniting her frenzy.

"Hurry." Katya tugged Michel's black silk shirt from her skintight
leather trousers, ripping the buttons open in the process. Her claws
punched out and she raked them down the center of Michel's torso. She
licked the scarlet streams and growled low in her throat.

Michel hissed and sliced into Katya's neck with practiced
penetration, injecting her feeding hormones into Katya's bloodstream.

Katya's first orgasm crested as her blood flowed into Michel's mouth, joining them in flesh and essence. The second followed as her bones melted, the third as Michel's consciousness joined with hers. Power blazed through her, and she felt Michel's pleasure as her own.

Katya whimpered, their union forcing a release so powerful her wolf broke her chains. Michel's face was pressed against her throat, her slender form shuddering as she climaxed. They were secluded but not alone, and Michel was helpless in the midst of her feeding, lost in bloodlust, bloodlust for *her*. Katya wrapped her arms around her, shielding her from the faceless forms gliding by in the dark. Protecting her. Katya's canines elongated and fire blazed in her blood. Her wolf demanded she make her claim. Katya bit Michel's shoulder, burying her canines and spreading her essence in Michel's flesh. Her wolf raised her head, howled. *Mine.*

CHAPTER SEVEN

Tell me, my pet," Francesca said from the height of her ornate gilded throne, her honeyed voice filling the opulent room with effortless command, "what happened in the dungeon."

Daniela knelt naked before the raised platform, her hands clasped behind her back, her head down, supplicant and shaking. "I...I don't remember, Mistress."

"Regent," Francesca murmured.

"Regent," Daniela echoed through a throat dry with terror. She had awakened in the dark dank cell, the evidence of her loss of control—blood and sex fluids—coating her skin. She'd been confused but oddly excited, her breasts and sex tingling as if someone had sent an electric current through her body. All her senses were alive, even though her memory of the last few hours was hazy. Strange images kaleidoscoped through her mind, fragments of sunshine and flowers, things she hadn't thought of since she'd been turned. Things she hadn't thought she'd missed until the dazzling light of the sun on her skin sent her reeling back in time. She'd awakened with tears coursing down her cheeks and the sensation she'd been dancing through fields of softly waving grass. The shackles lay in a tangle on the soaked sheets, and the door to the cell gaped like a mocking mouth. She'd stumbled to her feet, stared into the empty corners of the shadowy cell, and staggered into the hall. The other prisoners had been eerily silent, but she'd felt their eyes follow her as she struggled toward the heavy reinforced door that no one on this side—save her—should have been able to open.

When she'd tripped the lock with her palm and glided through into the lighted passage, the human servant guarding the door unsheathed a three-foot sword from the scabbard on his back and swung the lethal blade in a horizontal curve intended to behead. He'd aborted his strike with the shining blade inches from Daniela's neck and stared in horror.

"Mistress Daniela," he'd gasped, his sword clanging on the stone floor as he hastily lowered his weapon. "I'm sorry, I didn't see you return."

"Return? I…I haven't been gone," she said, barely recognizing the languid tone of her own voice. The taste of wine, something she hadn't drunk in a decade, lingered on her tongue. Had she been drugged? Poisoned? But how, when her Vampire nature should make her resistant to all those things? Alcohol, chemicals—had no effect on her blood now. But a gauzy curtain draped her in a delicate haze, as if she slumbered still in a daytime torpor. "What of the prisoner?"

"Prisoner?"

"The cell is empty. Where is she? Did someone come for her?"

The guard's color turned to ash. "I don't—no one has left after you."

She grasped him by the throat and pinned him to the wall, her incisors lengthening with fury. "I told you, I haven't left. What are you talking about?"

And he'd told her, but she couldn't make sense of it. She'd still been trying to piece together the fragments of memory when two of the mistress's private guards had come for her and dragged her to the throne room.

Francesca's voice cut through her reverie. "What do you remember, my sweet?"

Daniela flinched. The mistress's voice, soft, almost gentle, sliced through her like a blade, and she dared not raise her eyes. "I remember being hungry. So hungry."

"Of course you were. And I gave you permission to feed from the prisoner, didn't I."

"Yes, yes," Daniela said eagerly. "I took the Were to a recovery room, just as you said, and…and I went to the dungeon—I went to the prisoner's cell." And then, then she'd been so hungry and the Fae's blood was so sweet, like warm honey on her tongue.

"And then?" Francesca's voice whipped the air like a lash. "What happened?"

"I don't know, Mistress—*Regent*. I don't know."

Francesca glanced at her spymaster. "Charles? What is your opinion?"

Charles, an ascetically handsome blond with pale blue eyes, was a century or two younger than Michel, although he kept to the old ways and still dressed in the high style of court. He might have appeared delicate with his slender build and ruffled shirts, skintight trousers, and thigh-high shiny black boots, but he radiated masculine arrogance and sexual superiority. He also had an extensive network of spies and informants in the Praetern and human communities and was astute at both politics and strategy. Francesca relied on Michel as her primary advisor, but Michel was absent, as she had been more and more of late, and Charles was a natural successor, if circumstances warranted. His large and tireless cock wasn't altogether unimportant, either, even though she preferred Michel in her bed. Of late, though, even when Michel fed with her and later fucked her, she seemed partly absent. Francesca wasn't used to sharing, and she always kept those with power close. "Charles?"

"The facts, Mistress," he said in his cool, cultured voice that still held a hint of old Britain, "are that the Fae prisoner is gone, presumably having escaped while Daniela was feeding. Therefore, my conclusion is Daniela was enchanted."

"And the guard who swears the prisoner did not pass? He had no reason to lie, and we gave him every reason to tell the truth." She frowned. "I do hope he recovers soon."

"I wager he was also enchanted—perhaps with a forgetting spell. He did seem confused as to when he first saw Daniela appear." His expression grew disdainful. "Of course, he is human and more susceptible to influence."

"Very probably." Francesca's eyes flared scarlet and she stabbed a claret-tipped finger toward Daniela. "But what of her—how could the prisoner influence a Risen—even a young one? The prisoner was chained in iron. I thought that would prevent her from using her powers."

Charles shrugged and waved one hand indolently in the air. "Our knowledge of the Fae is centuries old. We have all evolved, and perhaps their magic is not as we once knew it. The iron should have been enough to suppress her magic, but if the Fae was strong enough, and…"

He paused as if reluctant to finish.

"Go on," Francesca snapped with such force every Vampire in attendance flinched.

Charles, however, appeared unperturbed. "It's possible if Daniela was deep in bloodlust, her shields would be lowered enough that the Fae's magic, *if* strong enough," he added almost apologetically, "could affect her."

He somehow managed to sound regretful while placing the blame for events completely on one of the Vampires closest to Francesca.

"So Daniela's carelessness set the prisoner free."

Daniela's head came up, her eyes wide with fear. "No, no, Regent, I would not—I would never—"

Francesca gazed down at her with a tender expression. "But you don't remember, do you, darling?"

"No," Daniela moaned, tears overflowing her lashes.

"You admitted you were hungry—and you fed from her."

"Yes, yes—with permission—"

"Of course I gave you permission—I trusted you, my pet. I gave you my prisoner as a reward."

Dread curled in Daniela's breast. She had failed the mistress's test.

"And you lost control, didn't you?" Francesca stepped down from the throne and walked slowly around Daniela, trailing her fingers over Daniela's naked body. "You lost yourself in bloodlust. And while you fed like a newling, with nothing on your mind except satisfying your own needs, you allowed the prisoner to escape."

Daniela cast imploring eyes toward Charles, who gazed back as if she were invisible.

"I understand how that might've happened," Francesca went on, her tone still reasonable. She placed one finger beneath Daniela's chin and raised her head. Flame leapt in her eyes. "How you could have forgotten all about me when—"

"No, Mistress!" Daniela sobbed. "Never, I would never—"

"But, darling," Francesca went on as if Daniela had not spoken, "you must understand, your transgression has had serious consequences. I think…I think you'll need some time to reflect on your error."

"I'm sorry, Regent." Trapped like a small animal in a cage, Daniela couldn't look away from Francesca's hypnotic power. Of course she must be punished. Anything, as long as she wasn't cast out from the heat of the mistress's gaze. "I will atone."

"I know." Francesca motioned to two of the guards standing attendance against the velvet-curtained wall. "Escort Daniela to her room."

Daniela sighed. She'd feared her punishment would be imprisonment, starvation.

"Until I decide otherwise, you will feed only from the blood slaves I provide, and you will be available for the entertainment of my guests whenever they desire." Francesca gazed at Daniela. "You will be sure to treat anyone I send you graciously, won't you, my sweet?"

"Yes," Daniela whispered. A sex slave, available to any Vampire or Were who wanted satisfaction, in any manner. The Risen, once they'd fed, would be potent, their sexual needs as ravenous as their hunger for blood. They would know she was disgraced, and they would take what they wanted however they wanted. She was being cast out from her mistress's inner circle and relegated to a level lower than a blood slave. She bowed her head. "Thank you, Regent."

Francesca flicked a hand and the guards lifted Daniela and half carried, half dragged her from the room. When the door closed behind them, she returned to the dais and dropped impatiently onto her throne. "Well, Charles? Your counsel?"

"We cannot let this affront go unanswered, Regent," he said immediately. "The loss of a prisoner from within your very lair suggests weakness to your enemies. The prisoner must be recovered and punished."

"I've dispatched a squadron of soldiers already."

He nodded and said nothing.

"What?" Francesca hissed impatiently.

"That may not be enough, especially since they cannot move in daylight."

"You have an alternative?"

"When I was advised of the…situation, I called upon a mercenary who might be useful," Charles said.

"Did you," Francesca said, wondering how long Charles had been aware of the escape, and who had told him. His sources obviously extended to within her very walls. Keeping him close was a very good idea. "Bring in your mercenary, then."

Silently, he nodded, and a moment later a door opened on the far end of the room and the Vampire guard he had summoned escorted a tall, muscular female with leonine features and tawny shoulder-length hair into the room. She wore skintight tan suede pants and a sleeveless shirt open between her full breasts. She exuded animal strength and sensuality. Her angled green eyes took in the room in one rapid sweep, passed over Charles, and fixed on Francesca. Her full lips curved into an arrogant smile as she stopped midway up the deep red carpet leading to the throne.

Francesca drew a breath as pheromones, wild and lush, drifted on the air. A wave of lust coursed through her, along with a spike of anticipation. She always did love feeding from Weres—their rich blood filled her sex more vigorously than any other host's, leaving her potent for hours. And she was more than potent now and still hungry.

"Regent," Charles said formally, "may I present Dru. She is an experienced tracker and an excellent hunter."

The cat Were tipped her head. "Regent. I am honored."

"We don't often see cat Weres here in the city," Francesca said. "What brings you to us?"

Dru's full upper lip curled briefly into a derisive snarl. "I have no desire to follow the bitch Alpha who seeks to unify the Prides. I am no one's bitch."

"Not even mine?" Francesca murmured.

Dru's shoulders tensed and the angular slope of her features sharpened. Her canines gleamed. "If I serve, I serve willingly."

Francesca laughed, pleased with her audacity. She grew tired sometimes of the servility of so many of her hosts. "Then I shall remember to ask before I take."

The female grinned.

"But first," Francesca said, "I have need of your services."

"I have told Charles I have no love for the wolf Weres, nor Raina. My services...all my service...are yours."

"Good." Francesca descended the throne and slipped her hand around Dru's muscular forearm. "Come with me and let me tell you what I need."

❖

Callan dropped from the top of the Compound stockade and landed in front of Misha's party. He wasn't as muscular as some of the males, but his growl was deep and powerful. Dark hair framed his long, lean face, blending in with his black T-shirt and pants, so he appeared as part of the night as he stalked around Torren, who stood still, facing forward, her posture neither aggressive nor subservient. Somehow, despite the heavy clouds overhead, she seemed surrounded by light. Misha blinked, trying to clear her vision.

"Who is this?" Callan blocked their path to the gate with his legs spread wide and his hands jammed on his hips.

Misha snapped to attention. "A prisoner, Captain. She was crossing Pack land in Were form—"

Callan stepped closer to Torren and sniffed. "She is not Were."

"I know." Sweat trickled down Misha's throat and she resisted the urge to whine and back away. It hadn't been that long ago that Callan routinely clamped his jaws on her throat and demanded she acknowledge his dominance in *sentrie* training. "But she was running in pelt. And she smelled like Were, until we got close."

Callan regarded her steadily, then looked to Gray. "And you, *Sentrie*. What say you?"

"We ran her down, and she was in pelt and looked like a Were." Gray sneered. "She isn't. She's not strong enough."

Torren smiled.

"Keep her here until I advise the Alpha," Callan said to Gray. "I'll send a squad to assist."

"I'll guard her," Misha said quickly.

Callan fixed her with a hard stare and she ducked her head. "Sir."

"You'll come with me to make a report."

"Yes, sir." Misha's wolf howled in protest and pain lanced through her middle. Overhead a hawk, hunting at night when no hawk should be hunting, gave a fierce, strong cry. Misha swallowed, and the clawing pain eased.

Gray pointed her rifle at Torren. "I have her."

Misha grumbled but jumped up onto the barricades after Callan. She followed him to a nearby Rover, and they drove beyond the encampment and into the forest, following the narrow trail to the Alpha's den.

"What do you think about her?" Callan asked.

Misha's skin tingled as if a host of butterflies passed all around her, beating their delicate wings against her bare flesh. Whatever Torren was, she was powerful. And power in anyone other than a wolf equaled danger. Misha answered as she had been trained, like the wolf she was. "I don't know who she is or why she's here, but I don't think we should trust her."

CHAPTER EIGHT

Drake's wolf dove off the moonlit trail into the dark underbrush and pressed her belly against the cool, pine needle–covered ground. The moment she and Sylvan reached the den, they'd wordlessly shifted, pulled by the call of the moon and their need for freedom, by their mutual need to run free of the pain of loss and threat of danger. To run until all that existed was their bond. They'd ordered the *centuri* to stand down, and they ran alone. Sylvan wasn't far behind her, had been shadowing her for miles, keeping pace, taunting her with her presence but never making a move. Waiting for Drake to show herself, to invite the final chase.

Drake's wolf understood this game. Sylvan fought every day to keep her natural instincts in check—she struggled to keep her Pack safe in a greater world that feared and reviled them. And in order to keep her Pack whole and healthy, she had to suppress her primal urge to hunt down and kill those who threatened her wolves. But out here, in the wild that sustained her, she did not have to chain her wolf. She could hunt, and chase, and conquer. She could take what was hers. But not without a challenge. Wolves liked games. And surprises. And Drake was good at playing.

Slightly smaller than Sylvan, she was ever so slightly more agile, and her speed was nearly a match for Sylvan's. And she knew how to use the shadows. She'd kept Sylvan at bay until they were deep in the heart of the forest, flitting in and out between islands of brilliant silver and deepest midnight, ghosting along ridges on twisting deer trails and bounding over streams, letting the icy mist rising from the water obscure her scent. She wouldn't lose her, Sylvan's senses were too sharp and she was too deadly a hunter, but she could make her work, make her blood race and her heart pound. Make her wolf long for the capture.

Drake panted softly, her tongue lolling, her ears perked. Listening for the telltale rustle of leaves shifting in the wind that let her know Sylvan's power rose to meet the moon.

The jaws that closed on her neck were strong, but gentle. The weight of Sylvan on her back unanticipated, but familiar. She'd expected Sylvan to take her while she ran, striking as Sylvan so often did like a bullet streaking out of the dark, pulling Drake down under her, pinning her with her greater weight, her lethal jaws clamped around her throat. The ultimate dominance.

This surprisingly tender claiming was just as exciting for its gentleness. Drake relaxed under the weight of Sylvan on her back, and her wolf, wary and interested, withdrew as she shifted from pelt. Sylvan shifted with her and loosely clasped her wrists, welcome manacles reminding her of where she belonged. Sylvan's skin was hot, slick with want.

"You didn't wait for the chase." Drake turned her head and kissed Sylvan's jaw.

"I missed you."

Drake laughed. "Afraid you couldn't catch me?"

Sylvan bit her shoulder. "Careful."

"Or else?"

"Or I might make *you* chase me."

"I would…but…" Desire swelled in Drake's belly, hard and fierce. She pressed her butt firmly into the arch of Sylvan's hips. Sylvan's swift intake of breath made her stomach tighten. "I like it when you chase me, and I like it even more when you catch me."

Rumbling softly, Sylvan kissed the mate bite on the curve of Drake's shoulder, and Drake moaned. They hadn't tangled all evening, and she'd been ready since before Sylvan left her alone to run and hunt. Too many others laid claim to what was hers. She gripped the rich untrampled earth in her fists, drew in the cool mountain air, and let her wolf rise—let her own power wrap around her mate. Sylvan growled and thrust against her ass.

"I expected you to come at me hard and fast tonight," Drake said.

Sylvan pushed up on one arm, grasped Drake's shoulder, and rolled Drake beneath her. Moonlight shone in her eyes, and they were still pure wolf. "Disappointed?"

"Never." Drake scissored her legs around Sylvan's hips and tugged her down, trapping her between her thighs, belly to belly, breast to breast. Sylvan was full and firm, as she knew she would be, as *she* was, distended with the essence of their unique joining.

Sylvan shuddered, her skin gleaming with a sheen of sex and power. She thrust slowly, possessively, sliding her clitoris over Drake's, readying her when she was already so close she wanted to give everything.

"I don't have the control to play," Drake warned.

Sylvan's smile was arrogant and all animal. She nipped Drake's lip, her canines lightly scoring the inner surface. "You don't have a choice."

She didn't, not because she was submissive or because she feared Sylvan's strength. She couldn't deny what she needed, and that was always and ever Sylvan. And she knew how to get what she wanted. Drake raked her claws down Sylvan's back, calling Sylvan's wolf with the aggressive move. The bones in Sylvan's face angled, her canines gleamed longer, and a growl reverberated in her chest.

"Be careful."

"Why should I be?" Drake pressed her canines to the mark on Sylvan's chest, igniting their bond and the fury that joined them. Sylvan's back arched and she pushed deeper between Drake's legs, notching her clitoris beneath Drake's. In a frenzy to join, Drake dragged her claws back up the length of Sylvan's back and locked her legs around Sylvan's. Her breasts and nipples tightened, her belly tensed. "Now, Sylvan."

"Mine."

Sylvan, at last, took her hard, driving into her with powerful thrusts of her hips, forcing Drake to explode over them both. Drake gave herself to the wolf in Sylvan's eyes, releasing in a pulsing rush of pleasure as Sylvan claimed her and was claimed.

"Mine," Sylvan growled again, wild for her mate, for the solace and blinding pleasure of joining, emptied hard and fast. Her hips pistoned until her breath gave way and her muscles trembled and she collapsed with her face buried in Drake's neck. The claws on her back soothed her now, gentling her beast, welcoming her to sanctuary.

"I love you," Drake whispered, stroking her hair.

Sylvan shivered, as weak as she had ever been and stronger than she could have believed. "You take everything. And give me more."

Drake twisted Sylvan's hair in her fist and pulled her head up to kiss her. Sylvan tasted wild, untamable, and hers. "You are my heart. I will give you everything until the end of time."

"If I asked, would you take the young and leave?"

"Never. Where you are, we will be." Drake kissed her again. "Ask as many times as you must, and the answer will always be the same."

Sylvan rested her forehead on Drake's. "Sometimes…"

"You won't lose us. I swear it."

Sighing, Sylvan finally relaxed and Drake tightened her hold. This was what Drake lived for—to drive Sylvan until she gave up control for these few seconds, to shield her, to protect her. For their joining to strengthen them both.

Sylvan stiffened, pushed up on her arms, scented the air. "Company."

Drake, her powers growing daily, sensed them then. "Callan and Misha."

Sylvan rose in one fluid movement and pulled Drake up with her. "Yes, and something's wrong."

❖

An hour later, Misha dropped from the barricade and landed lightly in front of the small group of *sentries* and soldiers congregated in front of the gates. Torren, still naked, stood in the center of the ring of armed Weres, and despite the cloudy sky and the intermittent flickers of moonlight that slashed the shadows and then disappeared, her skin seemed bathed in silvery light. Misha stilled as Torren's gaze slid over her like river water over slick stones, cool and fresh. With effort, Misha pulled free of the hypnotic sensation and strode to Beryl, the lieutenant Callan had placed in charge.

"The Alpha wishes to see the prisoner."

From above, Callan's deep voice called down, "Open the gates."

Misha kept her rifle on her shoulder and stepped next to Torren, aware that every other wolf held their weapons trained on Torren, even though she was without weapons and gave no indication of challenge. Torren was a stranger, and not even a wolf. Not even a Were. And she was about to be escorted into their sanctuary, where their pregnant females and young lived safe because no one encroached on their territory and lived. Not one Were would hesitate to kill Torren if she showed the slightest sign of a threat.

"Stay close," Misha murmured, gripping the back of Torren's neck and leading her through the gates into the Compound. Two Rovers idled just inside. Callan stood by the first one and motioned them toward it. Another squadron of soldiers milled around the second.

"I told you I would not resist," Torren said.

"I have no reason to believe you, and they even less."

"You know little of the world," Torren said, "so how do you know where to place your trust?"

Misha's wolf snapped in protest. "And you know nothing of me."

"You're wrong. I know you are strong and brave and loyal."

"And I know you are not what you seem." Misha spoke without real heat, realizing Torren sounded more curious than accusing. As they approached the first Rover, she said, "You can't know that."

"No?" Torren smiled. "I know your wolf loves sunshine and running through wildflowers. I know you like to chase, and not only to kill. That when you catch, you like to bite and ride your prey—"

Misha dug her claws into Torren's neck. Her canines punched down and her pelt bristled beneath her skin. Whatever Torren was doing made her sex pound, and she would not be played with—not by this female who shimmered with power she did not recognize. "I am not yours to call."

Beryl spoke from behind. "What is it?"

"Nothing," Misha said quickly, pushing Torren toward the Rover.

Gray stepped past them and yanked open the rear door. She motioned with her rifle to Torren. "Get in."

Torren climbed in and Misha followed. Gray sat opposite on the long, low bench, her rifle angled across her knees with the muzzle pointed at Torren's chest, her fingers hovering above the trigger. A gunshot probably wouldn't kill a Vampire and, unless it was a silver slug, probably wouldn't kill a Were, either. If Torren was human, a bullet at this range would surely be lethal. But she couldn't be human. Whatever she was, she had too much power to be human. Still, maybe she could be killed.

Misha struggled against the urge to put herself between Torren and Gray's rifle. Gray was spoiling for a fight, and Misha was ready to give her one, but not in the confines of the Rover when everyone was armed. Before the night was out, she would teach Gray her place. She'd given her enough time and enough room to find herself.

They bumped along over the narrow trail back to the Alpha's den and pulled up at the edge of the sparse clearing. A fire burned in the fire pit in front of the cabin, and the Alpha stood on the porch illuminated in flickering flames. She was shirtless in tight black combat pants, her arms folded across her chest, her gold hair glinting in the moonlight. The door behind her opened and closed, and the Prima came out dressed all in black. She stood to Sylvan's left, her expression alert but calm. The Alpha was the power that held them altogether, but the Prima gave them the safety to rest. The Pack needed them both to be whole. Being in their presence settled Misha's wolf.

The Rover stopped and the back door opened. Callan motioned them out. He pressed his rifle to the middle of Torren's back. "Walk forward."

Torren did as he asked and stopped where he indicated she should at the foot of the stairs leading up to the Alpha's den. Misha stood just to her right and the other Were *sentries* and soldiers fell in behind them in a loose semicircle.

"You are far from home," Sylvan said, taking in the prisoner. She'd scented her before they'd brought her through the gates. Not Vampire, not Were. Fae. She'd smelled something similar enough times at the Coalition meetings with Cecilia Thornton and her high-ranking emissaries to recognize the honeysuckle and spice scent that played across the surface of her consciousness like birds' wings riding on air currents, effortless and graceful.

Torren took a knee and bowed, a graceful and respectful greeting that did not diminish her. She slowly straightened. "Thank you for allowing me to interrupt your evening, Alpha Mir."

"And who might you be, Fae?"

"I am Torren de Brinna, of the royal court of Cecilia, Queen of Thorns."

"As I said, you are far from home."

"I'm afraid I am farther than you think."

Sylvan recognized the beginning of a negotiation cloaked in typical Fae innuendo and insinuation. "Callan, Misha, remain. The rest of you may go."

Gray rumbled unhappily, and Sylvan slowly turned her head, locking eyes until Gray flinched, ducked her head, and backed away with the others.

Callan looked over his shoulder at Beryl. "Take the Rovers and wait for me with the others at the first clearing."

Beryl saluted, and the Weres piled into the Rovers and pulled away.

Sylvan made no move to invite the Fae into her den. She brought no one into her inner sanctum except those she most trusted. She'd only brought the prisoner this far because the area was secluded and virtually impossible to find from outside the Compound perimeter. She would rather the Fae see an unadorned cabin in the woods than any more of the Compound itself than was necessary. If she determined the prisoner would not be executed, she would need to decide just how much she would disclose. Cecilia had made it very clear the Fae did not favor the Exodus and was reluctant to expose Faerie to humans *or* Praeterns. The Fae might not be enemies, but neither were they friends.

"Why are you here?" Sylvan asked.

"I seek sanctuary until I can return to Faerie," Torren said.

"Why do you need sanctuary?"

"I have this night escaped from the dungeons of Francesca, Viceregal of the Eastern Vampire seethe. She hunts me."

Sylvan stared at the slender, otherworldly beautiful female whose arrogance, even naked and surrounded by Weres, was only slightly tempered by her courtly manners. She read only truth in the blue eyes that returned her gaze—unchallenging but intimidated. "Holding a royal Fae prisoner is bold, even for Francesca. Is your queen aware you were imprisoned?"

Misha rumbled, unable to control the quick burst of fury from her wolf.

"Yes, Alpha," Torren said easily. "I owed the Viceregal a debt for encroaching uninvited in her territory and executing a Vampire under her protection."

"Why?"

Torren smiled. "I'm afraid I cannot say."

"You come to me and ask for sanctuary," Sylvan growled, "and yet you will not tell me of your crimes. I have no reason to involve my Pack in Vampire and Fae business. What is to prevent me from returning you to Francesca and putting her in my debt?"

"A safe and wise move," Torren said. "But I believe Cecilia, Queen of Thorns, would owe you a favor if you aided me in escaping capture and, in all likelihood, execution as punishment for my escape."

"And what need have I of a favor from the Faerie Queen?"

"For centuries, the Gates have been closed to all beyond the Realm, and the Fae have kept apart from the affairs of Vampires and Weres. Now the Exodus has opened wide the Gates. The Queen of Thorns values strong allies."

"Francesca and I already have a truce. If I harbor you, I will endanger that truce. In the morning, we will return you to her." Sylvan turned and draped an arm around Drake's neck. "Let's go to bed."

Torren had only one thing left with which to bargain. When Cecilia had ordered her to track the Crown Princess into the human realm, she had offered Torren certain protections to ensure the mission's success. Torren said quietly, "Have you ever heard of the Shadow Lords?"

Slowly, Sylvan turned, her wolf pushing to the surface. She leapt down the stairs and grasped Torren's throat. "I do not play Fae games. Speak plainly or I will execute you myself, here and now."

Sylvan's power cloaked Torren in moonlight, vast and impenetrable. But Sylvan's power was of the living, of the natural world, unlike the Vampires, whose power rose from the night and the dead. Torren opened herself to the moonlight, to the windsong, to the earth below her, and her magic flirted with Sylvan's power until her mind and Sylvan's slid past one another on the wind. She called up the image of a meeting under a bridge beside the Hudson where she'd watched from a boat with the other Fae royal guards.

Sylvan loosened her hold but kept Torren in her grip as murky images slowly swam into focus. Francesca with Bernardo, the rogue Were whose Pack had tried to kill her, and a human male—silver haired and superior, despite his human frailty. Others she could not quite see clearly. All of them meeting in secret. She opened her eyes, met Torren's, and released her. "You are more than a royal guard."

"I'm a tracker, of the House of Edric."

"Not just any tracker, then," Sylvan murmured. "You are Cecilia's Master of the Hunt."

Torren nodded.

"All the more reason for me to distrust you." Sylvan's canines gleamed. "Misha, Callan, take her to the barracks. Treat her as a guest, but put a guard on her room. If she attempts to escape, bind her in iron and bring her to me to kill."

CHAPTER NINE

Drake stood on the porch with Sylvan as the forest swallowed the red glow of the Rovers' taillights. Clouds moved in overhead, blurring the sharp edges of the gibbous moon, cloaking its brilliance with a murky haze. The clearing in front of the den descended into darkness for long moments at a time until a splinter of silvery light escaped the blanketed sky and arrowed down from above, only to be extinguished between one heartbeat and the next.

The dark was no deterrent to those who lived by night. Here and there bright eyes glinted in the underbrush—foxes and opossums and skunks, stealthily hunting for food. The soft rustle of owls' wings as they swooped down to capture mice was a whisper in the trees. Somewhere in the forest, *centuri* kept watch. Even inside the Compound, the Alpha pair was not without protection. Sylvan would have dismissed the guards, but to do so would have only created anxiety among the Pack. Drake had gotten used to the constant presence of others, even in her most intimate moments with her mate. Only when they hunted, when they outran everyone and everything, were they ever alone. The memory of where they had been only hours before, alone in the heart of their land—of how they had been together, free and completely joined—pierced her with a sense of longing she rarely acknowledged. As quickly as the melancholy rose, she pushed it away. She had chosen Sylvan, and with Sylvan came this life and all its demands.

"Are you sad?" Sylvan asked, her eyes as bright and sharp as those of the predators stalking the forest.

"No," Drake said quickly. And because Sylvan could read her moods, and her mind, with greater clarity every day, she added, "Never sad, and no regrets. But you're not the only one who worries." She brushed her fingers through Sylvan's mane, grown fierce and wild like her in the last few weeks. "I worry for you."

Sylvan leaned her bare back against the rough-hewn porch post and drew Drake against her, face-to-face. She held her loosely around the waist, her hands sliding under Drake's shirt for the contact all mated pairs needed, even more so in times of danger. "Do not worry for me. I have you, and now the young, and that gives me all the strength I need."

Drake knew better but didn't argue. Sylvan couldn't change who she was, nor would Drake want her to, but she still bore the scars where the bullets had entered her chest and belly, filling her with silver and nearly killing her. When Sylvan's wolf emerged, small dark patches marred the silver of her pelt, marking the wounds—badges of courage and a constant reminder that Sylvan, for all her strength and power, was not indestructible. Drake lightly kissed the mate bite on Sylvan's chest, and Sylvan rumbled, both a warning and an invitation. Just as quickly, Drake readied for her. Sylvan's call was impossible to withstand, for any wolf near enough to feel it. And perhaps, thinking of what she'd witnessed when Sylvan subdued the Fae, not just wolves. The Fae had done something to...*with*...Sylvan that was as potent as a touch. And no one touched her mate. Snarling softly, Drake leaned back in Sylvan's arms. "I almost challenged the Fae when she spread her magic over you. She is either very strong or very foolish to try that, especially in front of me."

"She is strong and far from foolish." Sylvan pulled Drake's T-shirt off and gripped Drake's ass, yanking her closer until their thighs met. Silver pelt, her wolf's call to join, slashed down the trench in the center of Sylvan's abdomen and disappeared under the waistband of her low-slung pants. "But no challenge to you. Your wolf can rest easy."

"My wolf guards what is hers." Drake slid her mouth down Sylvan's throat, grazing her with the sharp points of her canines, and Sylvan's rumble became a growl. Heat radiated from Sylvan's bare torso and pheromones glistened on her breasts and belly. Satisfied, Drake relaxed against her. "What did you see out there, in the clearing with the Fae?"

"Did you feel her magic?"

"Not feel it, exactly. I almost thought I could see it." Drake recalled the way the air glowed around Torren and Sylvan, as if the floating particles had come to life.

"You might have seen some of it—you are strong enough. She can project her magic and with someone weaker, enchant them. Her illusions would feel real in the body and the mind."

Drake snarled again. "Did she try to touch you?"

"Of course—she is not just Fae, she is the Master of the Hunt, one of the oldest and most powerful of the Fae royals. She tested me, as I would test her if I found myself a prisoner in her realm." Sylvan smiled. "But she cannot enchant my wolf—my wolf belongs to you."

"What about the rest of our wolves? Are even the mated wolves safe from enchantment?"

Sylvan sighed. "I don't know if any of them are safe. The mate bond prevents other wolves from approaching and trying to tangle. If the bond didn't exist—a kind of natural invisible barrier—our territorial instincts would force us to constantly challenge and fight. But Cecilia's hunt master has spent centuries enchanting weaker prey—human and Praetern. Centuries ago when the Were-Vampire wars raged across Europe, the Wild Hunt enchanted many Weres into Faerie, where the Fae bred with them to strengthen their lines."

"Was that Torren's doing, then, too?"

"The Fae are extremely long-lived." Sylvan shrugged.

"And now she's here, when another war is under way."

"The Fae are clever and wise. Torren might have been sent to gather intelligence, but she is capable of gathering much more than that."

"She needs to be watched," Drake said.

"She will be."

"What did she do to you?"

"She showed me a gathering." Sylvan described the murky images. "I couldn't tell when, but the meeting seemed to be under cover of darkness, and Bernardo was there." Sylvan's features grew sharp and angular. "And Francesca and Nicholas Gregory."

Ice filled Drake's chest. Not fear, but hard, lethal anger. They knew but could not prove Gregory was behind the recent attack. "Can you trust this vision?"

Sylvan swept her hand up Drake's back, spreading warmth wherever she touched. "I don't trust anything about the Fae. Until the Exodus, we had not dealt with them for centuries. They couch their truths in fable and riddles. Ancient lore says they do not lie—cannot lie—but I'm not sure I believe that. We've all changed."

"And this Torren," Drake said, "if she is who she says she is, what is she doing here?"

"Another question she managed to avoid answering while appearing to answer." Sylvan laughed shortly. "There are very few reasons why Cecilia would have allowed someone with Torren's status and power to leave Faerie for any length of time, so I can only guess some kind of emergency brought her here."

Drake stared into the forest, wishing she could see all the way to the Compound. Having someone with Torren's power inside their sanctuary had her wolf pacing anxiously. "If Torren is so important, why would Cecilia leave her in Francesca's prison?"

"You're asking me to think like a Fae," Sylvan said lightly. "An impossible task. However, I doubt Cecilia wanted Torren's true identity revealed, especially to Francesca. Plus time does not mean to the Fae what it means to other Praeterns, even to the Vampires. A hundred years, five hundred years, is nothing. And they love games—so who knows what Cecilia may have wanted Torren to do."

"Maybe Torren was sent to spy on Francesca."

Sylvan thought of the image of the gathering—the Shadow Lords, Torren called them. Cecilia or Torren must have been there, and if there was some secret plot being planned, Cecilia would have spies everywhere. "That might not have been Torren's original mission, but once she was captured…things could have changed."

Drake growled and the clouds fractured over the moon for an instant. Her canines gleamed as her wolf peered out. "So some of the most powerful Praeterns—and at least two members of the Coalition—are meeting in secret with a Were who wants you dead and the human we know conspires to destroy us."

"Cecilia, Francesca, Bernardo, and Nicholas Gregory," Sylvan murmured. "All opposed to the Exodus."

Fury, hot as flame, melted the ice in Drake's chest as her wolf raged. "How much longer can we wait to retaliate? How many more times will they try to kill you?"

"We don't know—"

"Yes," Drake said, refusing to be soothed when her mate was in danger, "we do. All of them are our enemies."

"Perhaps, probably," Sylvan said. "But Torren showed me the vision, and she would not have done that without Cecilia's permission. So maybe not all are our enemies."

"And Francesca? What of her?"

"Francesca's allegiances shift with the wind. She's a Vampire, and her only loyalty is to herself and her only goal to preserve her power."

"Then she is no ally of ours."

"Since we put down the rogues, Bernardo has gone into hiding. But he is a Were, and I can find him. He will tell me what I want to know." Sylvan clasped the back of Drake's neck and squeezed gently. "We are not yet ready to wage war."

"I am."

Sylvan kissed her. "Where is my mate with her voice of reason?"

Drake gripped Sylvan's bare shoulders, letting her claws extend enough to pierce her skin. "They threaten my mate."

"Yes," Sylvan murmured, "but they failed. And we will not."

❖

The gates swung open and the Rovers pulled back into the Compound. *Sentries* milled around the fire pits, eating and drinking coffee, their long shadows dancing over the red-brown earth like wraiths. Some turned, their wolves' eyes glinting in interest and suspicion as the Rovers drew up to the front of the barracks. Callan jumped down and opened the rear doors. "Misha, Beryl, take the prisoner inside. Secure her and wait for the guards to arrive. Then you are dismissed."

Misha climbed out and hurried to Callan, who started for the command post at the main entrance. "Permission to take the first watch, Captain."

Callan paused, his expression wary. "You've been on perimeter watch for five days and just ran down an intruder. You're due for relief."

"Yes, sir, but I'm fine, sir," Misha said, unable to explain the anger that escalated every time one of the other Weres took charge of Torren or the constant pressure in her head, as if someone was whispering words she couldn't make out clearly. All she knew was the clawing discomfort lessened when Torren was in sight. She took a breath. "I think the prisoner might talk to me, maybe tell me why she's here."

Callan folded his arms and stared. "Why?"

Misha shrugged. She didn't really know why. "Maybe because I was the one who subdued her. I didn't kill her, so she might trust me a little more than anyone else."

"And you think if you befriend her, she'll reveal why she's here?"

"It's worth a try." Misha tried to sound casual, but her heart was pounding so loudly she knew Callan could hear it.

"Maybe you're right," Callan said. "You take the first watch with Karl. I'll send him over in a minute."

"Yes, sir." Misha bounded to the barracks where Beryl had taken Torren. Gray leaned against the wall by the door, her rifle resting in one hand.

"Want to get something to eat?" Gray asked.

"I'm on watch," Misha said. "You go ahead."

"What happened with the Alpha?" Gray asked.

"Nothing," Misha said, although she wasn't really sure what had happened. The Alpha and Torren seemed ready to fight and then something...something had happened when the Alpha and Torren clashed, but her memory was foggy, like she'd seen it all in a dream. "I think the Alpha is waiting to see why Torren is here."

"She shouldn't be," Gray growled.

"You don't know anything about her," Misha said.

"Neither do you."

Yes, I do. But she couldn't explain exactly *what* she knew, or why she cared what happened to the Fae, so she didn't try. "I know how to follow orders. You should try it sometime."

"Yeah, right." Gray laughed, a harsh sound filled with anger, and vaulted over the rail. A second later the night took her.

Misha hurried down the long hall that ran the length of the barracks. Plain doors opened along each side. Soldiers returning from missions and adolescents in *sentrie* training used the rooms when off duty. Beryl, his rifle at arms, stood in front of a closed door at the far end of the building. Misha stopped short of pushing through the door into Torren's makeshift cell, even though her wolf clamored for her to find Torren. She nodded to Beryl. "Everything clear?"

"Not a word out of the prisoner," Beryl said. "She went in calm as you please."

"When Karl arrives, you're relieved." Misha knew she sounded sharp, but she didn't care. Torren wasn't a prisoner. They weren't like Francesca, putting her in a cell.

Beryl's brow rose but he shrugged. "Sure."

Misha finally gave in to the pressure to check on Torren and entered the room. The space was spartan, with a single bed, a straight-backed chair, a small chest, and plain hooks on the wall for clothes and gear. A square window high in the right corner was just large enough for a wolf in pelt to enter and leave. Misha had spent many nights in this room or one just like it and never felt confined, but looking at it now, imagining how Torren must feel, she wondered if "cell" wasn't the right word for it.

Torren stood below the window, her back to the room. Someone had given her clothes, but she looked nothing like a Were even in the same plain shirt and jeans they all wore around the Compound. The way she stood, the way her hair waved along her collar, the way her perfectly proportioned profile was highlighted in the faint yellow glow from the wall sconce spoke of elegance born, not bred. Torren spoke without turning. "Is there any way you can open that?"

"Yes, but if you go out through the window, the *sentries* on the far perimeter wall will see you and shoot you."

Torren glanced over her shoulder. "I won't."

"Even if you look like a wolf again, you won't smell like one."

"I thought I did."

Misha growled. "At a far distance, maybe."

"I'm not going through the window," Torren said.

Wordlessly, Misha pushed it open. She had no reason to trust her, but she couldn't stand to think of her locked away from the night. Torren would hate that as much as a wolf. Misha didn't know how she knew that, but she did. And she'd spoken the truth—if Torren tried to escape, the sharpshooters on the barricades would fire.

"Don't run."

"I won't. Not tonight." Torren tilted her head back and breathed deeply, and as if she had called the moon to her, her skin glowed.

A ripple of electricity raced along Misha's skin and her pelt prickled. Her wolf went on alert, intrigued and ready to play. Misha backed up a step. "Are you hungry?"

"Nourishment would be welcome. It has been...a while."

"Didn't they feed you?" Misha snarled.

Torren faced her and smiled. "Their idea of food and mine are quite different."

Misha searched Torren's neck for signs of scars. There were none, but that didn't mean they hadn't fed from her. "Who?"

"It doesn't matter."

"It does," Misha said, although she couldn't say why.

Torren tilted her head, studied Misha quietly. "If it ever does matter, I will tell you."

"Thank—"

"No," Torren said, "you are not in my debt."

"All right. I'll get you some food."

"I don't eat meat."

Misha frowned. "Then what?"

Torren's laughter was spring-fed water rushing down the mountainside, crystal clear and pure. Misha's neck tingled as if warm fingers brushed over her. Her wolf cocked her head and gave a soft, welcoming rumble. Blood pulsed in her loins. Pelt rippled down her torso. She'd tangled plenty, like every other young wolf, and she never gave it much thought. The call came over her and she found someone to answer. This...*thing*, whatever it was that Torren did to her, wasn't like any call she'd ever known. The need sprang from somewhere deep inside her, and even though her clitoris engorged and her glands swelled just like always, she didn't feel like tangling with the first available Were. She wanted something else—something that made her wolf snarl and pace. She wanted to run, to run and chase and catch and join.

"If you have any," Torren said from far away.

"What?" Misha asked hoarsely. She blinked sweat from her eyes. "What?"

"Bread. Any vegetables you might have. Cheese?"

"I'll find something." Misha hurriedly backed up and stopped at the door. Sex frenzy clawed at her. And Torren was the cause. "Don't test us, Torren. We're not Vampires. We don't lose our minds when we feed. Or when we fuck."

Torren inclined her head. "I'll remember if you do something for me."

Misha paused, suspecting a trap. But she'd told Callan she might get Torren to talk to her. "Speak."

"When you stop being afraid, let me in."

"I am not afraid. And I will never let you in." Misha slammed the door closed, ignoring the claws raking her midsection.

CHAPTER TEN

Veronica glanced at her watch for the third time in the past hour. Three hours until dawn. Three hours until Luce would disappear until sundown, slumbering in some hidden lair, safe from the ultraviolet rays that could destroy her unprotected flesh. But before Luce went to ground, she would need to feed, and if Veronica wasn't available, Luce would feed elsewhere. Someone else would feel the delicious slide of Luce's incisors into her throat, or her breast, or her groin just before the scorching heat incinerated every thought, burned through every nerve ending, and exploded into the most indescribable, exquisite pleasure imaginable. Veronica pushed back from her desk and stalked to the wide window that overlooked the black, roiling water. She'd been in the lab all day and night and hadn't seen Luce since the previous morning. And with every passing moment, her need grew.

The need to experience the euphoric transportation of body and mind when Luce's feeding hormones flooded her system was a constant demand—her stomach cramped with a gnawing hunger no food would satisfy, and her clitoris throbbed in a perpetual state of distension. No matter how many times she masturbated, the pulsing ache never abated. But even knowing she would find no satisfaction, she couldn't stop. The urgency was all consuming.

Only her work kept her even partly sane, but she was easily distracted and her concentration was brittle. The erosion of her efficiency was an annoyance when the remedy was so simple. All she needed was a few moments with Luce and she'd be back at peak performance again, stronger and mentally sharper.

She traced the outline of her breast beneath her emerald-green silk shirt, softly flicking her nipple with the edge of her nail until it was hard and tight. She could make herself orgasm, already had half a dozen times over the last few hours, but only Luce's bite gave her the kind of release she needed. Total mental and physical implosion.

Soon. She should finish the measurements she'd been taking and find Luce. Her clitoris twinged. Yes, soon.

A barge slowly moved upriver, pushing an empty oil tanker toward the dock, its lights blinking in the murky haze. Overhead, heating ducts clanged and the old building shuddered. A cold, damp draft seeped around the warped window frame. Nicholas had promised her a new laboratory after they'd had to abandon the previous one when Sylvan Mir had discovered them. This old pipe factory had been unused for decades, and Nicholas had been able to purchase it under the guise of manufacturing parts for a high-altitude surveillance system. The heavy security was explained by the sensitive nature of the product and the importance to national security. She had to admit, hiding in plain sight was infinitely preferable to spending her time driving back and forth to some isolated location in the mountains.

This wasn't what she'd had in mind, but at least she could resurrect her research. Her work. Her cause. She'd saved her data, of course, but she'd lost her specimens. Not that any of them were of all that much value. She hadn't yet been able to produce clear-cut reproducible results and had been about to abandon her protocols for a new avenue of study. She'd been trying to produce the Were mutation by injecting altered DNA into the human genome, but the results were unpredictable—or, unfortunately, too predictable. She could induce a condition in humans that closely resembled Were fever, the rare contagion that occasionally infected natural-born Weres and produced a lethal fever, but all her human subjects died without developing any sign of either immunity or adaptive Were physiology.

The fever itself was useful to an extent, especially when Nicholas cleverly suggested they deposit their failed specimens at human hospitals. They'd hoped to incite a public panic with the threat of a Were plague, perhaps creating a backlash against the Weres, but their plan was sidelined when Mir discovered their base of operations. Luckily, she and Nicholas had covered their tracks well. The Were didn't know their identity or the entire scope of their research. If Mir had known, she would have hunted them down by now. For a short time after the failed attempt on Mir's life at the governor's gala, Veronica had hidden with Luce's help. Now the danger seemed to have passed. The Were would not retaliate without proof.

Humans were not so particular. Public opinion was definitely shifting in favor of Humans First and their anti-Praetern sentiment, but Veronica wasn't interested in relying on chance to produce the outcome she desired. All her life, she'd been the one to control what was important to her, and since the day Sylvan Mir's father and representatives from the other Praetern species had gone on TV to announce their presence to the world, her sole focus had become preserving the natural order of the species. As the extent of the Praetern powers had slowly become apparent, her mission to ensure human supremacy had become even more urgent. She hadn't yet been able to replicate or manipulate the Were genome, but if she could induce errors in the mitochondrial DNA, she might be able to disrupt Were reproduction. And if they couldn't reproduce, they would eventually go the way of other inferior creatures. Extinction.

The work was progressing slowly. The Weres—in fact, all the Praeterns—kept the intricacies of their biology secret. However, once the Praeterns made their presence known, their secrets began to disappear. Exactly when in their life cycle the Weres began to shift and precisely what genetic sequence controlled their ability to transform were still unknowns, so of course, the logical solution was to study their life cycle. And where better to start than birth.

The barge passed out of view and a single blinking light cut diagonally across the wide Hudson River in the direction of her new laboratory, growing brighter as the seconds passed. Veronica's pulse skipped. The phone on her desk rang and she picked it up. "Dr. Standish."

"The delivery you've been expecting has arrived, Doctor," the Vampire security guard said in a smooth baritone.

"I'll be down shortly." Veronica smiled, the tension in her belly building. Her work had always been nearly as pleasurable as sex and often excited her in the same way. "See that the corridors are cleared and only your team has any contact with the specimens. Take the delivery directly to the holding area."

"Yes, Dr. Standish."

Veronica disconnected and dialed another extension.

"Church."

"A delivery has just arrived. See that the transport has been taken care of as we discussed." She couldn't afford to leave a trail directly to her facilities, and no matter how handsomely individuals were paid, silence was never guaranteed. Only one thing guaranteed that.

"Sure thing, Doc. Arrangements have been made."

Veronica gritted her teeth. The cat mercenaries were excellent when it came to carrying out orders no matter how difficult, dangerous, or distasteful the task, but they had no sense of respect. Their loyalty was as fickle as the wind and totally dependent upon how much they were paid, but since they never questioned her orders or even seemed to care what she asked of them, she was able to keep them in the dark as to what actually went on in the lab. She would have been happier with only Vampire security, but she needed forces that could operate in daylight. "Good."

She set the phone back in its cradle just as her office door opened. Her heart literally leapt, a sensation at once startling and exciting. Luce glided in, closed the door, and leaned back against it. Her coal-black hair blended with the collar of her black silk shirt, and her muscular body in black leather pants and boots looked like one continuous obsidian blade. She smiled, her incisors unsheathed and gleaming. "I know you're busy, but if you're as hungry as I am—"

Veronica flew across the room and grasped Luce's long cool fingers, dragging her toward the deep leather sofa against the wall. "God, yes. I didn't think I could stand it until morning. You're early."

Luce picked Veronica up and, in two powerful strides, carried her to the sofa and was upon her. With her mouth against Veronica's pounding pulse, she murmured, "I've been thinking of you since I roused at sunfall."

"You must have fed." Veronica wrapped her legs around Luce's slender hips and pushed up Luce's black silk shirt to grip her smooth, bare back. "I know you needed to."

"Food." Luce kissed the underside of Veronica's jaw and pressed her hips between Veronica's parted thighs. She slipped her fingers into Veronica's hair and kissed her mouth, sliding inside her, tasting her need, letting her feeding hormones tease over the surface of Veronica's tongue. Humans were such tantalizing prey, and so easy to ensnare.

"I can't stand it," Veronica gasped, her head thrashing. "Please. I need you inside me."

Luce didn't bother to enthrall her. Veronica didn't need to be seduced. The addiction was too powerful now. The human was physically and mentally a prisoner to pleasure. And Luce was hungry. She had fed from three humans in a row when she'd awakened in the secure chambers beneath Nocturne, enough to restore her strength and potency, but she'd wanted Veronica. Veronica's wild taste, her wanton need, was nearly as powerful as the rush of blood that coursed through Luce's body and revitalized her. She buried herself in Veronica's throat, a wave of lust tearing through her as Veronica stiffened with a cry beneath her. She could have dulled the stab of penetration with mental manipulation, but part of Veronica's pleasure was the pain before the orgasm. Luce swallowed rapidly while Veronica tore at her back and cried out again.

"Oh please," Veronica wailed. "Finish me!"

Luce forced more feeding hormones into Veronica's system, triggering the human's orgasm.

"Oh my God!" Veronica convulsed repeatedly in time to Luce's deep pulls at her neck.

Luce came with each shuddering swallow, riding the edge of bloodlust until Veronica grew limp in her arms. Finally she forced herself to stop and seal the punctures. Satisfied, she sat up and trailed her fingers over Veronica's breast. At some point while she'd been consumed in Veronica's taste, she'd opened Veronica's clothes.

Veronica moaned, her lids fluttering half-open. Her eyes, nearly the same color as her shirt, were dazed. Her mouth was slightly slack. She weakly grasped Luce's hand. "Again."

Luce laughed softly and lightly squeezed her nipple, watching aftershocks jolt through Veronica's sensuous body. "No. You've fed me enough."

"Never enough," Veronica murmured. Her hips undulated softly on the creamy caramel-colored leather. "I want you to fuck me while you feed."

"I will. Before I go."

Veronica sighed, her eyes beginning to clear. "I don't want to wait, but I must. I must go back to work."

"Something important?"

"What I've been waiting for," Veronica said, her voice low and heavy, nearly stuporous. "I have to go greet them."

"Them?" Luce said softly.

"My newest subjects."

"More humans?" Luce squeezed Veronica's nipple again and Veronica whimpered.

"Better," Veronica murmured. "Soon I'll be able to work from the source."

"Shall I wait for you?"

"Yes. Oh yes."

"I'll need you again before sunrise." Luce knew better than to push for more. Veronica was no ordinary prey, despite her blood addiction, and the mistress would not be happy if Luce overplayed her hand. Veronica was their conduit to Nicholas and his plans.

"Mmm." Veronica pushed herself up and straightened her clothes. She took several deep breaths, clearing the postorgasmic haze from her mind. She felt wonderful. Now that the need had eased, she could concentrate on her work. The need would come back, she knew, but right now, everything was exactly as it should be. She was at her full power. She kissed Luce, let her tongue slide over Luce's incisors, and smiled to herself when Luce hissed. Luce always thought she was in control, but Luce had come to her, needing her, and what was power if not creating need in others? "I won't be long."

"I'll be here."

Veronica left without a backward glance and hurried through the hall to the rear elevator. Her most important work was housed within a secret lab deep beneath the old pipe factory, in what had once been the boiler room. Every one of the key technicians and researchers who worked there had been handpicked and extensively screened. To further reduce the security risks, she made do with as few personnel as possible and fractionated the work between them so no one knew what the others were doing or what the greater project was meant to accomplish.

When the work approached a critical point, she would sequester them in on-site accommodations to prevent leaks. Right now they were at the beginning of a whole new phase, the most daring she'd ever undertaken, and one of the purest. Soon, she would have the perfect specimens.

She exited the elevator into a small bare antechamber and

unlocked the door to the research wing with retinal and palm scans. After passing through two more secure doors, she reached the holding area, which was set up like a pre-op area with curtained cubicles and monitoring equipment. The technician, a muscular human redhead in maroon scrubs, rose from a seat before a bank of monitors and met her at the door. "They just arrived."

"Do you have a set of vitals yet?"

"Yes. Both appear healthy." His pale green eyes glinted as they skimmed her body.

He probably thought he was being subtle, but his interest was pathetically obvious. Veronica smiled back, encouraging his attention. He was attractive enough, and she found sexual interest an effective tool for creating loyalty. She rarely fucked humans any longer. Without the bite, the release was so much…less. But they would do in an emergency, and she might as well make good use of him, since once the project was complete she'd need to dispose of him. "I want a full battery of bloods—chemistry, heme profile, serology, hormone levels. You know the drill."

"Under way." He grimaced. "They're both heavily sedated. I'm running a tox screen too."

Rage clouded Veronica's vision. She'd expressly instructed the wolf Were not to drug them. Not only would that interfere with her baseline tests, it might compromise their conditions. With effort, she regained her control. "Repeat the tests in twenty-four hours to make sure there's no contamination. Where are they?"

"Number three."

She passed through the curtained aisle to the isolation cubicles. The first two were empty, but behind the glass in the third ten-by-ten space, a dim light revealed the occupants of two narrow hospital beds. Her newest subjects. She smiled, taking in the two young females. They looked to be in their late teens or early twenties, but with Weres it was difficult to pinpoint age and she really didn't care. What mattered was their distended abdomens. Both pregnant and near-term. Soon, she could study newborn Weres before they had progressed to their first shift. If she could prevent the expression of the Were transformation genes, she would have accomplished the first step in eradicating them.

❖

Francesca stroked Dru's slowly softening clitoris and watched the monitors on the antique dresser across from her spacious bed. Dru was nearly slumbering, her heart rate slow and steady. Francesca rested her cheek on Dru's shoulder, absorbing the heat pouring from her body. Dru's muscular chest and belly were still faintly dusted with the soft tawny down that had burst out when she'd grown aroused.

The cats weren't always as potent as the wolves, but this one was. Dru had partially shifted while Francesca fed from her, growling and clawing and thrashing, coming everywhere with incredible force. She was very potent, and her sharp wild taste was an exciting novelty. So delicious. Francesca's sex twitched, but she'd have to wait until she'd tended to business to feast again.

The image on the screen was crystal clear. The young Were female wrapped her legs around Michel's hips, undulating as she threw back her head and pulled Michel to her throat. Michel took her for the fourth time, the fire in her eyes more intense than Francesca had seen in months. And the Were knew just how to control her, tempting her to feed over and over. Some Weres were so vital they could host until a Vampire lost control, and this one was young and potent. And dangerous. Michel had surrendered to bloodlust, drowning in the pleasure of the female's blood. A Vampire in bloodlust was open to attack, and a vulnerable Vampire was a security risk. Michel was walking a very sharp edge.

Francesca sliced a shallow groove up the center of Dru's belly with her nails as she watched the monitor, and Dru growled and twitched awake.

"What is it," Dru asked.

"Could you track a wolf?" Francesca idly dragged her nail over Dru's breast and around her nipple.

Dru hissed at the pain. "Of course."

"Could you catch one, without killing it, I mean?"

"Of course." Dru roused herself and rolled over onto Francesca, sliding her hand between Francesca's legs. She stroked her, entered her, and slowly thrust. "Who do you want me to track?"

Francesca smiled, rolling her hips to take Dru deeper, letting the orgasm build slowly. "No one, just yet." She buried her incisors in Dru's throat, formulating a plan as the pleasure burned.

Chapter Eleven

Misha bounded out of the barracks, her wolf still riding her hard. Her skin, lightly dusted with pelt, ran wet with pheromones and her sex pounded from the *victus* in her glands pressing for release. An image of moon-kissed skin, pale and silky, aglow with power, sprang into her mind as clear and sharp as a knife edge. Not the raw power of Were. The magic of wind and song and star. Misha shuddered and cut across the Compound toward the dining hall, skirting the fire pits to avoid the soldiers and trainees congregated around the simmering embers. Gray was there somewhere, and she didn't want to see her right now. Gray would sense her agitation, scent her need, and know she was aching to tangle. Any other night, Gray would be the perfect partner to answer her call.

They'd been tangling regularly since they were adolescents, at first no more or less than they'd tangled with anyone else. Nature had held sway when they were younger, and everyone played at sex and dominance games. Misha and Gray and Jazz and Katya all tangled at one time or another as they'd come into their power and sorted out their places in the Pack. No one had been interested in anything more serious than the thrill of release. Certainly no one had been thinking about a mate. Misha had never done more than give a teasing bite to trigger release. More and more as she left adolescence behind, she chose females to tangle with, and more and more, Gray had been the one.

After the Alpha freed Gray and Katya from captivity, Gray wanted a hard chase and a rough tussle before they tangled. Gray was always angry—always spoiling for a fight, but Misha didn't mind. They were close in dominance, and she liked the challenge and the furious sex. A quick, fast tangle with no worries about a few bites or claw marks or bruises helped defuse Gray's simmering rage, but even with the release, Gray's wolf never really settled.

Tonight, though, Misha didn't want Gray. She didn't want anyone, and that was as confusing as the need burning in her loins and the insistent ache in her clitoris. Angry and agitated, her wolf paced, pressing for control, craving to run and hunt and kill. Scenting the allure of the forest, tasting the tang of quarry on her tongue, Misha's wolf wanted to chase down some succulent prey and bring it back to her den. And present it to Torren.

Grumbling, Misha shook her head and shoved her way into the dark, deserted dining hall. She didn't have a den, and anyhow, why would she want to hunt for a Fae she didn't even know? Torren didn't even eat meat, and besides, she was a prisoner. Well, not really a prisoner, but a guest whose status was unknown. Misha's job was to guard her, not protect her. Her wolf didn't seem to agree and gnawed at her insides, driving her close to frenzy.

Misha stomped down the length of the long narrow room between rows of communal tables and rough-hewn benches and pushed through the swinging double doors into the big kitchen. The walls were unadorned whitewash with rows of windows beneath high ceilings. The dining hall was almost as central to Pack life as the nursery or headquarters. Everyone for miles around the Compound gathered there for morning meals, and those on cook detail always left plenty of food in the huge refrigerators for hungry soldiers returning from patrol. Tonight, though, the place echoed with emptiness that matched the hollow ache in Misha's midsection.

She flicked on a single bare bulb hanging from a cord over a prep island and checked the nearest refrigerator, staring at its contents without really seeing them. Her mind was far away. She was deep in the shadowy forest, bounding up rocky escarpments and leaping over icy streams, racing after prey, absorbed in the ancient cycle of life. The cool air from inside the refrigerator struck her, and the sweat drenching her skin frosted like morning mist on blades of grass. She shuddered and felt her canines drag across her lower lip. She had to think—had to pull her wolf back from the hunt.

What was it Torren had said? Cheese. Vegetables. The things that Misha ate without noticing. She pulled out a loaf of bread, collected a handful of vegetables from another drawer, and carried everything to a counter. For a few seconds she stood still, the objects before her fading as the memory of Torren shifting from wolf to skin underneath her claimed her awareness. The glow emanating from Torren's pale skin had radiated heat into her core, exciting her and rousing her wolf. She recognized the sexual call—she had grown up surrounded by Weres, bathed in the potent allure of their pheromones from the time she was old enough for her body to register the sensations. But Torren was not a Were, and for the first time in her life, she distrusted her body—and her wolf. To be at odds with her wolf was worse than uncomfortable—she was disoriented and unsure.

Blocking the tormenting uneasiness, Misha concentrated on assembling the sandwich, hoping the contents would be adequate. She wanted to make up for the mistreatment Torren had endured while imprisoned. A red haze obscured her vision—she wanted to stake every Vampire who had touched Torren. Take the head of every Vampire who had fed from her. Burn Nocturne to the—

"What are you doing?" a soft female voice inquired.

Snarling, Misha spun around. Elena, the Pack *medicus*, stood just behind her. Elena's dark eyes widened and she backed away, shivering. She was mated and submissive, but she was still a wolf, and the cloud of sex pheromones and aggression bursting from Misha was a call she couldn't totally ignore. Elena knew better than to confront a wolf in that state. Lowering her head, she said softly, "Misha. What do you need? Can I help you?"

"I am..." Misha shook her head, swallowed past the rage in her throat. She couldn't remember what she was doing. All she knew was want and a deep burning hunger to take and claim. "I'm..." She glanced behind her, focused on the array of food spread out across the chopping block. "Getting food for Torren."

Elena's gaze sharpened. "Torren. The prisoner?"

Misha shook her head. "Not a prisoner. A...guest."

"Ah." Elena edged closer, seeing with knowing eyes. "Did Callan tell you to feed her?"

Misha frowned. "No."

"You weren't ordered to bring her a tray of food?"

"No." Misha wanted to feed Torren because others had fed from her against her will. She wanted to erase the taint of her imprisonment, ease the pain of her incarceration. She wanted to protect her. Kill her enemies. Pelt burst down the center of her torso. She growled a warning.

Elena flinched.

"Sorry," Misha said. "I didn't mean—"

"I know. You don't need to be sorry. But..." Elena sighed. "You know how intimate offering food is for us."

"She's hungry." Misha's canines throbbed and her vision shimmered. Her wolf was about to take over. She had good control, hadn't shifted involuntarily in a long time, not since she'd shed the last vestiges of adolescence, but she had such a need to hunt and tangle she couldn't resist the pull. She gripped the table on either side of her hips, dug her claws in. The room fractured into flat intersecting planes of gray and white. Her wolf vision sharpened, her senses grew keener. Her voice became gravel on steel. "They kept her in chains."

"Who?" Elena asked softly, holding her distance but remaining perfectly still. "Who, Misha?"

"The Vampires."

"But she's all right now."

"She's hungry."

"Why don't I take the tray to her?"

"No."

"All right," Elena said. "If you have to."

"I'll feed her."

"Yes." Elena carefully stroked Misha's damp face. "Misha?"

Misha blinked. Focused on Elena's calm face. "What?"

"Can you control your wolf?"

For young dominants, control was a point of honor. Misha drew a shuddering breath. Nodded. "Yes, I'm all right."

"Good. Do something for me first, before you take Torren the tray."

"What?"

"Walk through the yard. Tangle if someone approaches. Calm your wolf."

"I don't want to."

Elena smiled softly. "I know. But try. It will be safer for Torren."

Reluctantly, Misha set the tray down on a table near the exit and walked out into the dark. She smelled Pack everywhere, males and females, dominants and submissives, all their power combining to send her spiraling toward frenzy. Jazz approached, a question in his eyes and a smile on his handsome mouth, but she shook her head. He shrugged, clapped her back, and went on his way. They'd come up together through *sentrie* training and were friends, but she didn't want him to quench the burning.

Gray stepped out of the shadows, gripped Misha's shirt, and dragged her close. Fabric shredded. Gray nipped her lip. "I felt your call across the yard. My room is empty." She grimaced, eyes flaring with rage and sex. "Katya isn't there."

Misha's skin burned, her guts twisted into aching knots of want and need. The pressure to release pounded between her legs. She needed to quench the fire scorching through her. "I don't…"

"Yes, you do." Gray stroked Misha's abdomen and cupped a hand between her thighs. "I want this. So do you."

Misha gasped. Her canines fully emerged. The barracks were too far away. Ten more steps was too far to go. She pushed Gray into the shadows and up against the stockade, grasped Gray's wrists, and pinned her to the wall. Scraping her canines down Gray's throat, she straddled Gray's thigh. "Jerk me off. Hurry."

Gray shoved her hand into Misha's pants, gripped her clitoris in her fist, and squeezed. The pressure was so intense, Misha howled. Gray milked her, hard, fast, furious strokes, and Misha's hips bucked. Misha bit her, couldn't stop herself, and the taste of Gray's powerful pheromones pushed her over the edge. She exploded in Gray's hand, drenching her with one hot pulsation after another until she was empty.

Not thinking, not even feeling, Misha dropped to her knees, opened Gray's pants, and took her into her mouth. She let her canines graze the rigid shaft of Gray's tense clitoris, and within seconds of sucking her, brought her to convulsing release.

Gray slumped in the twisting shadows, head thrown back against the rough logs. Misha got unsteadily to her feet, pushed her shirt into her pants, and shoved away. "I've got to go."

"You can't trust her," Gray gasped.

"How would you know? You don't trust anyone."

"Why should I, when anyone can make us want anything? Make us do anything?"

"You don't know that," Misha said.

"I know it wasn't me fucking you just now."

"And who was fucking you?" Misha asked softly, unable to deny Gray's accusation. She hadn't used Gray—their need had been mutual—but she hadn't wanted her either. What she wanted was the shimmer of moonlight on her skin and the sharp cry of the hawk soaring inside her.

Gray didn't answer, and Misha left in the shadows to retrieve the tray of food for Torren.

❖

Michel softly stroked Katya's breast. "Why are you here?"

"Isn't this enough?" Katya pressed her breast into Michel's palm. The hallway behind them reverberated with the sound of Vampires feeding and hosts, human and Praetern, crying out in the depths of thrall. Her shirt and pants were open, her thighs slick with *victus*, her neck burning from the bites that would be healed in another few seconds. She'd torn through Michel's silk shirt to get to her flesh. In the near dark, Michel's eyes glowed like perfect embers, ready to flare at the first breath of desire.

Michel kissed her, leaving behind the smoked-oak taste of her feeding hormones. "I could feed from you endlessly."

Katya growled as the rush of stimulants struck her sex and she readied again. Curling her fingers into Michel's hair, she kissed the bite she'd made on Michel's shoulder and smiled when Michel's lips pulled back in a grimace of pleasure, her incisors gleaming. Michel might be older and more powerful, but Katya felt the ache of Michel's hunger flare inside her. Michel was ready for her too. "Take me as often as you like. I'm here."

Michel shook her head. "You shouldn't be."

"I've felt your hunger," Katya murmured, tracing a line down Michel's throat with her tongue. She angled her hips between Michel's legs. "You wanted me to come to you."

Michel shuddered, her mouth against Katya's neck. "Yes. You're the only one who fills me."

Katya imagined Michel feeding from others—taking them inside her, drawing power and life from their blood. Filling them with her essence. Katya's canines throbbed. The pelt line on her belly thickened. She wanted to bite Michel again, claim her. "Then let me feed you when you need to be filled."

"Francesca will know if you come to me here."

"I'm not afraid of Francesca."

Michel laughed. "You should be. She is more powerful than you can imagine."

"What does she care if you feed from me?"

Michel pressed Katya to the wall, her eyes glowing like fire. "Because it's more than blood."

"Is it?" Katya ran her clawed fingertips down the center of Michel's chest and left a trail of scarlet on her pale skin.

"Be careful, Katya. My hunger is ancient and endless."

"I am stronger than you think."

Michel bent her head, kissed Katya's breast, filled her senses with the spicy tang of Katya's pheromones. Katya's blood, potent and rich, raced within her. She'd fed from her too many times already, and she hungered for her still. "You bit me."

"Yes."

"My blood flows in you now."

"And mine in you."

Michel looked up. "You must be careful not to do that again."

"Why?"

"If we exchange essence, you may become bonded to me."

"And then?"

Michel smiled thinly and traced her finger along the edge of Katya's jaw. "Then you will be mine."

"And you?" Katya pushed Michel's shirt aside and kissed the bite she'd left on her shoulder. Michel hissed. The marks were still visible, but fading. "What will you be?"

Instead of an answer, Michel jerked Katya's head back and kissed her hard. "You are not safe here."

"Then where?"

Michel should send her away—should protect herself and her Regent. Katya already sensed her need from afar, fed her without succumbing to thrall. The bonding had begun—and Francesca would never allow a Were that close to the center of her power. If Francesca suspected Katya might know what was in Michel's mind, she would kill them both.

"Where?" Katya asked again.

"I will send for you."

"When?"

Michel lifted her up and Katya wrapped her legs around Michel's hips. As Michel slid her incisors into Katya's flesh, she whispered, "Soon."

CHAPTER TWELVE

The edge of dawn trickled through the high window above the bed. Drake knew without opening her eyes she was alone. Sylvan never made a sound when she moved, in the forest or anywhere else, but even asleep, Drake had sensed the instant she'd left the bed. Their metaphysical connection was as strong as their physical bond, and whenever Sylvan left her side, she ached not from loneliness, but from the absence of a part of her that ran as deep as her soul. She imagined Sylvan running again, driving out her demons as her wolf paws pounded the forest floor and she leapt through crystal cold air, driven by instinct, unfettered by any law but that of nature.

The air stirred with anticipation a heartbeat before the bed sagged and Sylvan slipped in beside her. Warm lips moved over her neck. An arm, possessive and irresistible, banded around her waist. A hand, the contours of which she could trace in the depths of every cell, closed around her breast.

"Morning," Sylvan murmured against her ear.

Drake pushed back against her, settling her ass into the curve of Sylvan's hips, her back to Sylvan's chest. She covered Sylvan's hand and entwined their fingers. "Did you run?"

Sylvan nuzzled Drake's neck. "Not yet. Waiting for you."

"You could have wakened me."

"No reason for both of us to be restless."

Drake lifted Sylvan's hand and kissed her palm. "Where did you go?"

"To see the young."

Not running from them. Visiting the nursery. Drake's heart

lurched. Sylvan had never visited the young alone. Since Andrew died, she'd claimed her agitation would only frighten them, and she'd only visit when Drake was there to buffer her rage. Sylvan hadn't let her family, her Pack, be her solace. Instead she'd run, letting her wolf take her, but seeking to outrace her pain had been a futile task. Drake rubbed her thumb over the tendons in Sylvan's hand. Everything about her was bowstring tight. "How are they?"

"Sleeping soundly. Marta is with them." Sylvan bit down gently on the sensitive skin at the angle of Drake's neck and shoulder. "I didn't want to wake them, so I only stayed a second."

"Did they know you were there?"

"They sensed me, I think." Sylvan laughed. "Hard to tell. They were in a pup pile with some of the two-year-olds and there was a lot of ear-flickering going on."

"With the two-year-olds? Isn't it too soon?" Drake had images of her daughters being buried by bigger, stronger wolf pups.

"They're wolf Weres—not human. They won't follow the growth curve you're used to seeing. Our ancestors had to hunt to survive, and the only young who lived were those who grew quickly and learned to run within a few months."

"I keep expecting them to be like human babies," Drake said.

"They aren't human," Sylvan whispered, rubbing her cheek on Drake's throat—a possessive wolf gesture. "And neither are their parents."

"No. We aren't." When Drake had been turned, her cells, her DNA, had mutated. She had stopped being human. She was not a hybrid—she was pure Were, and her mate was the strongest wolf Were in existence. "When did you first speak?"

"In words?"

Drake laughed. "How else?"

"My mother said I could understand her mental commands in pelt right away. I didn't vocalize words until I was six months old. I was big enough to run with the Pack long before then."

Drake caught her breath. So soon. "Do you think ours—I know they have all your power, but—"

"Possibly. Probably," Sylvan said. "They're growing fast. And *I* think they both look like you."

"In case you haven't noticed"—Drake turned onto her back and pulled Sylvan on top of her—"one of them is blond."

"Other than that."

"I suspect they will both have a little bit of each of us." She tapped Sylvan's chin. "Although Kira already seems to be you, through and through."

Sylvan rumbled, a proud self-satisfied growl. "She does have the air of an Alpha already."

"Do you think it's a burden, that she's born to it, like you?" Drake would have caught the words back if she could have. She wasn't sorry she had borne the next Pack leaders. She only wished the future would be more certain. "I didn't mean—"

"I know you're only worried for them," Sylvan said. "But if I had been given the chance to change what I am, I wouldn't. I am proud to lead. Except..."

"Except what?"

Sylvan rested her forehead on Drake's. "When I put you in danger."

Drake twisted her fingers in Sylvan's hair and tugged hard. "I've told you I wouldn't have it any other way." She wrapped her legs around Sylvan's hips and coated her belly with a burst of *victus*, hot and thick and intoxicating. "And I wouldn't trade this for all the safety in the universe."

Gold flashed in Sylvan's deep blue eyes and a gleam of canine sparkled between her parted lips. Her grin was predatory as she pushed tight between Drake's thighs. Her clitoris was already distended, and her call brought Drake to instant readiness. "Your argument's convincing."

"Convince me more," Drake whispered, slowly rolling her hips in a way she knew pushed Sylvan to the edge.

Sylvan's face grew heavy and stark, her hunger a living force, and she thrust in time with Drake's teasing motions. "I don't need to run to be free," Sylvan murmured. "I just need this."

Drake scraped her claws up and down Sylvan's back, not deep enough to draw blood, but enough to heighten her pleasure with a whisper of pain. Sylvan was the ultra dominant, and challenge heightened all her responses, including pleasure. When Sylvan thrust harder and faster, pushing them both toward release, Drake gripped her shoulders hard and turned Sylvan onto her back.

Sylvan growled.

"Hush," Drake ordered against Sylvan's ear. "Let me."

Sylvan gripped the sides of the bed, struggling with her need to claim her mate. Giving her throat, exposing her belly, required the ultimate trust. Feeling Drake cover her, owning her, brought her pelt coursing to the surface and filled her glands to bursting. "Hurry."

Drake laughed. "I don't think so."

"I do—feel me." Sylvan's claws dug into the bed and she arched, pressing her clitoris against Drake's belly. "I'm ready."

"I know. I can scent you, feel your hunger like my own." Drake braced her arms on the bed and rocked downward, kissing her way along the cleft between Sylvan's taut abdominals. "I will make you come. Just wait."

Sylvan panted, needing to empty. Needing Drake even more. She whispered the word no one but Drake would ever hear. "Please."

Drake gripped Sylvan's hips and took her into her mouth, stroking her length with her tongue, teasing the rigid, silky core of her. Sylvan's need was her pleasure, Sylvan's release her satisfaction. She pulled her deeper, felt the first sharp spasm.

Sylvan jolted, a howl of pleasure torn from her throat. Drake's hips bucked at the sound, poised to release when Sylvan did. She sucked harder, drawing forth Sylvan's essence in long powerful waves. Pleasure as bright as sunlight burned through her.

"More," Sylvan groaned, her hands in Drake's hair, slowly thrusting between Drake's lips as she crested and then languidly continued to empty. "I love when you claim me."

Drake rested her cheek between Sylvan's thighs, slowly licking the last drops from her still-turgid flesh. "I love making you mine."

"I'm always yours."

Drake rose above Sylvan and straddled her thigh. As she kissed her, she thrust several times and finished emptying over Sylvan's leg. Marking her with her scent. Sighing with contentment, she tucked her face into the curve of Sylvan's shoulder, cradling Sylvan's breast in one hand. "You are everything."

Sylvan stroked her hair and closed her eyes. "Let's go wake them up—they could use some playtime."

"All ri—"

Sylvan jerked as her wolf snapped to attention. "That will have to wait."

"I think we're going to have to move the den farther into the mountains," Drake said half-seriously. "Callan, isn't it?"

"Yes."

A knock sounded on the door and they both sat up.

"I'll go," Sylvan said swinging out of bed.

"No, I'll come too." Drake joined her and they both pulled on clothes. "If he's here this early, it's something serious."

Sylvan opened the door and Callan ducked his head quickly. "I'm sorry to disturb you, Alpha, but I've had a report of an attack on one of our border outposts."

Sylvan's eyes flashed. "Where?"

"At the northern Massachusetts line."

"Cats?" Sylvan's growl filled the air with menace, and Callan backed up a step.

"No, Alpha. Wolves." Callan snarled. "Blackpaws, we think."

"Bernardo," Sylvan spat. "Do we have prisoners?"

"No, but we have wounded."

"Then we can't waste time. I want whoever attacked us caught."

Sylvan sent out a mental call for the *centuri* standing guard in the forest, and Jace, Max, and Dasha appeared in the clearing a few seconds later. They looked to Sylvan, who called, "We hunt!"

A howl split the air and a great silver wolf bounded off the porch into the clearing. Milliseconds later a midnight wolf joined her, and the others, drawn by Sylvan's power into pelt, shifted in the second wave. Spreading out into a phalanx behind the Alpha pair, they raced to the hunt.

❖

Torren watched the moon slide behind the clouds for the last time as dawn broke. She drew in sweet morning air through the open window, letting the morning mist cleanse her body and soul. After weeks underground, in the dark, the moment was as sweet as any she could remember. The door behind her opened and closed, and another fragrance—crushed leaves and simmering pine—soared through her like morning song.

"I brought you some food," Misha said quietly.

Torren turned and took in the tray. A plate of fruit and some kind of bread and filling. Misha eyed her warily, as if expecting her to do something threatening, but some of the tension had left her. The angry press of wolf was gone. Torren tilted her head, studied her. "You've been pleasuring."

"What is it to you?" Misha said defensively. She had spent hard, but the gnawing pressure remained. She could control it now. She was a wolf, after all.

"Nothing, other than I like the taste of it on your skin."

Misha dropped the tray onto the small table next to the cot with a clatter. She folded her arms and spread her legs in challenge. "What are you talking about?"

"Your pleasure"—Torren drew in a breath—"tastes of wild berries and rain."

Her words struck Misha like a spear piercing her belly. Her thighs tensed. Softly, almost against her will, she said, "How do you know?"

"Your taste is everywhere in the air—you're powerful and strong," Torren murmured, "and young."

Misha growled. "Not as young as you think."

"No, perhaps not. War has a way of aging us."

"How old are you?"

Torren lifted a shoulder. How could she explain to this creature of the earth what it meant to occupy an ethereal plane, where light was as solid to her as the stones beneath their feet. "We don't judge time the way you do. Not in years, not even in seasons. But I have seen more than a few cycles."

"Have you had many lovers?" Misha asked abruptly.

"Yes."

Misha growled again.

"But none of the heart." The admission surprised Torren. The Hunt ruled her life, and she never thought of what else she might want. Or need.

"What does that mean?" Misha asked.

"Have you pleasured with many?"

Misha gave her an arrogant nod. "I am a wolf. We tangle whenever we want."

"I'll take that as a yes."

"I haven't had as many…cycles…as you."

"And have you…tangled…?"—at Misha's nod, Torren continued—"from the heart?"

Misha stared at the plate of food. "No."

"Then you know what I mean."

Misha raised her head, glared at Torren. "Why do I know what you taste like?"

Torren jolted, surprised. "Do you?"

Misha stepped closer, ran a finger along the edge of Torren's jaw, brushed her thumb over Torren's mouth. "Yes. Honeysuckle and spice."

"I hadn't intended that." Torren's eyes were incandescent, glowing silver deep enough to drown in.

"What are you doing to me?" Misha gasped.

"Only hoping to convince you to trust me."

"It's not my place to trust you or not. The Alpha will decide."

"And that's enough for you? Your Alpha's decision?"

"Of course."

Torren regarded her curiously. What would it be like to have total trust in another being? She'd never encountered that. Allegiances, loyalty, perhaps. But trust? Never. "Why? Why do you trust her?"

"Because she would die for us," Misha said instantly.

"Would she?" The concept was curious and foreign. The Fae, at heart, were selfish. Life was a game to be played and won. Self-sacrifice was unheard of, a weakness to be exploited. "And you? Who would you die for?"

"Any of my Packmates."

"Why?" Torren asked again.

Misha straightened, her chin lifting proudly. "Because I am a wolf."

Torren laughed softly. "Your reasoning is circular."

"I do not have to reason. I only have to feel."

"And what do you feel right now?"

Misha shivered in the sunlight that slanted through the window. The scent of honeysuckle enveloped her and silken wings played across her skin. Her pelt ruffled as if in a morning breeze. The cry of a hawk urged her wolf to run. She panted softly. "Freedom. The thrill of the hunt."

"Your Alpha is hunting now."

"Is she," Misha murmured, her vision swimming in pools of iridescent blue and silver.

"Yes. Do you want to follow?"

"No. I want you."

Torren slipped closer until their bodies touched. She cupped Misha's jaw and tilted her face upward. Her mouth hovered over Misha's. "You are very beautiful."

Misha's wolf leapt forward, eager and jubilant. Misha grasped Torren's shoulders.

How can you trust anyone when they can make us do anything?

This wasn't real. Torren was other. Not wolf.

"No," Misha whispered, gravel tearing at her throat. She stumbled back, and her wolf howled in protest. "I don't know you."

"Don't you? You knew I was hungry. You brought me food." Torren spread her hands at her sides, opening herself to Misha's wolf— exposing herself. "You know my scent. You hear my blood."

Misha stared at the food, heard the call of the hawk, scented honeysuckle. Her nipples tingled, her belly tightened. She backed against the door. "How do I know any of it is real?"

"What is real?" Torren whispered.

Chapter Thirteen

Just before dawn, Sasha had turned the Rover onto the unmarked, single-lane trail leading to the Compound.

"Let me out," Katya said.

Sasha slowed. "Are you sure? I'm supposed to be your escort."

"We're on safe ground. And I want to run. Don't you?" Katya jumped down and peered at Sasha. She looked as if she'd just come back from a week's patrol and was in need of a long night's sleep. Katya felt anything but tired. Her wolf clamored to hunt.

"I...I'm fine." Sasha smiled wryly. "Just a little hungry."

"Go get a meal and then some sleep."

Sasha still looked unsure, but drove on.

Katya's wolf burst free, energized, her senses sharper than she could remember since the Alpha had freed her from captivity. She chased down a small prey, killed it swiftly, and fed. Then she ran just for the joy of running, watching the sunrise crest the trees, breathing in needles of frosty air until her muzzle ached. And with every step, she felt Michel's power coursing through her. Michel was everywhere—the heat of Michel's mouth on her skin, the sharp pleasure of her bite, the piercing ecstasy of her hormones exploding through her—every sensation was defined by Michel's presence.

Katya bounded across the Compound, vaulted through the high narrow barracks window, and landed on her cot, shifting to skin as she settled down in the center. Michel shouldn't worry about how often or how long Katya fed her. She felt stronger than ever.

"Where have you been?" Gray sat cross-legged on the adjacent cot, her back against the wall. She wore charcoal fatigue pants and a matching T-shirt, both stretched tight over thick muscles honed every day with hours of running and solitary workouts.

"Out." Naked, Katya stretched back on the plain wool blanket. The unheated room was cold despite the early morning sun that had followed her inside. Her nipples tightened and gooseflesh pebbled her skin, but inside she was hot. Her blood still burned. Michel's smoky taste lingered on her tongue. Her sex beat in time with her heart, full and tense. She could never remember feeling so alive, even after a hunt.

"Where?"

"You know where." Katya sighed, her hand trailing down the center of her torso. Now she was tired, but even the fatigue felt wonderful. She pressed her hand to her bare abdomen, the last vestiges of pleasure tingling under her fingertips. Michel would be deep in the lair by now, possibly asleep. Katya looked forward to sleep—Michel would come to her then.

"You smell different," Gray grumbled.

Katya turned her head, read the anger in Gray's eyes. "You smell like sex."

"At least I smell like Were."

"Why do you care who I'm with? You never have before."

"Because I watched them torture you."

"You remember?" Katya sat up, fatigue falling away. "Tell me."

"You don't?"

Katya shook her head. "Only pieces. A few more now than before, but mostly, I remember...pain."

Gray sneered. "Yes, I think that's all we were supposed to know."

"Elena and Drake said they poisoned us with silver—in the air, so our minds would be clouded and our bodies weak. I remember feeling heavy, like a blanket of snow and stone was piled on top of me. And sometimes..." Katya looked away.

"Sometimes what?" Gray leaned forward intently.

Katya met her gaze, saw something she rarely did in Gray's eyes. Fear. "Wanting. Wanting...*needing*...to release so badly. Just wanting someone, anyone, to take me and make me come."

Gray shuddered. "Do you remember the shocks?"

Katya frowned, searched the murky haze of her fractured memory.

Pain was the final common pathway—all she could conjure clearly. That and the pleasure wrenched from her. She shook her head. "No. What do you mean?"

"It doesn't matter."

"It does. What did they do to you?"

Gray stared at her hands, pressing her palms so tightly against her thighs her fingers dug into the flesh. "When they wanted to punish me, they would shock me over and over until I...They would force me to release. I didn't want to, at first. But then I did. Sometimes I think I fought just for the punishment." Gray's shoulders shook. "Like a coward, I did what they really wanted me to do."

Katya drew a slow breath that seared her lungs, as if she still breathed poison, but the sensation came from deep inside her. "We should kill them all."

Gray's lips drew back in a feral grin. "Yes. All of them."

"Do you remember who they are?"

"No. I keep trying, and sometimes I'm so *close*." Gray jumped up, started to pace. "I see faces sometimes, but I can't make them out clearly. I recognized the human the Alpha captured once I saw him again, but before then...only the pain." She snarled. "I should have killed him."

"Martin. I remember him too now. He tried to help us."

"Maybe." Gray's claws punched out. "But he was with them, when they came for us. When they did...things."

"Sometimes we can't do what we want to do right away. Like on a hunt, we have to be patient before we can strike."

"Not if we hunt alone."

Katya rose, pulled on her fatigues, grasped Gray's shoulders to stop her pacing. "You're not a lone wolf. Just because you're angry, and you think no one understands you, doesn't mean you've been turned out."

Gray yanked away and stalked to the window, her back to Katya. Outside the sky was crystal blue, clouds of ice ribboning the sky. "Winter is coming."

"So?"

"If I want to find a den so I can last through the winter, I have to leave soon."

Katya jerked her around and snarled in her face. Her wolf was so close her pelt streaked her forearms and chest. "What makes you think you're so special?"

Gray's eyes widened. "What?"

"You weren't the only one in those cells. I was there too. And there are probably others—still imprisoned somewhere. So why do you get to run away? Why is your pain so much worse than mine or anyone else's?"

Gray's lips drew back and her canines flashed. "You don't know—"

"Yes, I do. Maybe they didn't do to me what they did to you, but every single thing they did was just as bad. I remember the pain, and I remember—" She hesitated, lifted her chin. "I remember the pleasure too. And I wanted it. I wanted what they were doing, just like you."

"No, you didn't." Gray sagged and wrapped her arms around Katya's waist. "They just made you think you wanted it. We can't help what our bodies feel."

Katya clasped the back of Gray's neck and massaged the steel-banded muscles. Gray's breasts pressed to hers, their thighs met, strength on strength. This was what Gray needed, what every wolf needed. Pack. "Then why do you torture yourself?"

Gray was quiet for a long time, her forehead pressed to Katya's shoulder. Finally she spoke, her voice muffled, almost apologetic. "Because I still want the pain."

"So?" Katya dragged Gray over to the cot, pushed her down, and flopped next to her. Their shoulders and sides and thighs touched as they stared straight ahead. "We're wolves. We're predators. Pain is part of our life. When we hunt, when we run with the Alpha, when we take our prey, don't you ready? Don't you want to release when we're done?"

"Yes, but—"

"But what? Why is one feeling right and the other wrong? Do you want to submit, is that what embarrasses you? Because you're dominant and you want someone else to take control?"

"Sometimes." Gray drew a shuddering breath. "Sometimes I want to be forced, taken, made to hurt so the pleasure's even greater."

Katya laughed softly and Gray stiffened beside her. Katya rapped her fist lightly on Gray's thigh. "Don't take yourself so seriously. If you want someone to bite you, so what? I like being bitten too."

"Yeah," Gray said sullenly, "by a Vampire."

"Why does that bother you so much?"

"I saw her take you that first time, in the labs. You didn't want her then. She just took you."

"That first time," Katya said, remembering the terrible pressure in her belly and the torrential release when Michel bit her, "I only wanted someone to take away the need. But now…now I want more. I want her."

"But she's…not us. The Vampires are our enemies."

"Not all of them. The Alpha has a treaty with the Vampires."

"For now."

"Lara is a Vampire and a wolf," Katya said. "She's still *centuri*. Still one of us. Maybe we can be more than what we think."

"Vampires can't be trusted. They can make us want things."

"She does," Katya murmured, and just the memory of Michel's mouth on her neck made her nipples tighten all over again. Sex pheromones burst on her skin. Beside her, Gray grumbled, her wolf scenting Katya's excitement. "I want her to make me want. I like the way it feels. But you forget, she wants too. She wants *me*. I am not without power."

Gray tilted her head against the wall and stared at the ceiling. "Everything is changing."

"Maybe. But some things will never change. We will always be wolves. We will always be Pack. And we will always be loyal to the Alpha, and she to us. You need to be here, you need to fight."

Gray turned her head, gazed at Katya with vulnerable eyes. "I don't want to go."

Katya slid her arm around Gray's shoulder, pulled her close, kissed her. "Good. Because I'm not letting you."

Gray sighed and rested her cheek against Katya's shoulder. "Does the Alpha know you were with her tonight?"

"She gave me leave to see her."

"Why?"

Katya hesitated. The Alpha thought she might be able to learn from Michel who was involved in the attack on the Alpha and the Prima. But that's not why she had gone. She had gone because Michel's call lived inside her, a need that was always with her. "To find out more about the attack."

"You need to be careful," Gray said.

"Yes," Katya said, an image of Francesca sliding through her mind.

❖

Sylvan's wolf scrambled up a rocky slope downwind from the trio of raiders they'd been tracking since dawn. Drake bounded up at her side, the heat of her breath warming Sylvan's face. The raiders had gotten a good start on them after their blitz attack on a cadre of young soldiers at a border outpost, but the raiding wolves were Blackpaws and had slowed down the deeper they'd traveled into the Berkshires, Blackpaw territory where they felt safe. They should have known they wouldn't be safe from the Timberwolf Alpha, no matter how far they ran.

Sylvan halted along a ridge covered from the sight of those below by a line of scraggly mulberry bushes and crawled forward on her belly, panting softly. Drake inched up beside her. Two hundred yards downslope, three wolves trotted along a narrow forest path heading northeast, toward the Blackpaw stronghold. Sylvan couldn't see them, but she scented other Blackpaws ranging in the forest around them. The Blackpaw Pack was smaller than the Timberwolf and led by an Alpha far less experienced and powerful. Bernardo, the wolf Were she'd seen in Torren's vision, had seized power after the last Alpha had challenged Sylvan's mother and lost. Bernardo had been meeting in secret with those Torren called the Shadow Lords. Cecilia, Francesca, and others Sylvan could not name. Bernardo was her enemy. Did that make all of them her enemy?

Drake nosed her shoulder. They were in Blackpaw territory, and as soon as these wolves sent out a call for reinforcements, they would be outnumbered. Time was short. *We should take them before they get closer to their Pack.*

Yes. The answers to her questions would have to wait. *Take Max and Dasha and block their forward escape. I'll strike from the flank. Wait for me before you show yourself.*

Drake flashed her teeth, her wolf happy to be hunting with Sylvan again. *Go.*

With a flick of her ear and a tilt of her muzzle, Sylvan signaled to

Jace and Callan to come with her. Drake waited until they disappeared and called Dasha and Max to follow her. Trusting Sylvan's group to outflank the trio of raiders, Drake arrowed straight northeast to intersect the path of their quarry if they should try to outrun Sylvan and the others. Before they reached the trail, she picked up the sounds of fighting and running wolves approaching fast. She burst out of the forest with Max and Dasha as the raiders, a big gray male with black slashes on his muzzle and a pair of smaller black and whites, one male and one female, bounded onto the path.

The heavily muscled gray male charged without slowing.

Drake crouched, waiting until the last second to dart to one side, slashing at his shoulder with her teeth as he passed. She caught flesh but not deep enough to slow him down. He scissored around and launched himself at her, clearing the distance between them in one powerful lunge. She managed to twist away, his claws raking a line of fire down her side. Dasha and Max rolled on the ground with the other two, snapping and clawing. Two more wolves burst from the forest and joined the fray. One landed on Dasha's back, burying his fangs in the thick muscle at the juncture of her neck and shoulder. She howled in pain.

Drake spun and snarled at the fifth Blackpaw, and the big gray wolf hit her from the side and took her down. She brought her rear legs up to protect her belly, clawing and thrashing to keep him from grabbing her throat. Pain raked down the center of her belly and warm blood soaked her pelt. In a rage of pain, she clamped onto his throat, closing her jaws like a vise. She kept his snarling teeth away from her neck but she couldn't crush his windpipe through the thick layer of muscles. She'd never defeat him strength on strength, but she was quicker and more agile. Twisting as she clung to his throat, she raked at his loins with her rear legs. Her assault was enough to put him on the defensive, and he rolled off her, his teeth still buried in her shoulder, hers in his neck. With his greater mass, he dragged her with him as he tried to throw her off. She hung on stubbornly, and more and more blood drenched her belly. They were at a stalemate. Eventually he would win if she couldn't shake him loose or damage him in some vital place.

Summoning all her strength, Drake wrenched her head from side to side, burying her canines deeper in his throat. He roared and raked her unprotected side again. Her muscles quivered, weakening. Breath rasped from her locked jaws, misted with red. He'd punctured her lung.

A mad howl sliced the air, striking at the primal core of her, so raw and powerful she would have been paralyzed with fear if she hadn't recognized the raging war cry. Sylvan. The Alpha more powerful than any living wolf.

Sylvan landed on the back of the big gray wolf as he tore at Drake's exposed belly. Sylvan's jaws closed over his spine in one massive strike, and the crack of bone rifled through the air like gunshot. He went limp instantly and fell onto Drake, carrying her down under him and pinning her to the forest floor with his weight. Forcing down the pain that seemed everywhere at once, she panted for air and struggled to drag herself free. Then the weight was lifted and all she could see was the huge silver wolf, snarling and circling her in a fury. Protecting her.

See to the others, Drake signaled.

No. You're hurt. They all must die.

I'll be all right. Don't kill them all. We need living prisoners.

Sylvan's slanted gold eyes burned over her before she leapt away. Snarls and growls and howls of anguish filled the forest and, just as quickly, trailed off. Drake rolled onto her belly and got her legs under her. Weak, and losing blood, but she had to stand. None of them would be safe until they reached Pack land.

Sylvan landed beside her and licked her face. *Can you run?*

Yes.

We chased off a scouting party earlier. More will come.

Do we have a prisoner?

Sylvan snarled. *One. The others are dead.*

Drake steeled herself and took a few steps. Her legs held, but her breathing was wrong. She wasn't going to be able to run at full speed. *Dasha is hurt, and we need to get the prisoner to Pack land. Leave Callan and Jace with me. Take Dasha and Max and go ahead with the Blackpaw.*

I'm not leaving you. Sylvan's expression, lips pulled back, ears flat, was as close as a wolf could come to sneering. She signaled to the others to take the prisoner and go. Callan, Dasha, and Jace herded the black-and-white wolf between them into the forest and disappeared.

Max, limping from a bleeding gash in his shoulder and a tear in his front leg, shook his head and fell back by Sylvan's side. *You and the Prima need a guard.*

See to the Prima, then, Sylvan ordered as they headed into the forest behind the others.

Drake met Max's flat dark stare as he loped beside her. His ear flicked as he read in her eyes the truth every Were was born with. *Protect the Alpha above all others.*

Satisfied that Sylvan would be safe, Drake leaned on the strength of their mate bond—and the power of the Alpha enveloping her—and ran.

CHAPTER FOURTEEN

Dru pushed farther into Timberwolf territory than she had ever dared penetrate before. Usually she crossed into wolf territory along the border between the far northern Catamount Pride land and the sparsely patrolled and undeveloped wolf wildlands. When she did, her forays were short—just long enough to chase down a deer or mountain goat. Her need to hunt outweighed the slim chance of running into a wolf patrol party. Since the Exodus and the rebellion within the Pride, she'd joined a few raiding parties in pursuit of Raina and those loyal to her. The raids had skirted into Pack land, but most cats knew better than to challenge the wolves. The cats were outnumbered and far less organized than the wolves. One-on-one, the cats were superior fighters, but the wolves fought in packs. Cowards that they were.

Now she deliberately forayed deeper and deeper into the heart of Pack land, following the distinctive scent of Francesca's escaped prisoner. She loved to track almost as much as she loved the kill. She'd expected the prey to go to ground in some hidey-hole along the riverfront as quickly as possible, but this one seemed unconcerned about staying out in the open. She'd been tracking since dawn, and this trail was still fresh, leading directly to the river from the dank cell where Francesca had kept the Fae prisoner. No rain had fallen in the forest to dilute the distinctive spicy taste that coated her lolling tongue.

She'd been surprised the first time the prey circled back on itself to divert first into a park and then a second time under a bridge. She couldn't detect anything unusual about the sites. The park had been deserted. The area under the bridge was just as barren—no dock, no evidence of an encampment, nothing to distinguish the trash-strewn ground from any other area along the riverbank, and yet the prey had deliberately traveled there. She could scent nothing out of the ordinary and filed the location away in her memory before putting her nose to the ground again and racing after the distinctive scent of wolf cut through with something distinctly not-wolf—spice and honeysuckle.

The wolf scent was another surprise. She hadn't expected the Fae to be running with a wolf escort, but the evidence was clear. She tasted, smelled wolf. Francesca appeared not to know the wolves were accomplices in her prisoner's escape. That information would certainly be of interest to the Vampire Regent. The monitor in the Vampire's bedroom had shown images of dozens of wolves upstairs in the club—some were probably involved. With luck she could identify the exact wolf and perhaps earn a bounty. As it was, she had proof the wolves were harboring the escapee.

She savored the knowledge that her report would drive a wedge between the Vampires and the wolves, and anyone the wolves called friends. She'd love to see Raina chained to a wall in the Vampire Regent's dungeon. If Raina disappeared, the cats would be in complete disarray and those who *should* lead would be able to, in the old way—where strength, courage, and power were the only things that mattered. Compromise, alliances, politics, and planning—what did they need of those? They were human constructs, human concerns—all the cat Weres needed was finding and holding enough land to feed themselves, to sustain their Pride, and to provide prey for their young. And the wolves had plenty of all that—with an Alpha willing to go to war, the cats could expand their territory and take their rightful place at the top.

As she ran, the sun rose and warmed her back. She covered the miles easily, savoring the stretch of her muscles after the cramped confines of the city. The trail lay out before her as if a visible ribbon wended through the trees. Following it was almost too easy, or it had been until the prey turned toward the heart of Pack land. Perhaps her prey had thought to lose herself among the morass of scents left by countless wolves crisscrossing the forest—hoping her scent would become just one note among many. But then her prey had underestimated her skill. She was a master tracker. She could pick out the different refrains left by each member of a herd of deer, or identify the path of an intruder with nothing more to go on than weeks-old spoor. All the same, she was uneasy. She was alone in wolf territory.

If she came across a wolf patrol or even a hunting pair, she'd be instantly attacked. She was disadvantaged in combat against more than one opponent—she might be bigger than a wolf, but they were almost as quick as cats and relentless fighters. She could outrun even the strongest of them, however, and if they dogged her until she reached Catamount territory, they would soon become the prey and not the predators.

The wind shifted and she caught the pungent scent of fresh blood. Slowing, she swung her big head around and sniffed the air. Her mouth filled with the remembered taste of prey. She hadn't eaten in a long time, and something was losing a lot of blood. Something was weak, and the weak were easy prey. A wounded animal was easy to cut from the pack, easy to chase down.

Judging the direction the prey was moving, she took to the trees and, flattening her belly on a wide branch twenty feet above a narrow trail, eased forward until she could peer below. Sunlight dappled the ground although the air remained cool. A perfect day for hunting. She scented wolf—a number of them had passed this way recently—and then the blood scent grew stronger. She growled deep in her chest, gauging the distance she would have to cover, and flicked her tail in anticipation. She could easily drop onto the back of her prey as it passed beneath her.

A great silver wolf bounded from the underbrush and Dru's hackles rose. A wolf that huge, radiating such power and strength, could only be one wolf. The Alpha wolf. The Alpha searched the trail and circled the small clearing just ahead, her golden eyes glaring and seeming nearly mad. After a second, she glanced back and barked a soft command. A black female, nearly as large as the silver one, shadowed by a muscular male, limped from the cover of the trees and passed under Dru's perch. Every step was marked by a patter of blood falling like rain on the needle-covered ground. Not prey. Wolf.

Dru pressed tighter to the limb, her head resting on her paws as she watched the trio move into the small clearing. The blood trail was visible even at a distance. The black wolf was bleeding heavily, and if the Alpha was a personal escort, the black wolf was of major importance. More interesting news to take back to her new employer.

She hissed softly, her breath a mere whisper on the breeze as she recalled the moments she'd spent in Francesca's bed. She'd fed Vampires before, but never one as powerful as the Regent—the pleasure that had been forced upon her was beyond description. And dangerous. She'd been weak after, not from blood loss—she could host a dozen Vampires and not feel the effect—but from pleasure. Whatever the Vampire Regent had done to her had clouded her mind and drained her body of strength. And even now, she craved more. For one mad instant, she contemplated stalking the wolves and ambushing the wounded wolf. If she brought the black wolf back to Francesca as a trophy, she would secure her place in the Regent's bed.

But Sylvan was said to be invincible in a fight, and even the promise of pleasure vicious enough to drive her cat to her belly was not enough to banish all reason. Dru backed down off the limb, dropped softly to the ground, and turned to go back the way she had come. Francesca would be grateful to learn that her prisoner was hiding in Sylvan's territory, and for now, gratitude was enough.

❖

Drake stumbled to a halt. *I'm delaying you and it isn't safe for any of us. Send Max ahead to bring back a Rover. I don't think I can run the rest of the way.*

Sylvan circled her anxiously, whining unhappily in the back of her throat. She nosed Drake's neck and licked the wound on her shoulder.

The bleeding is slowing, but the wound isn't closing. The more I run, the more I'll bleed. We're in Pack land—it should be safe to stop now.

Sylvan paced. *We might be pursued. They were foolish enough to attack us once in our own territory, they might be again, especially if a patrol found the dead we left behind.*

Drake stiffened. *I will not run or hide from a fight. If we are attacked on our own land, we must fight.*

Sylvan's lips drew back. *There is no hiding from a wolf, even if we wanted to. They'll smell us. But we can at least choose a place to fight to our own advantage.*

I'm sorry.

You're wounded. There is nothing to be sorry for. Sylvan spun around, and Max, surprised by her quick movement, flattened on the ground in automatic submission. Sylvan lifted her muzzle, calling him to her. *Go on ahead. We'll wait here. Bring back a Rover and a medic.*

Yes, Alpha.

Run faster than you've ever run.

Max's eyes gleamed. *You can count on me, Alpha.*

Sylvan watched him go, raging, barely able to resist charging back to Blackpaw territory and killing anyone in her path. If she didn't have to look after Drake, she would lead a raiding party back there without worrying about explanations. They had violated her territory, attacked her soldiers, wounded her mate. There was no answer for what had been done but swift and lethal retribution.

Drake curled up against a rocky escarpment that rose to the tree line thirty feet above her head. No one could come up behind her, and unless they dropped from the sky, she was safe from above. She watched the narrow path they'd taken out of the woods and readied what strength she had left in case of attack. Sylvan stood guard in front of her, her legs planted wide, her head swinging from side to side, fury in every quivering muscle. *I'm going to be all right.*

Sylvan didn't acknowledge her, although Drake knew she felt her words. Sylvan's rage was as formidable as it had been after Andrew had been killed, and Drake doubted anyone other than her could penetrate Sylvan's cloak of fury. But Sylvan would always hear her, even when ruled completely by her wolf. Even half-feral, Sylvan was hers. *We can't fight them now. We don't even know what happened—why our patrol was attacked. When we retaliate, we will have a plan, and we will attack with purpose. Come lie down with me.*

I must watch the trail.

You can watch it from here. I need your heat. Come.

Sylvan hesitated for only a few seconds, then spun around and dropped down by Drake's side. She pressed close, putting her body between Drake and any enemy who might approach. Drake rested her muzzle on Sylvan's shoulder, her breath a soft trickle of heat against Sylvan's ear. *We'll be home soon. Safe.*

Sylvan growled.

Drake nipped softly at her muzzle. *I know you're worried. Just stay by my side.*

I will never leave you.

Drake closed her eyes, certain of the truth of Sylvan's words.

❖

"Can't you get any more speed out of this thing?" Max grumbled from the passenger seat, aggressive hormones flowing off him in waves.

Niki gritted her teeth and fought the wheel as the Rover rocked over the uneven ground, its oversized tires crushing the underbrush, and the fenders peeling bark from trees as she squeezed the vehicle through passages where no trail existed. "Not if I want to get us there with the undercarriage intact. I can feel the Alpha. We're close."

What she felt was rage, a terrible fury that pounded through her, heating her blood to a fighting frenzy Sylvan was ready to go to war. Max was barely holding back his wolf. If he made any sudden moves, she was going to be at his throat.

A cool hand wrapped around the back of her neck. Sophia's lips caressed her ear. "You'll get there in time. I need you to keep everyone else calm. Max—and the Alpha."

Niki snarled but nodded. She could sense Sylvan but not the Prima, and her stomach clenched. Her wolf clawed for freedom but she had more experience than any other wolf at absorbing the Alpha's call. The Alpha needed her to be in control now, and she would be. "All right. But stay in the Rover until I tell you it's safe."

"She won't hurt me," Sophia murmured. "But I'll wait."

After what seemed like an eternity, the Rover's headlights slashed across an opening in the treeline and Niki edged into a small clearing. Sylvan rose naked in half-form from the shadows, her jaws elongated, her limbs ending in huge lethal claws. She strode directly toward them, snarling a warning. Niki slammed the Rover to a halt and sucked in a breath. Pheromones so potent she almost choked flooded her system. Shuddering against the onslaught, struggling not to shift, Niki pushed out through the door and stumbled a few steps toward Sylvan. Dropping to her knees, her arms outstretched on either side of her body, she tilted back her head and exposed her throat. One swipe of Sylvan's massive claw would tear out her throat, and even if she shifted instantly, she would probably die.

"We've come to help the Prima," Niki said softly, her gaze downcast. "We offer no challenge."

Sweat dripped from Sylvan's pelt-streaked body and a low continuous rumble emanated from her heavily muscled chest. Niki heard the sound of the Rover door creaking open behind her but dared not move.

Go back!

Sophia, her white-gold hair shimmering in the waning sunlight, slipped up beside Niki with the med kit in her hand. She knelt, her shoulder brushing Niki's. A soothing calm quieted Niki's clamoring heart.

"Alpha," Sophia said gently, her voice steady and strong. "Will you let me help the Prima?"

"No one touches her," Sylvan snarled.

Sophia flinched at the fury emanating from Sylvan and glanced up. "I must touch her to care for her."

Niki grasped Sophia's arm. "Go back."

Sophia pulled slowly away. "Please, Alpha. Let me help her."

Sylvan knew Sophia was no threat, but her wolf was beyond control. She'd been hunted, attacked, her mate seriously injured. She was beyond reason. Sylvan breathed deeply, drew on the strength of Pack and the unwavering loyalty of her closest Packmates. "Don't. Hurt. Her."

"Never," Sophia whispered.

Sylvan turned, knelt by the slumbering black wolf, and motioned for Niki and Sophia to edge forward. "She's been deep in sleep for the last few hours. The bleeding is better, but she's not strong enough to heal everything on her own."

"How safe are we here?" Sophia asked, opening her kit and removing fluids and medication. "I don't want to move her until the bleeding has slowed."

Niki stood over them, Max at her side. "You're safe to do whatever you need to do. The other *centuri* are here. We'll keep the Alpha and Prima safe."

Sylvan scented Dasha, Jace, and Jonathan in the forest and focused on Sophia, who parted the pelt around the gash in Drake's shoulder. Drake twitched and Sylvan growled. Niki crouched next to Sylvan, easing slightly between Sylvan and Sophia.

"Alpha, Sophia is a medic. She'll take care of the Prima."

Sylvan looked on the verge of attacking. Niki shuddered but kept her gaze fixed on Sylvan's cheek, avoiding direct eye contact but keeping her head up, exerting the strength of her position as Sylvan's second. When Sylvan needed a cool head in the midst of battle, she was there. And this was a battle to define all battles.

"You must see to the prisoner when we return," Sylvan said, her voice so contorted by the partially transformed vocal cords her words were barely distinguishable from one another. "If I see her I will kill her."

"I've given orders for her to be placed in a cell under guard. I will interrogate her as soon as we return."

"I want to know why. I want to know who gave the order." Sylvan rose to her feet, power flooding the forest, and tilted back her head to howl at the rising moon. "I want to know who I should kill."

Chapter Fifteen

Francesca lounged in the center of her broad bed, human twins—both young, blond, beautiful, and naked—curled up on either side. Idly she stroked the somnolent brother and sister and watched the monitors set into the Louis XVI armoire on the opposite wall. At just after sunfall, Vampires and those who hoped to host for them before the next dawn streamed into the club. Underground in her lair, human servants, blood bound, and blood slaves fed her court, handmaidens, and guards. Once the Vampires had fed, they were sexually potent and most lingered in their quarters, satisfying their urges with each other—with or without a coterie of their blood hosts. Ordinarily, she would have spent the early evening enjoying half a dozen hosts along with the sexual skills of her favorites, but tonight she had fed alone. Michel was absent from her bed again.

As she often did, Michel had spent the daylight hours in the offices Francesca kept in the lair beneath Nocturne, dealing with the business of running their various enterprises up and down the eastern seaboard. Like Francesca, Michel did not need to sleep during daylight hours and, like her, did so less and less as the decades wore on. But usually when it came time to feed, Michel was at her side. The one power Francesca still held over Michel, the oldest and most formidable Vampire of her line, was the ability to enhance Michel's sexual pleasure with her own erotic allure. If she lost that hold on Michel, all that remained between them was history. Loyalty was a fleeting concept for immortals. The world around them changed, allegiances and alliances disappeared as death claimed others. She held dominion over those she ruled through only two means—violence and passion. She smiled to herself as the female beside her murmured and pressed close, her full breasts warm and heavy against Francesca's arm.

"Again, please," the female whispered.

Francesca circled her nail around the female's nipple, leaving a thin trail of scarlet. The female keened softly, her hips rolling, and the scent of need teased Francesca's senses.

Violence and passion. So little really separated them. Violence, though, was a much simpler weapon.

If one of her Vampires angered or challenged her, she imprisoned them and didn't let them feed. They wouldn't perish, but eventually they would long for true death, going nearly mad from hunger. If a Vampire threatened her rule or broke her commandments, she would take their head. Immortality, even for them, was relative. Swift, violent judgment. But those she ruled by passion, she did so only from her bed—the bed Michel had abandoned in favor of a series of Weres and blood slaves.

Beside her, the female whimpered, and the male stirred. Francesca stroked his chest and abdomen, smiling at his instant arousal. She'd fed from each already but hadn't been inclined to satisfy her sexual urges with them. Humans had so little stamina, and their blood, while adequate to replenish the absent elements in her own blood, failed to invigorate her sexual interest. She studied the two of them, amused by their blatant craving. They were slaves to their passion, while hers was her most potent weapon.

"Please, please," the female gasped.

"Yes. Soon." Flowing over the naked form, Francesca guided the female until the blonde faced the sleekly muscled male. Stroking them both, Francesca enveloped them in her sexual thrall. Easily entering the female's mind, she teased her with images of unbearable pleasure and laughed softly as the voluptuous blonde straddled her brother, taking him inside with a wild cry. He groaned, his open eyes dazed and unseeing, as bloodlust swept him up in his own thrall-induced fantasy. He cupped the female's breasts as she rode him in long frantic thrusts, her head thrown back and her belly heaving. Francesca leaned over and took the male's throat. Hot sweet blood flooded her mouth and she pulled deeply.

"God!" he cried, his abdomen rigid. Half rearing off the bed, he pumped his essence in long hard jolts into the convulsing female as Francesca swallowed.

When she'd finished with the male, he slumped back in a stupor and the female fell across his body, whimpering as her orgasm tailed off. Humans were interesting to toy with, but they only whetted her appetite in bed. Francesca rolled onto her side and reached for the teacup on the silver tray beside her bed. She sipped the fragrant concoction and sent a mental call for Charles. With Daniela still in the dungeons and Michel absent, Charles would have to satisfy her needs for now.

A moment later a rap sounded on the door and Francesca rose, pulled on a gauzy, champagne-gold dressing gown, and called, "Enter."

Charles came in, leading Dru. The cat Were looked leaner and edgier than when Francesca had last seen her. Her facial bones stood out beneath taut skin. Her green eyes were stark. She looked hungry.

"I'm sorry to disturb you with business, Regent," Charles said with a courtly bow, "but I felt you would want to hear what our tracker has discovered."

Francesca raised a brow. She hadn't expected the cat Were to return so soon. "You've had a successful hunt?"

Dru flicked a glance at the bed as a spark of gold flashed through her eyes. Francesca drew a breath, scenting the potent Were pheromones. Yes, humans were amusing, but Weres were so much more satisfying. The cat was hungry, and not just for food. She hadn't satisfied herself after her hunt.

"I hope you'll think so, Regent." Dru tipped her head in greeting, but her eyes held Francesca's.

Francesca sent a call to the guard outside her bedchamber and the door instantly opened. A tall, slender dark-haired Vampire slid into the room. "Yes, Regent?"

"Take these two away, would you please, Richard."

"Yes, Regent."

Francesca motioned to Charles and Dru. "Let's move into the sitting room."

She led the way and indicated that Dru sit beside her on the blue brocade sofa. Charles took the one opposite, carefully crossing his long legs, his thigh-high boots gleaming over his form-fitting black trousers.

His white ruffled shirt was open at the throat, the full sleeves falling to wide ornate cuffs. In his time he would have been thought a dandy. Now she found his nonchalant masculinity refreshing. Francesca reclined with one arm stretched out along the curved back of the sofa and stroked Dru's cheek. Dru's canines gleamed as her lips drew back in a soft hiss.

"Tell me," Francesca said, toying with the tawny curls at Dru's nape.

"I've tracked your prisoner almost as far as the wolf Were Compound."

Francesca stilled. "Which wolves?"

"The Timberwolves."

"Really." For the first time in weeks, Francesca was glad for Michel's absence. "And her flight into wolf territory wasn't by accident? They have a vast holding. Perhaps she was lost."

Dru snarled. "The path was no accident. The prisoner had a wolf escort."

"You're sure?"

"The scents were clear," Dru said confidently. "Were and Fae, running together."

"You weren't able to intercept them?"

"I wasn't close enough to overtake them before tonight," Dru said, "and I thought it more important that you have this information immediately."

"Yes." Francesca stroked Dru's neck and the cat's pheromones spiked. Indeed, the cat was hungry, and no doubt good for several vigorous rounds, but Francesca didn't have time to indulge. "You've done well. Before you rest, you might like to visit one of my handmaidens. Daniela. She hasn't fed today, and when she does, I think you'll find the experience most"—Francesca drew a finger down the center of Dru's chest—"satisfying."

Dru shuddered, her skin shimmering with golden pelt and sex-sheen. "I'm sure I will."

"Indulge yourself. You've earned it." Francesca nodded to Charles, who led Dru to the door and instructed one of the guards to take Dru to Daniela's quarters. She waited until they were alone again to speak. "That is unexpected."

"Yes."

Francesca poured claret into two crystal glasses and handed one to Charles. "Your assessment?"

If Charles was surprised Francesca sought his counsel rather than Michel's, her usual advisor, he didn't show it. He took the wine and settled back on the sofa, his posture relaxed. "It would appear the wolves have broken their treaty with you."

"If one can believe appearances." Francesca rearranged her gown, crossing her legs and allowing the flimsy material to slide up her thighs. Charles's gaze sharpened. He had fed as well by now and would be potent. And all the more eager the longer she made him wait. "On the face of it, that's true. We don't know that the wolf involved acted under Sylvan's orders, however."

Charles laughed shortly. "Any wolf who doesn't is a dead wolf."

"As that may be, we have seen that the wolves can be tempted— look at the one who became blood addicted and nearly managed to kill Sylvan and her mate, for instance."

"How do you propose to determine the truth?"

"Sylvan is not capable of subterfuge. If we have the right leverage, she will tell us what we need to know. If not in words, by her actions."

"Leverage?" Charles asked softly.

"Mmm." Francesca looked at the monitors again and studied Michel bent over her desk in the offices. The time had come for her *senechal* to prove her allegiance. "I believe I know just the thing."

❖

Sylvan sat on the floor of the Rover with her back against the side wall and Drake cradled in her arms. Drake had shed pelt halfway back to the Compound, but she hadn't awakened. Sophia had put a needle into her arm and fluids ran in, helping to restore her lost blood volume. Sylvan's wolf prowled, hungering to fight, images of death and carnage consuming her. Sylvan caressed Drake's face and nuzzled her pale cheek.

Drake, can you hear me? Mate?

The silence was worse than a bullet in Sylvan's heart. Drake should be getting better. Her wolf should be healing her. Sylvan growled, and her fury filled the Rover.

Niki tensed on the seat beside Sophia, ready to jump between her and the Alpha if the Alpha lashed out in her pain. Sophia stroked Niki's arm and said softly, "Now that the bleeding has stopped, she will begin to heal. She is strong, the strongest of us all. She just needs rest."

Sylvan looked up, her wolf's eyes blazing. Had it been anyone other than the Omega, she might have snapped. "Are you sure?"

"Yes, Alpha."

Sylvan went back to stroking Drake and did not look up again until the gates of the Compound opened and the Rover roared through, cutting across the yard to the infirmary. When the back doors opened, flickering light from the fires flooded in. Sylvan's eyes burned brighter than the flames. Elena appeared in the open doorway.

"Bring her inside, Alpha. Let us care for her."

Sylvan hesitated, her wolf wary, distrusting. Her mate was injured, defenseless. She wanted to secrete her away, protect her until she was well.

"Alpha," Sophia whispered, kneeling on the corrugated metal floor next to Sylvan. She kept her hands folded in front of her, unthreatening. "You can stay with her and see her safe. Please."

With a low rumble, Sylvan picked Drake up and climbed down. "Where?"

"Come with me," Elena said.

All activity in the Compound stopped as Sylvan stalked across the yard and pounded up the stairs into the infirmary. Whenever the Alpha was out of sight, the Pack was uneasy. Now every Were within miles of the Compound resonated to Sylvan's rage. All across the yard, Weres snarled at each other or pressed close to the shadows, the submissives uncertain, the dominants restless and edgy.

Misha rose from her seat on a log in front of the fire pit where she'd been eating her evening meal, suddenly so agitated she couldn't sit any longer. The Prima was hurt. The Alpha was in a fury. Drenched in pheromones, Misha's wolf circled, hungry to hunt. Rubbing her belly, the burn burrowing deep inside, Misha headed for the barracks without questioning why.

Inside, Jazz guarded Torren's door. His eyes gleamed as Misha approached, his expression hungry. "What's going on out there?"

"The Alpha has returned. The Prima is hurt."

He shivered and tilted his head toward the shadows a little ways away. "The prisoner has been quiet. I can watch her door from the end of the hall."

Jazz had always been a fun tangle—sleek and playful. He'd satisfied her restless urges before, but tonight the ache went too deep. She shook her head. Like the last time she'd refused him, he shrugged and grinned.

"The prisoner refuses to speak with anyone but the Alpha," he said. "Even the *imperator* couldn't change her mind."

Misha snarled softly. "Did she—"

Jazz gave her a curious look. "Why do you care?"

"I'm going to talk to her."

"Just talk?" Jazz asked.

"Yes." Misha reached for the door, ignoring his unspoken challenge, and let herself inside.

Torren sat on her narrow cot, looking elegant enough for a royal court. Her gaze was steady, and a small smile lifted the corners of her wide mouth. "No dinner this time?"

"Are you hungry?" Misha leaned back against the door and tried to settle her wolf. *She* hungered. Craved contact. Or a fight.

"I find that I am." Torren rose, her skin as luminous as moonlight. Her turquoise eyes glittered as if shot through with diamonds.

Misha took a deep breath and honeysuckle flooded her senses. She growled softly, her canines and claws extruding as her sex pulsed.

"I wondered when you would come," Torren said softly, crossing to her.

"What made you think I would?"

Torren traced her thumb over the slanted arch of Misha's cheek, absorbing the wolf's call as her hawk took wing. A hunter called to hunt. "Your taste has been in my mouth all day."

Misha growled, wrapped an arm around Torren's slender waist, and yanked her close. She kissed her, gentling her mouth at the last second, holding back her wolf's need to claim. Spice and flowers exploded in her mouth, and every fiber of her body burst to life. Her wolf bounded through fields of wildflowers, chasing white-tailed deer in the spring sunlight. Joy and power flooded through her. She drew Torren's lower lip into her mouth, nipped the inner surface with her canines.

Torren laughed, her long-fingered hands raking through Misha's hair. The wind ruffled her wolf's pelt while the clouds overhead streamed through her blood, bright and cool as spring water racing down a mountain face. Earth and wind and sky filled her until she overflowed.

Misha and her wolf were one. The chase was on. Hunt fever flooded through her. She cupped Torren's ass, pulled her tight between her thighs, kissed her neck, the arch of her collarbone. "Your scent torments me everywhere I go."

Torren pulled her to the cot, dragged her down until they lay face-to-face. Thousands of stars shimmered in her eyes. "Taste me, then."

Misha rolled on top of her, slanted her mouth over Torren's, and the forest enveloped her in deep green and dappled sunlight. Torren's fingers entwined with hers and suddenly she was soaring, carried by the hawk over the mountain ranges. The forest swirled away beneath her and she pulled back, gasping for breath. "What are you doing to me?"

"Only what you desire," Torren whispered.

Misha trembled, drunk on spice and honeysuckle. Her wolf lunged for freedom, and she let her run.

CHAPTER SIXTEEN

Niki paced up and down the long empty hallway, her skin prickling uneasily. The closed door to the treatment room was as potent as a predator in her territory, a threat that had her wolf on the verge of erupting. She was locked away from the Alpha and Prima when both were injured, but worse, her mate was in that room, unprotected and in danger. The Alpha was beyond reason, enraged and likely to strike out at anyone who seemed a threat. Niki's wolf gnawed at her insides, wanting out, wanting to snap and snarl and stand between Sophia and anything—anyone—who might harm her, even the Alpha. She didn't care if the odds were insurmountable. Her wolf had no concept of suicide, only the innate imperative to protect. She would fight for what was hers even if the Alpha dragged her down and tore out her throat. Even if the choice between mate and Alpha tore her soul apar—

Behind her the door opened, and Niki swung around with a warning growl, canines jutting down and a haze of fury clouding her senses.

"Hush now," Sophia said, closing the door gently behind her. "Everything's all right. There's no need for you to fight. No harm will come to me." She opened her arms. "Come here. I need you."

Niki bounded to her and pressed her face into the curve of Sophia's neck. She breathed deeply, steadying herself in the sweet power of her mate's clear mountain scent. "Are you all right?"

Sophia stroked her hair. "Of course I am. Maybe a little tired. As you must be."

Niki held her tight, afraid to let her go, afraid her strength would desert her if she didn't have Sophia's to lean on. This need would have shamed her before, but was precious to her now. Sophia, with her steely calm and tender strength, banished the darkness from Niki's heart and made her twice the warrior she had been for knowing she had a reason to come home. "I...I missed you."

"I'm here." Sophia raked her fingers through Niki's long auburn hair, kissed her cheek. "Always, right here."

Shuddering, Niki straightened, keeping Sophia in her arms. "The Prima?"

Worry settled in Sophia's deep blue eyes, but she smiled faintly. "She's very strong. She's still...resting."

Niki frowned. "She hasn't awakened? She should have by now—her wounds were many and she lost blood, but none appeared lethal."

"I know." Sophia's voice was a low murmur even though any Were nearby could hear them. "But Elena says the Prima may not heal the same as other wolves, because she is...different."

"Different," Niki said flatly. The Prima was neither born Were nor turned—she was genetically altered by some man-made agent. Just as Sophia was. Even though they both appeared to be completely Were in every way, no one knew the extent of their alterations.

"The Prima may need more time, that's all. But Elena is a wonderful healer—"

"So are you," Niki said gruffly.

Sophia's smile widened and she kissed Niki softly. "Thank you, but I am just a pup compared to her. Elena says the Prima needs only to shift and draw on the strength of the Pack, and she will heal."

"And the Alpha?"

Sophia rested her cheek against Niki's shoulder, one hand stroking Niki's chest. "She is a little more settled now that the bleeding has stopped and the Prima seems to be without pain."

"I must speak to her. Can I go in?"

Sophia nodded. "Just step cautiously."

"When I'm done, I'm taking you home."

"Elena will need—"

Niki shook her head. "She'll have plenty of help. And you need to rest."

Sophia gripped Niki's shirt, pressed tightly against her, her breasts supple and warm against Niki's, her thighs cleaving to Niki in seductive welcome. Against Niki's mouth, she murmured, "I need you. Not rest. Just you."

Niki snarled, her canines brushing Sophia's throat. "Yes."

"Come," Sophia said and eased open the door.

Niki followed slowly. The square timber-sided room held nothing more than a treatment table, shelves laden with medical supplies, a few tall metal stools, and a single bed beneath the sole window. The air vibrated with the lingering scent of the hunt, a vicious fight, and the Alpha's rage. The Prima lay naked and motionless on the bed with a snowy white sheet, for warmth more than modesty, covering her to midchest. Sylvan, wearing only jeans, sat on the floor, her back against the bed, her arm stretched out protectively over the Prima's body and her feral gaze tracking every movement in the room. Her eyes glowed golden in the dim light from a shaded bulb on the wall beside the door. The push of her power nearly brought Niki to her knees. Shuddering, on the verge of shifting, Niki stared at a spot on the rough wood floor midway between them. "Alpha, I've come to report. I interrogated the prisoner."

Sylvan said flatly, "Tell me."

Niki checked for Sophia out of the corner of her eye. The Alpha was not herself, and Niki feared what would happen if she angered her by mistake. Sophia stood by Elena next to a counter on the far side of the room, where Elena, her face strained with fatigue, prepared medication. Sophia nodded imperceptibly to Niki, and her faith settled Niki's wolf. She was Sylvan's second, and she was needed now more than ever.

"She's a Blackpaw, like we thought." Niki hunkered down in front of Sylvan, keeping her head slightly below Sylvan's, her gaze fixed in the center of Sylvan's chest. She did not look at the Prima. "She is injured and weak, but so far refusing to say much."

"I should see to her injuries," Elena said.

"Leave her to heal on her own or die," Sylvan snarled. "She does not deserve our mercy or our care."

Elena pressed her lips together but did not argue.

"Who orchestrated the attack?" Sylvan's voice was little more than crushed glass and gravel.

Niki whined low in her throat and fought not to shift. "She claims the three acted on their own, on no one's orders."

"No." Sylvan's eyes glowed above hatchet-carved bones grown heavy and broad. "Bernardo does not tolerate independence among his

Pack—none would attack without orders from someone above, if not their Alpha, then one they believed was acting for him. And why would the three cross into our territory and strike for no reason?"

"She and the younger male are siblings. The one who attacked the Prima an older cousin. She swears they were retaliating against us because we attacked first."

Sylvan's brows drew down. "That makes no sense."

Niki drew a breath, choosing her words carefully. "She says we killed or kidnapped several of their wolves."

"Who told her that?" Sylvan's canines lengthened and silver pelt blanketed her torso. "If she will not speak willingly, you have my leave to force a confession—"

"Alpha," Sophia said gently. "The prisoner is a wolf, and she might have believed she acted on good information. If we help her, she might—"

"They attacked *my mate*."

Sophia shivered, and beside her, Elena gasped. Niki slid a few feet toward Sophia, ready to block Sylvan's path should she leap.

"I will question her again," Niki said.

"This is Bernardo's doing," Sylvan growled. "He is inciting his Pack to attack us." She shook her head, the demands of leadership forcing her wolf to retreat, letting her think. A welcome quiet settled in her depths, the first since she'd seen Drake locked in mortal combat and covered in blood. "But why? We must know what games Bernardo plays."

"The prisoner may not know any more," Niki said.

Sylvan stroked Drake's face, and in the recesses of her mind, a gentle hand returned her caress. "No, but we have another prisoner who does. Bring the Fae to my headquarters."

Niki backed away, closed her fist over her heart. "Yes, Alpha."

Gray slung her rifle off her shoulder, cradled it in her arms, and squatted down in front of the cell. Callan had awakened her at midnight and assigned her to guard duty. She hadn't been to the prison area in months. They rarely had use of the cells, but cleaning the detention zone was one of the regular duties of soldiers assigned to the Compound.

She'd never thought very much about it as she'd swept and, wearing protective gloves, checked the mechanics of the silver-impregnated cages. Now, she viewed everything in the long narrow room with its three cells differently. Without windows, and only weak bulbs interspersed along the ceiling, it was impossible to tell day from night. The air smelled stale and unused—nothing like the mountain air full of the scents of life everywhere else in the Compound. She expected to smell fear, but the air was impregnated with rage.

The prisoner, a slender redhead with tangled auburn curls down to her shoulders, had deep gouges and bite marks on her chest and arms. Glaring at Gray, she hunched against the back wall, her knees drawn up and her arms wrapped around them. She looked to be a little older than Gray and not as well fed. Her bones showed tight beneath her angular cheeks, and her ribs tented out the pale bruised skin under her breasts. Her hipbones were sharp blades capping narrow hips. Callan hadn't given Gray any instructions—only to stand guard. She'd done that until the silence became as oppressive as the dead air.

"What's your name?" Gray asked, somehow feeling that was important. She remembered how anonymous—how invisible—she'd felt in captivity. If Katya hadn't been there to remind her of who she was, she might have lost herself completely.

"What do you care?" The redhead's voice was low and angry.

"I don't."

The redhead frowned. Her golden brows, thick and gracefully arched, drew down over eyes the color of spring grass. "Then why did you ask?"

"I don't know."

The prisoner's jaw jutted out. "What's yours?"

"Gray." She didn't know why she answered, either, but with just the two of them alone in the dark, with only silver-impregnated bars between them, it was difficult to tell which was the prisoner.

"I'm Tamara."

"Tamara," Gray murmured. The name tasted a little like fall leaves on her tongue—deep and mysterious. "You should shift, your wounds will heal faster."

"I will," the redhead murmured, "as soon as I can."

"There's nothing wrong with the air. There's no silver in the walls. Nothing will poison you."

"What are you talking about?"

Gray remembered the acrid bite of the poisoned air she'd been forced to breathe, the burning in her back where her skin touched the tainted wall they'd shackled her to. She felt anew the torpor in her muscles, and the way her wolf had been chained deep inside her. Her body had functioned—she'd felt pain and hunger and excruciating release—but she couldn't shift. Being cut off from her wolf, from the source of her strength and power—from her self—was worse than the chains. "We're wolves. We have honor. You're a prisoner, but we won't torture you."

Tamara snorted. "Your *imperator* made it pretty clear she planned to kill me."

"Did she use those words?"

Tamara shrugged. "She didn't have to. You already murdered my brother and my uncle."

"You attacked us first. Retaliation is justice—not murder."

"*We* retaliated," Tamara snarled, and her wolf, weakened from her wounds but proud and strong, showed in her eyes. Amber sparked deep beneath the green, and her angular face took on a fierce warrior glow. She was a dominant, young but, even injured and weak, powerful.

"You're wrong," Gray said. "Our patrols were within our perimeter when you attacked without provocation. The Alpha has every right to execute intruders."

Tamara folded her arms over her small, tight breasts and stared hard at Gray. Her canines gleamed against her full lower lip. "You lie, just like your *imperator*."

Gray growled, and red-gold pelt flared down the center of Tamara's hollow abdomen as she rose to the challenge. In her weakened state she couldn't possibly fight, but her wolf refused to belly down.

"That is not wise." Gray rose, shouldered her rifle, and stalked to the far end of the room. She opened a narrow closet set into one corner and pulled out a set of plain gray cotton clothes. Returning, she pushed them through the bars and tossed them to the center of the cell. "Get dressed."

"Why?"

"Because I told you to." Gray moved away from the cell until her back was against the far wall. Tamara's wolf, even injured, was strong enough to interest Gray's. Had the bars not stood between them, they would have circled one another, scenting, testing, challenging. Under other circumstances, they might have tussled, and imagining it, Gray's skin misted with sex pheromones.

Tamara started to push herself up and lost her balance. Breathing hard, she sat back down heavily. The shadows beneath her eyes darkened as her skin grew paler. In the few seconds she'd been nearly upright, Gray had glimpsed the wall behind her, dark and slick with blood.

"What's wrong with your back?"

"Nothing," Tamara gasped.

"Now who lies? Did the *imperator* know you were that badly wounded?"

"I don't know, but I'm sure she wouldn't care."

"I'm coming in." Gray put her rifle down against the far wall and took the key from the hook. She unlocked the bolt, pocketed the key, and stepped inside. The door clicked closed behind her, and they were alone in the cell together. Amber glowed in Tamara's eyes again, and Gray smiled thinly. "If you try, you will lose."

"Maybe," Tamara whispered, and Gray could see her wolf preparing to spring.

"If you hold your wolf, you might have a chance to live. If you attack, you will either die now or later."

Tamara trembled, her pelt thickening as her wolf struggled to ascend.

"I won't show mercy."

"I would ask for none." Tamara gasped. She held her wolf in check, too weak to shift, or maybe wise enough not to provoke a fight she couldn't win.

Gray approached slowly, her arms loose at her side, her gaze holding Tamara's without challenge.

"What are you doing?" Tamara asked.

"Turn around."

Tamara hesitated.

"Truce," Gray murmured.

"Truce." Tamara awkwardly shifted on her knees, giving Gray her back. It was a position no wolf, dominant or submissive, would willingly assume, and the fact that she did only spoke of how weak she was. Or perhaps, that she trusted Gray not to snap her spine.

A surge of anger caught Gray by surprise. Deep bite marks scored

Tamara's right shoulder down to bone, and a steady stream of bright red blood trickled down the center of her back. She'd been bleeding for hours. No wonder she was too weak to shift. "I'm going to get a medic."

"I heard your Alpha say I wasn't to receive any treatment."

"Why did you do this? You must have known you would lose."

Tamara slumped against the wall, her face not even registering the agony she must be feeling from the pressure against her damaged back. "What I had to do. What any wolf would do. Why did you take our pregnant females?"

Gray jerked. "What? That's not possible."

"Ask your *imperator*. Ask your Alpha."

"Just stay quiet. You'll bleed less." Gray reached through the bars to unlock the bolt, slipped out, and locked the cell again. "We would never harm a pregnant female. You're a wolf. Don't you know that?"

Tamara's lids closed, and she struggled to open them. She was weakening by the minute. "I've seen crueler things done to wolves by other wolves."

"Then I'm sorry for you. I'll be back with help."

Tamara's gaze found hers and held. "Why?"

Gray gripped the bars, the silver searing her flesh. "Because we are not like them."

Tamara's eyes widened. "Like who?"

"I only wish I knew," Gray whispered.

CHAPTER SEVENTEEN

Francesca tracked Luce on the monitor as she wended her way though the club's hidden passages down to the lair, a lean shadow slipping between the feeding Vampires and their lust-ridden hosts. When the knock sounded on her office door, Francesca set aside the accounts she'd been reviewing and bade her enter.

"Mistress," Luce said, bowing her head. As usual she was in black—a body-hugging silk shirt, leather pants, and low boots. The glow from the wall sconces on either side of the door haloed her thick black hair and gave her the illusion of an unholy angel.

"I didn't expect to see you tonight," Francesca said. "Something important to report?"

"I believe so, Mistress. I thought it best to tell you in person."

Francesca smiled. "In person and in private."

Luce nodded ever so slightly.

Ordinarily, Francesca would have sent for Michel to sit in on Luce's report, but instead she pushed away from her desk and came around to take Luce's arm. She slid hers through the crook of Luce's elbow and drew her down the connecting hallway to her sitting room. She guided her to the sofa and sat beside her, resting one hand on Luce's leather-clad thigh. "News of Dr. Standish?"

"Her lab's up and running again, and from what I can tell, she is close to resuming full operations."

"Nicholas has influence with those with funds and power, and he obviously used his connections to restore Dr. Standish's facilities." Francesca hadn't heard from Nicholas since the unfortunate events of the governor's gala. Although he publicly denied any involvement in the attempt on Sylvan, she had no doubt he was behind the attack. He hated the Weres for some private reason and pursued his own agenda, which made him not only a useless ally, but a dangerous one. "So tell me, what is the doctor doing?"

"She's very careful to keep some sections of the lab secluded from almost everyone, but she received an interesting delivery last night. When she left to oversee the details, I slipped outside. Two wolf Weres had delivered something by barge. Something requiring cages."

"Living specimens," Francesca mused. "Yes, that seems to be Veronica's pleasure. But why would wolves be involved? Surely not Sylvan's?"

"Doubtful," Luce said immediately. "I'm not certain, but I think they were Bernardo's. I heard one of them object when a security guard told them to wait for paperwork from the lab. They said they wanted to get back to New Hampshire before dawn."

Francesca's incisors gleamed as she hissed. "Bernardo. He is as stupid as he is untrustworthy. Now he seeks to forge a secret alliance with the humans, and he has no idea that Nicholas's only goal is to destroy him and every other Were on the planet."

"Veronica seeks no alliance," Luce said darkly. "A squad of cat Weres murdered the wolves before they could leave. That must have been on her order."

"She thinks to eliminate witnesses, but she is not reasoning clearly," Francesca mused. "Bernardo overestimates his own power, but he will know she is responsible for their deaths."

Luce flashed her incisors with a satisfied smile. "She thinks only of blood pleasures but deludes herself she is in control."

Francesca stroked Luce's cheek. "She doesn't know you observed the execution of the wolf couriers?"

Luce shrugged. "I had no reason to stop it, so I watched unseen from the shadows."

"Veronica, leaving no trail." Francesca smiled. "She is admirable, for a human."

"What would you have me do next?"

Francesca leaned over and kissed Luce. "We must know what experiments she is planning. I'm sure you can think of a way to find out."

"And Bernardo?"

"Leave him to me." Francesca opened Luce's shirt and cupped her breast. "You have done well. I am pleased."

Luce's eyes blazed scarlet and she tilted her head back, allowing Francesca to drink from her throat. She shuddered as her pleasure escaped on a whisper. "Yes, Mistress."

"Go now," Francesca murmured after a moment. Her need was unsatisfied, but she had business to attend to first. Then she would find Michel—it was time Michel returned to her place and proved herself worthy of her Regent's trust.

❖

Misha's heart pounded like thunder, and the breath rasped from her lungs in staccato bursts. The kiss was like running with the Alpha on a midnight hunt, the excitement driving Misha's wolf in a headlong rush through virgin forests over trails thick with fallen leaves. Not wanting the chase to end, she pulled back, and Torren's pale perfect features slowly came into focus. They were still lying face-to-face on the narrow cot beneath the open window. Her shirt was on the floor next to them, Torren's torn open down the center. She didn't remember how they got that way. All she remembered was falling into the heat of Torren's mouth and drowning in the intoxicating taste of her. She hadn't released, neither had Torren, and she should have been wild to by now. Her body was primed, pulsing and full, but all she wanted was to bask in the silvery glow that surrounded Torren, content just to touch and taste, seduced by her mystical allure. She pressed her palm between Torren's breasts, captivated by the cool beauty of her luminous skin.

"Is it true you can do magic?" Misha asked.

Leaning on one arm, Torren traced the sharp angle of Misha's jaw, marveling at the strength beneath the soft, smooth skin. The wolf was so close to the surface, Misha's face burned with power and a magic all her own. "Yes, but probably not the way you think of it."

"I don't know what you mean." Misha frowned, distracted by the electricity spreading through her from the light caress and the scent of Torren's nearness. She nipped at Torren's finger, gave it a shake. "Magic is magic, isn't it?"

"What is magic to one might be ordinary to another."

Misha laughed. "Do you know you talk in circles?"

"Circles are only an infinite series of straight lines joined together."

Growling, Misha bit Torren's throat gently. "More riddles. I know only the earth beneath me, and the scent of prey, and the thrill of the chase."

"Then we are not so different," Torren murmured, easing her fingers through Misha's dark silky hair. "I too am of the earth and the moon, and my soul thrills to the hunt."

Misha's wolf perked up her ears, her gold eyes glittering. "You're a hunter."

"Yes."

"And you can shift. That's why I thought you were a wolf at first."

"I was."

"Not an illusion—not magic?"

"Magic, yes, but real." Torren settled along Misha's length, her thigh between Misha's, her arms caging Misha's shoulders. "As real as this."

Torren pushed the fingers of both hands into Misha's hair and lightly held her head. She kissed her, and moonlight streamed through Misha's blood. Misha rumbled deep in her chest, unused to the unfamiliar position, unused to being comfortable with anyone above her. Torren was unlike any dominant she'd ever been with—her power was as strong as, stronger even than, the dominant wolves', but as elusive as the shimmering shafts of moonlight splintering over them. A wolf's power was of sinew and muscle and primal force—Torren's was of the wind holding the clouds aloft and the moonlit glades where time stretched to eternity. She broke the kiss, wanting, needing, to know more. "What do you hunt?"

Torren grew still, her mouth a whisper above Misha's. Her eyes were the midnight blue of a night sky, deep and fathomless and filled with diamond pinpoints of starlight. "Souls."

"Of the dead?" Misha's heart stuttered, but she didn't pull away, even though a chill threatened to freeze her breath in her chest. She was of the earth, of the flesh of her Packmates, of the blood of her prey. Of sex and passion and instinct. Her world was life.

Torren shook her head, staring into Misha's eyes as if trying to read *her* soul. "Not the dead, the living. I return the lost and the missing, and sentence the unruly, to Faerie."

"You're like the *imperator*."

"Somewhat." Torren smiled. "I am called the Master of the Hunt. I serve the Queen, as your *imperator* serves your Alpha."

"Why did the Vampires imprison you?" Misha's canines bulged when she thought about Torren in captivity, being bled for pleasure or punishment.

"I violated the Vampire Code. The Vampire Regent extracted her punishment."

"And your Queen didn't come to rescue you?"

"Would your Alpha?"

"Yes," Misha said instantly. "The Alpha would never abandon us."

Torren kissed her. "Then you are lucky indeed."

"Could you take me?" Misha eased one leg around Torren's calf, anchoring Torren to her. She had told the Alpha she might be able to learn why Torren had been imprisoned and why she was on their land, but she didn't see how that mattered any longer. Torren had willingly accepted the Alpha's decision to detain her, and she could have escaped. Her power was greater than anyone knew. She was no threat, but she might be in danger, and Misha would not let her be hurt.

"Take you where, my adventurous wolf?"

Misha tugged at Torren's lower lip hard enough to draw a tiny drop of blood. She licked it away and nectar flooded her throat. She growled in pleasure. "On a hunt."

Torren smiled and her smile was sad. "Yes, but if I did, I might not want to bring you back, and you would not be happy in Faerie unless I made you Faerie-kissed."

"I'm not afraid of your kisses."

"Not these, perhaps." Torren kissed her, a slow slide of breath and flesh that brought their hearts beating as one. When she drew back, she shook her head again. "But the kiss of Faerie would make you forget this world, and all you have known here."

"Like Vampires can make you forget." Again Misha felt an instinctive rush of cold fear, but her wolf did not retreat. Her wolf did not see Torren as the enemy, and she trusted her wolf.

"A Vampire can blur the mind, steal the memory of pleasure or pain. But in Faerie, time has no meaning, and once Faerie-kissed, you would long only for the scent of spring flowers and the taste of moonlight." Torren stroked Misha's face. "You would be lost to this world."

Misha traced the delicate arch of Torren's cheek where shadows played with her fingertips. Her wolf was wise. Torren would never hurt her. "Do you miss it?"

"Sometimes. Not tonight."

Growling, Misha wrapped both legs around Torren's hips, the clothes between them suddenly an unbearable barrier. "My wolf knows you—recognized you from the first. Why is that?"

"I don't know," Torren murmured, "but I know you too."

"When you hunt, how do you do it?"

Torren sighed. "You ask me to share secrets I have kept for centuries."

"I can keep a secret."

Laughing, Torren lowered her head and kissed the hollow at the base of Misha's throat. "You taste of moonlight and desire."

"I taste of you." Misha gripped Torren's hair, pulled her head back, bit lightly at her neck. "You hunt as a wolf?"

Torren gasped. "No."

"As a hawk?"

"I search as a hawk, I hunt"—Torren gazed down, her pupils wide and black, eclipsing the blue—"as a Hound."

Misha stilled but her wolf sat up, instantly alert. "Can you show me?"

"No one has ever dared ask of me. Why do you?"

"I want to see what lives inside you."

"And I, I…" Torren shuddered and rested her forehead on Misha's. "I want to *taste* what lives inside you."

"Yes, I want you to."

Torren's weight was gone even before Misha's wolf sensed her move. Misha knelt on the cot and stared as the room filled with mist, curling from the floor in swirling silver clouds that dazzled her eyes. And then she was pushing back against the wall, her heart hammering wildly. A beast twice as big as the Alpha crouched on the floor, regarding her with cold eyes darker than midnight. The orbs would have appeared empty of life except for the fire raging in their depths. Not a dog, not a wolf, but a beast with four legs, massive paws tipped with talon-like claws, and a huge head with a broad muzzle harboring teeth long enough to sever a limb in a single bite. The leathery brown head was capped with short sharp ears and a wide snout. The heavy shoulders and lean haunches were designed for running long distances, leaping over obstacles, hunting down prey. The long tapering body was a machine made of power, to chase and capture and drag quarry back to the Otherworld—or to kill.

Inside, Misha's wolf stilled, regarding the great beast with curiosity and interest. She had no urge to challenge, even with a massive predator within her territory, only inches away. The Hound crouched, its great ribs rising and falling evenly as it watched Misha.

Misha eased forward, held out a hand. Her heart swelled, and the cry of the hawk filled her with joy. "You are magnificent."

The Hound tilted its head until its great muzzle rested against her palm. The hide was warm and soft, lightly furred like a newborn pup's. Its—*her*—breath was warm and her body strong. Misha slid her palms down the huge neck, leaned closer until she felt the steady heartbeat deep within the broad chest. "I want to run with you."

The next time I hunt, you will come with me.

The words, the voice, were Torren's, streaming through Misha's mind as clearly as if spoken. She had only ever heard the Alpha's voice in her mind when the Alpha called the wolves to hunt, but she knew this was right. Somehow, she was Torren's to call too. Her wolf did not question it, and neither did she.

"Yes."

The Hound growled softly, as if pleased, and the mist drew around them and settled a foot above the floor, an ocean of cloud pulled from the sky and brought to earth. Misha rose, and the Hound pressed against her leg.

"I like you better as a Hound than a wolf."

Torren's laughter echoed through her mind, and Misha gasped as the huge beast rose up to rub its head against her chest.

The door behind her swung open, and she heard a startled shout. She pivoted, saw Jazz and the *imperator* framed in the doorway, saw the glint of metal as Jazz's rifle barrel jerked up.

"No!" Misha jumped between Jazz and the Hound as a blast shook the air. The blow propelled her back against the wall and she couldn't see, couldn't catch her breath. Her ears rang with the howl of an enraged beast, and then the splintering pain carried her into darkness.

CHAPTER EIGHTEEN

Sylvan was halfway across the Compound on the way to her headquarters when she heard the shot. Her wolf went on instant alert and every wolf within ten miles followed. The dominants outside the barricades shifted to pelt and took up protective positions along the perimeter. Those inside rushed to their posts along the walls. Nondominants hurried to safeguard the young, prepare arms, and secure the communication lines and emergency escape routes. Sylvan bounded across the yard in two powerful leaps, landed on the barracks porch with enough force to make the building shake, and crashed through the door. The scent of rage, fear, and blood tore a warning growl from her throat as she searched for an enemy.

Two wolves in pelt crouched in an open doorway at the far end of the hall. The red-gray, the smaller of the two, blocked the doorway, keeping the younger black wolf from leaping inside—Niki, the general, controlling her soldier, and probably saving Jazz's life. From within the darkened room, the sound of hell poured forth like volcanic flame—a deep-throated roar that spoke of fury and madness. Sylvan had found her enemy. She covered the length of the hallway in a single leap and gripped Niki's pelt at the base of her neck.

I am here. What happened?

Misha is hurt. That thing *is a threat.* Niki quivered, her wolf verging on the edge of attack.

Wait.

Niki whined, her shoulders bunched to spring.

Wait! Sylvan barred Niki and Jazz from attacking until she was sure she faced an enemy set on battle.

Across the room, a huge beast crouched over Misha's bleeding body. The open maw was cavernous, spreading across a foot-wide muzzle, the thick black lips drawn back from dagger like fangs as long as Sylvan's hand. Its deep-set ebony eyes beneath a broad heavy skull glowed with crimson swirls of molten lava. The leathery mahogany hide was drawn tight over a muscle-bound body as large as a grizzly. The beast roared and the air glowed with power. Sylvan had never seen its kind before, but her wolf recognized a supreme predator and snarled a warning.

You have violated my territory, and I will give you no quarter if you don't stand aside now. I've come for my wolf.

The beast's head slowly swiveled back and forth, its claws scraping the floor as it took one step forward. A direct challenge. *You are not trustworthy. Your minions hurt her.*

Behind her, Niki growled and paced. Sylvan stared into the Hound's fathomless eyes. *No, they would never hurt her. Now I will have what is mine.*

I will take her to Faerie. She is mine now.

No. Sylvan snarled and let her wolf rise. She partially shifted, her claws and canines extending. Her muscles thickened and her pelt flowed heavily down the center of her chest and abdomen. *She is mine and will ever be mine.*

She is dying. The poison has spread too far. If I don't take her quickly, she will be lost. Even I cannot resurrect a soul from beyond the mists.

I can remove the bullet.

The Hound shook its head again, its claws raking the floor. *Not soon enough.*

Sylvan feared the Fae spoke the truth. The wound in Misha's chest ran black with poison. Guards routinely loaded their rifles with silver shot when a Were was imprisoned, and Jazz's shot not only damaged Misha physically, the silver prevented her from shifting and healing. Removing the silver might be too late if the poison crippled the cells throughout her body. If the bullet had struck her heart or a major artery, Misha had very little time left.

I will not let you take her to Faerie. I will not lose her. Sylvan let her power roll, filling the room, drawing on the will of every member of her Pack with the legacy of generations of Alphas. The Master of the Hunt shuddered under her will. *You will do what needs to be done here.*

The Hound stalked to Sylvan, their heads nearly level. Its flaming eyes roiled with fury. It caught Sylvan's gaze and issued a challenge. *I will try, but if she dies, I will have your soul instead.*

Sylvan smiled thinly. *You will have to kill me first.*

I will.

Shouldering the Hound aside, Sylvan strode to Misha and lifted her into her arms. When she straightened, Torren stood beside her, her eyes a glacial blue. She was luminescent, glowing with power that cascaded over Sylvan's skin like frigid mountain water. The Fae's cold rage crashed against her own burning fury. If they fought, the clash of their powers would level the forests.

"I cannot feel her wolf," Sylvan murmured, locking eyes with Torren. If she could not call Misha's wolf, Misha would not have the strength to heal even if she removed the silver.

Torren rested a palm over the wound and closed her eyes. A shudder passed through her. "The bullet is in her heart. I can slow her heart and slow the bleeding, but that may not be enough. If you let me take her to Faerie—"

"If you can quiet her heart, I can remove the silver," Sylvan said.

"Can you guarantee she won't die?"

"Can you?"

"In Faerie, she would live."

Sylvan pressed Misha's pale, cool face to her chest and let her wolf warm her. "But not as a wolf."

"Faerie is a world unto itself. She would be happy."

"Happy?" Sylvan asked softly. "Are you?"

Torren's face shuttered closed. "I will wait to take her as long as I can. But if you fail…"

"I will not fail."

Sylvan loped down the hall, signaling Jazz and Misha to follow. Jazz drew back, whimpering softly as Sylvan stalked past him. Niki shed her pelt and rose, blocking Torren's path.

"You will never touch the Alpha," Niki said. "I will tear your throat out first."

"You are welcome to try." Torren swept through the building and joined the Alpha as she bounded across the courtyard into another log building. The acrid scent of blood and the chemical aroma of drugs flooded the corridor. A dark-haired female stepped into the hall, her eyes widening as she took in Misha in Sylvan's arms.

"Oh no. Alpha—"

"The Prima?" Sylvan growled, and the female shrank back a step from the wave of power undulating in the air.

"She rests. All is well."

"Stay with her. I will see to Misha." Sylvan signaled Niki to guard Drake and kicked open the door of the nearest room. It banged against the inside wall with a crack like thunder. The dark-haired female quickly disappeared back into the room opposite them and closed the door behind her.

Torren followed Sylvan as she laid Misha on a narrow table covered with a plain sheet in the center of the nearly empty room. The shadows were alive with the pain and bravery of a hundred injured warriors, and Torren sent her respects to the souls of the fallen.

"Are you ready?" Sylvan asked.

"Yes." Torren took Misha's hand in one of hers and placed her other hand on Misha's forehead. She let her magic rise, a melody carried on a warm summer's breeze infusing Misha's blood, easing her pain, diverting the flow of poison away from her vital organs like river rocks channeled a roaring stream.

"I must get to the bullet," Sylvan growled. "Her wolf is fading."

"Wait." Torren gathered all that remained of her magic. With a burst of power, the hawk screamed and dove for earth. Misha's heart slowed to a stop, her blood stilled, and the silver settled in torpid streams swirling without direction in her veins. "Now."

Sylvan plunged her claws into the wound in Misha's chest. Misha's lithe body bowed upward as Sylvan slowly eased her hand deeper and closed around her wolf's silent heart. Torren concentrated on keeping Misha's heart calm, channeling the life force of the earth and the sky into Misha's struggling mind and body. Her vision dimmed and a crushing pain filled her chest.

"I am almost empty," Torren gasped. "Hurry."

"I feel the bullet." Sylvan's words rolled through Torren's mind on a ferocious growl. "I need time. Can you dilute the poison?"

"No, but I might be able to draw some of it forth," Torren murmured, winding the spidery black strands around the filaments of her magic and pulling them across the psychic chasm toward her body. She gripped them in her fist and scattered them into the midnight sky where the night winds carried them away.

"I have it." Sylvan dropped the bullet into a basin near the table and pressed her hand to the gaping wound. Sylvan threw back her head and howled, calling every wolf in her Pack to send her their strength.

Torren sensed Misha's spirit surge. As the Alpha's power claimed Misha's wolf, Torren withdrew, carrying all that remained of the black death with her. Misha's heart began to beat faster. After a minute, Sylvan moved her hand from Misha's chest. A healing wound appeared between Misha's breasts. Only a trickle of bright red blood escaped. At the same instant, the inky thread snapped free from Misha's body, and Torren pulled it inside her. Her magic nearly exhausted, she fell to her knees, struggling to destroy the poison.

"What do you need, Torren?" Sylvan gripped the back of Torren's neck. Her wolf raced beneath the wavering hawk, and the night wind lifted its wings.

The pressure in Torren's chest eased. "Just food and rest."

"You shall have both. I am in your debt."

"No. We will call ourselves even this night." Torren grimaced faintly and pushed herself to her feet. Misha's breathing was even and unlabored, a light bronze hue returning to her ashen skin. Torren met Sylvan's golden gaze. "She is young and strong, and your power is great. She will be able to shift soon and finish healing. She will not journey to Faerie yet."

"I will not let you take her, healthy or not," Sylvan said.

Torren brushed her fingers through Misha's hair. "I won't, unless she asks."

Dru jerked upright on the narrow bed as the door to the cell-like room swung open. The hall beyond was dim, and a faceless shadow glided inside. She'd been half-asleep in a pleasant torpor after the human servants had brought her food and the Vampire blood slave had satisfied her physical needs. Her cat was at full strength now, and she crouched, ready to attack. The shadow took form, and Dru recognized the icy floral scent. Francesca. Her cat relaxed only a little. The Vampire

Regent was a powerful predator, and even though her bite was filled with pleasure, it was still deadly.

"I see you're well." Francesca set a glowing torch that appeared as if by magic out of the darkness into the sconce on the wall and closed the door behind her. Her blood-red gown was cut low, hugging her breasts and draping over her hips and thighs in luxurious folds. Her flawless skin pulsed with a faint ruby flush. She'd fed recently and well. Her thrall spread through the room on a wave of heat and honey.

Naked, Dru stood, a light dusting of golden pelt streaming down her belly as her sex filled to Francesca's carnal lure. Beside her, the Vampire slave Daniela whimpered and struggled to her knees on the bed, her head bowed in supplication.

"Regent," Dru said, keeping her cat on a tight leash. Her beast wanted to fuck or fight or both, and either would do. "How may I serve you?"

Francesca suddenly misted to the bedside and traced her fingertips along the curve of Daniela's breast. The blood slave on the bed hissed quietly and her hips rocked in urgent invitation. "I trust my Vampire was pleasing to you?"

"Most pleasurable, thank you."

"Did you fuck her?"

"No, Regent, but I fed her and she answered my needs." The Vampire had been more than hungry—she'd been starving. When Dru walked into the room after Francesca's guard unlocked the door, Daniela fell upon her like a cat on a fawn. The first strike had been so deep and so potent, Dru had instantly spilled her essence over her thighs in a hot torrent. Reeling from the force of the Vampire's bloodlust, she'd staggered to the narrow bed where Daniela had taken her throat again and again, each time driving her to an explosive climax. Now that the urgent pressure of the hunt had been relieved for the moment, her cat was supremely satisfied.

"Good, because I will need you at full strength tomorrow."

"I am ready to hunt again now if you so command."

Francesca smiled. "Soon. I think first I'd like to watch you fuck my Vampire. She's fed, and now she hungers for satisfaction of another kind."

Dru's skin prickled as another pulse of Francesca's thrall flowed over her. Her clitoris lengthened. Her cat's night vision cut through the shadows and the room leapt into sharp focus. Francesca glowed with power.

"Yes," Daniela crooned, her hands over her own breasts. She lay back, opening herself to Francesca's view. Her gaze, blind with lust, fixed on Francesca's face as she reached for Dru. "Fill me."

Dru didn't hesitate. Her cat was in control, and the need to couple rode her hard. She fell on Daniela, one hand between Daniela's thighs and her mouth at Daniela's breast. She bit, tasting the sweet warm tang of Daniela's hormones mixed with the blood she had given her. Her sex clenched, and she rode Daniela's thigh in wild thrusts while she fucked her.

Daniela writhed on the crest of orgasm, her eyes a scarlet sea of madness. Her head thrashed, her incisors scoring Dru's shoulder. Dru roared.

Murmuring encouragement, Francesca stroked the tense muscles in Dru's ass until Dru exploded in a hot shower over Daniela's thigh. Francesca saturated them both with her thrall, driving Dru's cat into an unquenchable heat. "Take her again." She leaned down and kissed Dru's straining jaw. "I want you hungry tomorrow. I want you to catch me a wolf."

Chapter Nineteen

Sは is healing," Sylvan murmured. As the moments passed, the wound in Misha's chest closed completely.

Torren sat beside the narrow bed, the long pale fingers of one hand resting lightly on Misha's forearm. Her eyes had lost the ice of winter and held the soft brilliant blue of an early spring morning. "Young and strong."

Sylvan reached out in search of Misha's wolf and found her curled up quietly in the shadow of a great pine. A hawk perched high above her, its wings tucked, its eyes sharp as it scanned the skies above. Sylvan's wolf settled down beside Misha's and nudged her shoulder to let her know she wasn't alone. The small gray-and-white wolf took a deep breath, shook herself, rumbled quietly, and then settled back to sleep. Sylvan withdrew, leaving her under the protective watch of the hawk.

"How is it I can sense you?" Sylvan asked.

Torren smiled. "Misha is the link."

"And can you—touch my wolf? Through Misha?" Sylvan frowned. She was the link to all her wolves, and if she was vulnerable, then so might they be. Her dealings with the Fae had been limited to her meetings with Queen Cecilia or her emissaries, and she'd never detected any attempt to intrude in her mind. Her wolf would recognize any invasion, warn her of the threat, but Torren's hawk appeared as naturally to her wolf as one of the Pack.

"Do you mean, can I see your thoughts?" Torren laughed softly. "I do not need a link for that, Alpha Mir."

Sylvan snarled softly. "What are you talking about?"

"Your wolf never hides, and the greater the threat, the more she emerges, even when you are not in wolf form. Right now, you're not happy about trusting me. You're also worried about whoever rests in the room across the hall. And this one"—Torren stroked the length of Misha's arm—"she's special, and you want to see her safe."

"They're all special."

Torren nodded slowly. "Yes. I can see that too. She will heal."

"And then what? What will you have of my wolf?"

Torren regarded Sylvan steadily, seemingly unconcerned that holding Sylvan's gaze would send a challenge. When Sylvan snarled softly to warn her she was stepping close to danger, Torren's lips moved upward as if amused, but her eyes held no humor. "I will have whatever she will give me, it seems."

"She is a wolf. Tangling is natural, and Fae magic is seductive. She will want to dance with you, and if she does..." Sylvan shrugged.

"But you are not concerned about a pleasant few hours, are you?" Torren asked quietly.

"You touch her wolf, even when she sleeps, and her wolf lets you. If she gives her heart, once given, she will be bound."

"And I am Fae. You think I have enchanted her?"

"Have you?"

"See for yourself."

Torren met Sylvan's gaze, and Sylvan's wolf padded into the shadows of the deep forest. The aroma of pine and earth surrounded her. A cool breeze ruffled her pelt. She lifted her muzzle, caught the scent of a foreign creature in her territory. A strange not-wolf ran through her land, weary and hungry and alone. Misha's wolf pursued and caught her in the clearing where Sylvan watched. The not-wolf, her power a gleaming halo pushing outward to where Sylvan crouched, did not fight back but let Misha take her throat. When Misha brought her down, the wolf and the not-wolf touched.

"You could have overpowered her," Sylvan said. "You could have trapped her in an illusion."

"My goal was to reach you," Torren said. "Had I needed to, I would have enchanted her, but her wolf called to my hawk. Her wolf heard my song."

Sylvan sighed. "These things should not happen."

"I agree, but the world is not as it once was," Torren said. "Time changes all."

"Soon we shall discover just how much." Sylvan walked to the door. "You are no longer under house arrest. Do not leave the Compound, but you are free to move about."

Torren's fingers closed lightly around Misha's hand. Misha's fingers twitched and entwined with hers. "I'll stay here."

"As you wish. I'll have food sent. She will be very hungry when she awakens."

"I'll see that she receives what she needs."

Sylvan gave her a long stare. "Don't forget, she is mine."

"I understand." Torren's smile was as light and sure as the breeze that carried the hawk's proud call to Sylvan's wolf. "For now."

❖

Sylvan found Jazz and Niki waiting outside in the hall, their anxiety a palpable weight in the air. "She will live."

Jazz's shoulders slumped and he dropped to his knees before Sylvan, his head bowed. "I am sorry, Alpha. I saw...I saw the beast and I thought...I thought—"

"You couldn't have known. None of us have ever seen the Hunt Master's Hound." Sylvan threaded her fingers through Jazz's hair and pulled him close. His arms came around her waist and he pressed hard into her heat. She stroked his hair and regarded Niki over his head. "Where is Sophia?"

"She is seeing to the Were prisoner."

"Why?" Sylvan tensed. "By whose order? I said the prisoner should not—"

"My order, Alpha." Niki's shoulders straightened. "Gray talked with her, learned things I had not. Things you need to know. The prisoner was more badly injured than I realized, and I did not want her to die."

"Where are they?" Sylvan couldn't fault Niki's decision, but she didn't want the renegade wolf anywhere near Drake. She still wanted to kill every last Blackpaw for the attack on her lands and the injury to her mate.

"In the detention center still." Niki's canines flashed. "Max is standing guard while Sophia treats her."

"Good." Sylvan knew how uneasy Niki must be with Sophia so

close to a prisoner. Only Niki's loyalty to Sylvan and her imperative to protect her Alpha could keep Niki from her mate. "Go to her. When Sophia is done, have her tend to Misha. She is healing, but I want to be sure."

Niki glanced at the door. "What about the Fae?"

"She is free to move about the Compound."

Niki's lip curled. "Without a guard?"

"She has shown no evidence of hostility, and she saved Misha's life."

"It is because of her, Misha nearly died. She trespassed and has brought nothing but trouble."

"She escaped imprisonment and sought sanctuary with us. She shared knowledge with me. And she risked her life for Misha. She has earned trust."

Niki grumbled in her chest but didn't protest. "I will not leave Sophia alone with her."

"I'm not asking you to. But do not provoke the Fae just so you will have a chance to fight."

Niki's brows rose and her forest-green eyes sparked with an instant of amusement and mischief. "I cannot know what will provoke one such as her."

"Use your imagination." Sylvan growled the order but her heart lifted. Niki was as ever-unchanging as the mountains that guarded their lands. Strong, stubborn, unyielding, and unrelenting in her loyalty. She would punch through the clouds on the coldest, harshest winter day so the sun could warm them all. Sylvan gripped her neck and yanked her close. Jazz curled between their two bodies. "I need you whole and unharmed. Now and always."

"I am always and ever yours." Niki rubbed her face against Sylvan's neck, their scents mingling, strengthening their bond. Her breath was warm against Sylvan's throat, her body hot and hard against the length of hers.

Sylvan slid her arm down around Niki's shoulders. "Thank you. I must see Drake, then we will find out what the prisoner knows."

Jazz stood, his expression imploring. "I want to guard Misha."

"Granted." Sylvan squeezed his shoulder and eased open the door to Drake's room. The sun had risen while she'd been caring for Misha, and soft golden light streamed through the window.

"There are no signs of fever," Elena said from the bedside. "Her heart beats strong and steady. She is in some kind of deep healing sleep."

"Are you sure?" Sylvan stroked Drake's hair. They'd been apart for hours now, longer than any time since they'd been mated. The separation bruised her heart. "If she hasn't shifted, how is she healing the deeper wounds?"

"I've been charting her vital signs carefully." Elena rubbed Sylvan's arm. "I've never seen anything quite like it, but she is healing as if she *has* shifted, even though she has not."

"As if her wolf has taken control without showing herself?"

"It seems that way, Alpha," Elena said.

"How?" Sylvan's wolf could ride her even when she wasn't in pelt, but the effort not to shift with her wolf ascendant required tremendous strength and control. Only a few Alphas ever managed it. Drake should not have been able to draw on her wolf's power without shifting.

Elena hesitated. "It might be the result of her genetically engineered biology."

"Do not speak of it. This is not something we want our enemies to know."

"Not to anyone. My word."

"Thank you." Sylvan drew Elena near. "You are tired. Go. Rest. I will stay here."

"You might need me—"

"We all need you." Sylvan kissed her forehead. "Go, find your mate, let Roger care for you. I will call, if there is need."

Elena leaned into Sylvan for an instant, drawing strength from her strength. "I will, Alpha."

Once alone, Sylvan stretched out beside Drake, settling her mate against her body the way she often did after they'd tangled or when they awakened in the quiet before dawn. Her wolf sought Drake's and found her lying quietly in a pool of sunlight, her head on her paws, her eyes closed. Sylvan pressed close against her, resting her head on Drake's. *Mate?*

Drake's wolf opened a sleepy eye, nipped at her muzzle. *You worry too much. What are you doing here? Don't you have business to attend to?*

I missed you.

Then stay for a while. I am here.

When their wolves settled down to sleep, Sylvan buried her face in Drake's hair. "I love you."

Drake's hand moved slowly over her abdomen, her breath a whisper against Sylvan's throat. "I love you. Rest now."

Sylvan's heart eased and she closed her eyes.

❖

In the mess hall, Katya heaped food onto a metal plate, carried it to one of the long tables, and sat down next to Gray. "I thought you had guard duty."

"Sophia is with the prisoner. I've been relieved."

"Huh." Katya shoveled stew into her mouth and swallowed. "I can't believe those wolves attacked us. No sense of honor, I guess."

"They thought they had reason," Gray snapped. "Where have you been?"

Katya raised a brow at the accusing tone. "Running with Eric. That's why I'm starving. Why?"

"Did you tangle?"

Katya laughed and shook her head. "Is that all you think about?"

Gray's brows furrowed. "Don't you?"

"You don't want me to answer that, not really. You only want to know what you want to hear."

"I do want to know." Gray stared at the rough surface of the plank table and picked at a splinter of wood. "It's just…I'm afraid, and I'm afraid of being afraid."

"There's nothing wrong with being afraid." Katya slid close until their thighs touched. "The only thing wrong is letting your fear hold you prisoner."

Gray wrapped her arm around Katya's waist. The softness of Katya's breast against her arm, the strength of her embrace, reached deep inside and comforted Gray's wolf. She had been so lonely for so long and sometimes forgot that always when the darkness closed in, Katya had been there. "I know you're right, but the anger is so much safer."

"I'm angry too, and you're right, anger is better than fear." Katya straddled the bench and pulled Gray into the circle of her arms. After an instant, Gray relaxed into her hold. Katya kissed her cheek and nuzzled her hair. "Keep your anger," Katya murmured, "but let the Pack take your fear."

"I think we will be fighting soon," Gray said. "The prisoner—she told me things."

"What things?"

"Bernardo lied and told his wolves we captured some of their pregnant females. He's the reason they attacked us."

"You believe her?"

"Yes," Gray said, thinking about the blood, and the pain, and the strength. "She's too proud to lie."

"If that's true, the Alpha will challenge Bernardo."

Gray grinned. "Yes, and if he doesn't turn tail and run, she will destroy him."

"I bet he starts a war because he's too cowardly to stand to a challenge, and he'd rather see his wolves die than lose face," Katya said.

"If Bernardo is the reason the Prima is hurt, the Alpha will paint the forest with his blood. And soon."

"The Alpha will need soldiers. She'll call us, don't you think?"

Gray nodded. "We have proven ourselves. The Alpha has said so."

"Good." Katya was as eager as any wolf to protect their territory, and she might not have much time before the coming battle. She hadn't tangled with Eric when he'd offered. She hadn't tangled with any wolf since she'd been freed from captivity. She'd only given herself to Michel, only tasted Michel, and the need for her was a constant drumbeat in her body and her blood. She kissed Gray's cheek quickly and stood. "Finish your breakfast and get some sleep. If we're going to battle, we'll have to be ready."

"Where are you going?"

"Not far."

Katya hurried outside and through the gates. Within seconds she'd shifted, and her wolf raced toward the city. Time was short, but Michel didn't sleep, and she would know Katya was coming.

CHAPTER TWENTY

Sylvan pushed open the cell door, ignoring the flash of pain in her palm as the silver burned a stripe across it, and stepped into the cramped dim space. Sophia knelt by the prisoner, a med bag open by her side. Max stood off to the right, his scorching glare riveted on the Blackpaw. The young female, wearing only gray fatigue pants, writhed on the narrow cot in an attempt to rise.

"Don't. You'll make the bleeding worse." Sophia pressed her hand to the center of the prisoner's chest. The prisoner snapped and thrashed, her claws shooting out, red-gold pelt flaring down the center of her taut, slender abdomen.

"Stay still," Sylvan roared, and every wolf in the vicinity shuddered and ducked their heads. The prisoner cringed and backed against the wall in a defensive position. Blood trailed across the stones beneath her. The prisoner's scent, full of pain and fury, nearly obliterated the undercurrent of fear. Any rational wolf would fear an Alpha, but this one wanted to fight more than she wanted to run. In any other wolf, Sylvan would have admired the trait. Now she didn't even regret that she would have to kill a brave fighter.

Sophia glanced over her shoulder, her face pale, her eyes imploring. "Please, Alpha, she needs to be in the infirmary. She is bleeding and I—"

"Let her bleed." Sylvan stalked across the narrow cell and stared down at the injured renegade. The female would not meet her eyes, but her posture bordered on aggressive. She was brave, the bravery of the young and inexperienced. Sylvan could tear her limbs off in one strike.

"Move away," Sylvan said to Sophia.

Sophia hesitated.

"Now," Sylvan growled, and Sophia quickly retreated to the cell's open doorway. Sylvan's wolf was in a killing rage, and all she wanted was to bring a swift end to the one who had threatened everything that mattered to her. Through the frenzy, she could almost hear Drake admonishing her to use all the power the Pack brought her, sound advice she had trouble remembering when her Pack and her mate were in danger.

"Gray says she is not to blame," Sophia said softly from behind her.

"Gray was not there."

"No, but Gray has talked with her. If you listen, you might learn more than if she is dead."

Sylvan wanted to ignore her, but her wolf knew better. Every Pack needed an Omega, but not all had them. Sophia was a rarity. She brought balance and reason to those whose first instinct was to fight. Sylvan shuddered and her wolf backed off a step, wary but willing to wait for the kill. Sophia's strength and calm washed over her like a warm oasis in a raging storm, and she took a minute to let her wolf absorb the soothing energy.

"Tell me what you told my wolf about Bernardo," Sylvan said.

The prisoner's head snapped up and she glared in defiance. "Why ask when you won't believ—"

Sylvan grabbed her by the neck and jerked her into the air. Sophia gasped but no one else made a sound. Sylvan lifted the female until their eyes were at the same level. Through vision gone wolf shades of gray, she saw terror in the eyes looking back at her. Her hand, tipped with claws, dwarfed the young female's throat. Sylvan's wolf smelled her mate's blood, sensed her pain. One squeeze and she would have her retribution.

We are not savages. You are not Bernardo.

Her mate's voice teased through her awareness and an imagined hand stroked her rigid back. Her wolf's blind need to dominate, to destroy her enemies, to protect all that was hers, gave way to the reason that kept her from feral madness. She focused on the place inside her where Drake's love gave her strength, and held back her wolf from the killing strike. She snarled close to the female's throat. "I have no patience. Tell me what I want to know or die now."

The female held Sylvan's stare longer than Sylvan would have believed possible before lowering her gaze and going limp in submission. Sylvan shook her once, hard, and let her fall back onto the cot. A low continuous rumble of warning sounded in her chest as she folded her arms and stared down. "What's your name?"

"Tamara."

"Why were you on my land?"

Tamara drew a long shaky breath. "We were trying to track our missing wolves. When we crossed paths with your patrol, we had to fight."

"Did you follow a scent trail into Timberwolf territory?"

"No, but Bernardo told my uncle, one of his lieutenants, that our missing females were in your territory. That you wanted the pups."

"Your uncle led the raiding party?"

Tamara's canines flashed, but she kept silent, only nodding her assent again.

"How many are missing?" Sylvan could easily imagine undisciplined wolves in a frenzy over missing females, especially pregnant ones, and attacking without thought. Bernardo was either too weak an Alpha to control them, or he didn't want to.

"Two that I know of, but I think there is at least one other."

"Whose mates?"

Tamara's brows drew together. "I don't understand."

"Whose pups are the missing females carrying? Are they Bernardo's young?"

"No," Tamara said quickly. "Bernardo has no mate, and the females he tangles with never breed."

"Then who bred these pups?"

"Two I know of for sure—one by Rona, a *centuri*." Tamara was silent for a long moment before her gaze met Sylvan's before flashing away. "The other by Franco, a captain in Bernardo's guard."

Dominant wolves, high in the pack hierarchy. Their young would strengthen the power of whoever led the Pack. "Are these wolves loyal to Bernardo?"

"I don't know. Bernardo…" Tamara hesitated, rightly reluctant to criticize her Alpha.

From the door, Niki said softly, "Those pups would be a threat to Bernardo's rule if they or whoever bred them challenged him."

"Yes." Sylvan held her rule by strength and loyalty. She would sooner die in a challenge than kill an unborn pup to hold her power. She growled and Tamara flinched. "How many others know of this?"

Tamara shrugged. "I don't know. All the lieutenants—at least half a dozen—but who they told…? We didn't wait to start the search. One of the missing females is my uncle's sister."

Others would be coming. Bernardo's lies were meant to incite his Pack into attacking, and a guerrilla war along her borders could go on for years. Her forces would be divided and Bernardo would be safe in the heart of his territory. Unless Sylvan stopped him now. She motioned for Sophia. "Tend to her."

"Not here," an unexpected voice said.

Sylvan jerked around.

Drake, standing just outside the cell with Niki, said gently, "If Sophia thinks the prisoner needs to be cared for in the infirmary, we should listen to her."

Sylvan's wolf leapt joyously. The air around her sprang to life. "Mate?"

"Yes." Drake smiled and rested a hand on Sophia's shoulder. Sophia drew a deep breath, as if replenishing her depleted strength from Drake's touch. "Let's leave our *medicus* to do her job."

"How are you—" Sylvan stopped, aware of those listening. Drake was healed, completely healed. Her wolf was whole, her power a shining force obliterating the darkness that had shadowed the edges of Sylvan's soul these last hours. She nodded, her throat tight. "Fine." She gestured to Max and Gray. "Move the prisoner to the infirmary. Take up post there."

"Yes, Alpha," Max and Gray said with simultaneous salutes.

Sylvan wrapped an arm around Drake's waist and pulled her away from the cell to the far end of the detention area. Once they were alone, she cradled Drake's face between her hands and kissed her. Shaking with the effort to contain her wild need to taste her, she asked hoarsely, "How are you here?"

"I woke up alone and I missed you," Drake whispered, sliding her hands up and down Sylvan's back. "You haven't eaten and you haven't slept. Why can't I trust you to take care of yourself?"

Sylvan laughed shakily. "I had other things on my mind."

"No excuses. I'm going to feed you, then we're going to see our young, and then I am taking you to the den and putting you to sleep."

"There is much we must do."

"And we will. But first we both need this."

Sylvan crushed Drake to her, afraid she was imagining Drake's presence. Drake felt so strong, so healthy and vital. The heat of Drake's body was real. The surge of renewal that coursed in her blood was real and could only have come from her mate. Sylvan licked Drake's neck, drew deeply of her scent. "You shouldn't be healed by now."

"But I am." Drake raised Sylvan's head until their mouths met. She kissed her, tugged sharply at her lip, teased her until Sylvan's wolf forgot about injury and danger and fear and knew only the joy of their union. Drake pulled away, gasping for breath and hungry for the comfort of her mate. "I'm fine. And I want you."

"You have me," Sylvan murmured, "but we may not have much time."

Drake dug her claws into Sylvan's ass until Sylvan snarled. Smiling, she pulled Sylvan toward the light shining beyond the dark corridor and the now-empty cells. "We will always have time enough."

❖

Katya trotted around the perimeter of the deserted-appearing building. Nothing moved except the desultory breeze off the slowly churning Hudson, carrying the pungent scents of diesel and decay. Nocturne, in the hour before sundown, looked like every other abandoned warehouse along the waterfront, its windows boarded over, its single weather-worn door padlocked closed, the huge expanse of concrete surrounding it cracked and uneven, weeds and rubble scattered over its surface. But she knew beneath the concrete, deep under the club, Francesca's Vampires, their human servants, and the blood slaves slumbered or fed or fucked. And she knew Michel was waiting for her. The closer she'd come, the stronger the insistent hum in her veins, the more urgent the pulsing beat in her sex. Michel was not slumbering, and she had not fed.

Katya skirted low along the side of the building, using the scraggly bushes and clumps of weeds as cover until she reached the rear of the building facing the river. A shed roof extended along half the length of the building and provided cover for a raised concrete loading dock underneath. Adjacent to the platform, a huge metal roll-down door marked the entrance to a garage. At the far end of the building, a single weathered metal door marked the only other entrance. She trotted over and rubbed against the door, still warm from the sun, and crouched to wait. Less than a minute later, the door opened a few inches and she slid inside, shedding her pelt as she entered. She'd barely gotten to her feet when two hands gripped her shoulders and slammed her back against the wall. Her naked back scraped on cold stone. A figure loomed over her and a torrential downpour of rage flooded her skin.

"What are you doing here?" Michel hissed.

Katya gathered Michel's shirt into her fists and tore it from her shoulders, her claws scoring Michel's alabaster chest. She licked the streaks of blood even as Michel's flesh healed. "I came for you."

Michel's hand slid down her abdomen, between her thighs, and inside her at the same instant as Michel's incisors struck her throat. Katya's body arced as if electrified, and she muffled her howls against Michel's shoulder as she released hard once, twice, then again. Michel thrust against her, inside her, as she fed and came. Katya gripped her hair, held her face to her throat.

"All," she murmured as lust and pleasure stole her reason. "All of me. Yours."

Michel sagged against her, her chest heaving, one hand still buried in her depths. "I told you it's not safe."

"You're starving."

Michel's head whipped back, her eyes ablaze with scarlet fury. "I can survive without you."

Katya raked her claws over the bite she'd left in Michel's shoulder the last time they were together, and Michel shuddered, her throat convulsing as feeding hormones drove her toward bloodlust again.

"You can't," Katya said, "and neither can I. I had to see you."

Michel glanced up and down the dark, deserted corridor. "Francesca will expect me soon, and the others will be rising. I won't let them feed from you. I have taken your blood, and you mine. Will you let me claim blood rights?"

"Oh yes," Katya murmured. "But I can't stay. We might…"

Michel's eyes narrowed. "What?"

Katya shook her head.

"You don't trust me." Michel laughed harshly. "I am more helpless before you than I have been for a thousand years, and still, you do not trust me."

Katya ran her fingers through Michel's hair. "I trust you, but not Francesca."

"I will not betray you."

"And when she enthralls you and steals your mind? What will she see?"

Michel kissed her, let her hormones merge with Katya's. "Our bond grows daily. I won't let her in."

"And then she'll know you are resisting, and you will be in more danger." Katya shook her head. "If you don't know the plans, you don't need to shut her out, and you will be safer."

"I don't need a wolf barely out of adolescence to protect me," Michel said archly.

Katya bit her, burying her canines in the mark on Michel's shoulder. Heat blasted through Michel's body as their blood fused and their bond was forged. Groaning, she straddled Katya's thigh as the orgasm swept through her.

"I forgot you can bite," Michel gasped when the brutal orgasm faded.

"Tell me again you don't need me," Katya growled, "and I'll do more than bite you."

"If you accept my claim, I will never let you leave me."

"I already have accepted, and I won't be leaving."

"Go—before the sun is down and this place is surrounded by the Risen," Michel said. "I'll send for you as soon as I can."

Katya stroked her face. "What are you going to do?"

Michel shrugged, faced with choices she hadn't considered for centuries. "I don't know."

"You may be ancient and powerful, but you must still be careful. I want you to come back to me." Katya kissed her hard. "And if you don't, I will find you. I promise."

Chapter Twenty-one

Sylvan, resting on one arm, stroked Drake's face and throat. Somewhere nearby a hawk called for its mate, the sharp cry floating through the open windows above their bed. She was reminded of Torren's hawk communing with her wolf in a way she'd never thought possible. So many things she hadn't expected—most of all this love that gave her strength and taught her to fear in a way she never had before. She leaned down and kissed Drake's chest where her heart beat. "I'm not sure even I can heal as you did."

"What do you mean?" Drake pulled Sylvan down on top of her and wrapped both arms tightly around her shoulders. The worry in Sylvan's eyes and the pain she still carried around her heart tore at Drake the way no physical damage ever had. She smoothed the tight muscles in Sylvan's back until she felt Sylvan relax into her. "Tell me."

Sylvan drew a deep breath and let it out with a sigh. "How much of the fight do you remember?"

Drake snarled. "I remember the ambush, and the black wolf we killed."

"Yes," Sylvan said, the satisfaction of the kill still rippling in her depths. The wolf had deserved to die—he had invaded her territory and attacked her mate. The scent of Drake's blood still assaulted her senses, and her wolf started to pace, her fury returning.

"I'm fine because you came when I needed you, as I knew you would," Drake whispered. "Let your wolf have some peace."

Sylvan nodded and drank in Drake's pure, strong scent. "Do you remember anything about being in the infirmary?"

"No, I only remember waking up and missing you."

Sylvan tensed. "I'm sorry I wasn't there. I needed—"

"I know what you needed to do and where you needed to be." Drake let her claws drag up and down Sylvan's back, the small slivers of pain reminding Sylvan that theirs was a love and a union built on strength and trust. "But then I sensed you nearby, and I wanted to see you."

"When I left, you were deeply asleep, so deep that for a long time I couldn't find you."

Drake caught her breath. "I'm sorry. I don't remember very much, but I always knew you were near."

Sylvan kissed Drake's breast. "Good."

"I wasn't hurt that badly, so I don't understand why you're surprised that I healed."

"Your wounds weren't fatal, you're right. But you lost a lot of blood very quickly and you were weak. Weak enough that you weren't able to shift right away."

"That happens sometimes, but usually with treatment, a Were can shift and finish the healing at an accelerated rate." Drake frowned, her physician's mind turning over the issues. "And even if they can't, as long as supportive therapy is provided, healing should progress—"

Laughing softly, Sylvan kissed her again. "Dr. McKennan, you don't understand. You've healed faster than any other wolf could, other than a powerful Alpha drawing on a large Pack. And you didn't shift."

Drake stilled. "At all?"

"No. Your wolf was weakened during the attack, and by the time we got back here, you'd shed pelt. Even with Elena's treatment and my wolf transferring power, you never shifted."

Drake took in the information, sorting through everything she knew about Were physiology, which was far less than she wished. The ancient Praetern imperative to guard the details of their biology from outsiders was not always to their benefit. "It seems I can access the enhanced healing powers of my wolf without actually shifting."

"Yes," Sylvan said.

"That is likely because I'm not a born Were," Drake mused. "Have you never seen this is in other *mutia*?"

"No, but not many lived long, and they all resulted from Were fever. You and Sophia did not."

"But Sophia has never shown the same ability to heal, has she?"

"Sophia is not a warrior—she's never sustained a near-lethal injury."

"And let's hope she never does." Drake closed her eyes, letting her subconscious work on the problem. "We don't really know if the two of us share the same alterations, but at least in me, whatever they've done to genetically engineer the transformation has inherently altered the balance between my forms."

"Allowing you to call on your wolf without actually shifting," Sylvan said.

Drake opened her eyes, the enormity of the conclusion suddenly clear. "They set out to produce a viral contagion to terrify the population into quarantining and possibly destroying the Weres, and instead, they may have created a vehicle to transform humans into enhanced Weres."

"And if they were to discover that," Sylvan said, "they would almost certainly try to raise an army against us."

"They won't," Drake said decisively. "We must put a stop to this. Subverting Were natural biology can only lead to other unpredictable and potentially dangerous mutations. Who knows what else they might be able to alter."

Sylvan growled softly. "What if the primal urges are enhanced as well? With no Alpha to control them, these engineered Weres could become killing machines."

"We have to find the labs, and we have to destroy them."

"First, I must find Bernardo."

"What are you going to do?"

"He has left me no choice." Sylvan sat up on the bed, her face and eyes all wolf. "I'm going to kill him."

"What of his Pack?"

"If no new Alpha emerges, I will annex his Pack. They need a strong leader. One who does not lie to them and lead them to their deaths for his own purposes."

"Not all of them will come willingly."

Sylvan shrugged. "They are wolves. They will follow the Alpha."

"Some will fight for the old Alpha until he is defeated."

Sylvan smiled. "Then I will kill him swiftly."

"When?"

"Tonight."

"I can be ready—"

"We have young, and they have not yet hunted." Sylvan's voice was that of the Alpha, full of command. "We cannot risk them losing both of us."

"They will have a better chance of having two parents if I come with you."

Sylvan grasped Drake's shoulders and loomed over her, pinning her to the bed. The golden light from her eyes blazed as brightly as the sun, and Drake struggled not to look away. "Our Pack cannot be without a strong leader now, and our young cannot be without a mother." Sylvan kissed Drake, her canines scoring the soft inner surface of her lip. "Let me go into battle with your strength at my back, and my heart safe."

Drake lay perfectly still for a long time, then kissed the hollow of Sylvan's throat. "This one time, and only because our young are as yet untrained. But they will learn to lead by our example, and we will show them a united, mated Alpha pair. I will not stay behind again."

Sylvan let out a long sigh and rested her forehead against Drake's. "Agreed."

"And you will not ask or command otherwise."

Sylvan sighed again. "As you wish, Prima."

Drake rolled her over and settled between Sylvan's legs. Grasping Sylvan's wrists, she held her arms to the bed and Sylvan relented, even though she could easily have broken Drake's hold. Drake kissed her slowly, her body molding to the stark planes and soft valleys of Sylvan's body. Pelt shimmered beneath her belly as Sylvan readied under her. Heat poured over her thighs and Sylvan's clitoris rose against hers. Her need for Sylvan was a living beast consuming her from the inside— ferocious and insatiable. She thrust hard between Sylvan's thighs and pain and pleasure warred within her. Her vision wavered until all she saw were the deep craters of Sylvan's pupils, inviting her to burn. She punctuated every word with another thrust. "Do. Not. Take. Chances."

"I won't." Sylvan turned her head, offered her throat. "I will always come back to you."

Drake kissed down Sylvan's throat along the path to the bite on Sylvan's chest. She covered her mark with her mouth and slid her clitoris against Sylvan's. Then she sank her canines into the deep muscle over Sylvan's heart and claimed her mate.

❖

Misha opened her eyes and found the turquoise ones that had been haunting her dreams for hours. She swallowed past the dryness in her throat. "You should be hunting. Hawk is hungry."

Torren smiled. "She will hunt now that you are awake."

Misha stretched, touched her hand to the center of her chest. "You weren't hurt?"

"No. Only you." Torren leaned over and kissed her. "That was a foolish thing to do, even for a wolf."

Misha growled and nipped at Torren's lip. "What would you have had me do? Let you be shot?"

"I would not have been shot."

"What would happen if your Hound were shot?"

Torren's eyes gleamed. "It would take more than one bullet and very lucky aim."

"My wolf doesn't think that way. You were in danger, that's all I cared about."

"I'll remember that the next time we're faced with an enemy." Torren stroked Misha's hair. "I have food here. Are you hungry?"

"Starving." Misha grinned and started to sit up.

Torren stopped her with a hand on her shoulder. "No. I'll see to it."

Deep inside, Misha's wolf rumbled with satisfaction and settled down to wait. "You're pale."

"I'm not a wolf."

Misha snarled softly. "I know what you are, and you're never pale. You're…like moonlight."

Torren smiled and the air around her glowed. She pulled the cart near and sat on the side of the bed, sliding one arm behind Misha to help her sit up. "How do you feel?"

"A little weak. Nothing a good meal won't cure." Misha leaned against Torren's side and stilled Torren's hand when she reached for the tray. "You didn't answer me. What happened to you? Are you sure Jazz didn't hit you?"

"I am just a little drained. I…helped your Alpha with your wound."

"Drained." Misha's wolf whined unhappily, and an image of a dense black web of poisonous tendrils formed in her mind. She stiffened. "You absorbed the silver."

"Silver doesn't affect me."

"But inside me it turned to some kind of poison, and you...you took it into *you*." Misha twisted around and grasped Torren's shoulders. "Are you hurt?"

"No," Torren whispered, amazed at the fearlessness of the young Were who challenged the Master of the Hunt. "I am well."

"Don't do that again."

Torren arched a brow. "Or?"

Misha flashed her canines. "Or I will be very angry."

"I'll remember that, then." Torren gestured to the heaping platters of food. "You should eat. A few days' rest and you'll be fine."

Misha frowned. "The Alpha has called the warriors. I felt it—I think that's what woke me. There will be a battle. I must go."

"No," Torren said calmly, carving a thick piece off a slab of roast and offering it to Misha. "Not right away."

Grumbling, Misha took the meat and nearly swallowed it whole. Her wolf was so hungry she couldn't think of anything else for a few minutes. With every bite Torren fed her, she felt stronger, and more certain than ever that Torren was hers.

"Better?" Torren asked when everything that had been delivered from the kitchen was gone.

"Much better." Misha rested her cheek against Torren's shoulder. "You smell like the breeze—so cool and so...alive."

"You fill me with the lightness of the clouds." Torren cupped her chin and kissed her. "Tired?"

"A little. If I shift, I'll heal faster."

"Then call your wolf. There will be no battle for you for a while."

Misha wanted to protest, but Torren was right. She felt as wobbly as she had when she was first learning to shift and every transformation would leave her weak. When she took a deep breath, a dull pain radiated through her chest. She was not yet healed. "Will you stay?"

"Until you tell me otherwise." Torren stretched out beside her.

"Rest with me, then." Misha shuddered and a gray wolf with white patches on her chest and forelegs curled up against Torren's side.

Torren ran her fingers through the thick soft pelt. Dark eyes watched her face with curiosity and trust. For an instant her hawk dropped from the sky and her Hound roused from its slumber and they welcomed the wolf. The wolf barked a sharp greeting, the hawk let out a shrill cry of acknowledgment, and the Hound rumbled deep in its great chest.

"Sleep," Torren whispered, and the wolf closed its eyes. Torren loosed the hawk to hunt and the Hound to keep watch and, draping one arm around the wolf's powerful shoulders, settled down to rest.

❖

Francesca closed the doors of the armoire, hiding the monitor from sight. She'd seen what she needed to see, what she'd been expecting to see for weeks. She turned to Dru, who lounged on her sofa, her eyes faintly hazy from her recent sexual pleasures with Daniela. "Can you track her?"

"Of course."

"I want her in a cell by daybreak."

"She'll fight."

"She's young and alone. You are the experienced fighter." Francesca smiled and draped the arrogant cat in her thrall. As she expected, her faint challenge to the Were's ego and the subtle blood kiss caught the cat's interest.

"I'm not worried about a fight." Dru smiled and ran her hand down the center of her chest. Her blood was still high from her recent coupling with Daniela and the chiseled muscles were still brushed with soft pelt. "If she resists, I can't promise you she won't be injured."

"As long as she doesn't die."

"As you command." Dru stretched, her nipples tight and tingling. Her clitoris was tender from the repeated releases, but her sex still throbbed with urgency and need. Her heat seemed to be never ending. She couldn't remember any longer what mattered beyond her service to the Vampire Regent and the rewards for pleasing her. She would welcome a hard run and a successful hunt. She would welcome the taste of her victim's blood in her mouth when she brought her down. And then when she returned—

"When you return," Francesca said smoothly, "I will see that you are amply compensated, as always. As many times with as many partners of any nature as you desire."

"And if I desire you?"

"Then you may find yourself with more pleasure than you can stand."

Francesca was suddenly looming over Dru. Francesca kissed her, and Dru's body reacted as if the Vampire had bitten her. She groaned and released her essence in a blinding explosion. When she caught her breath, she met Francesca's laughing gaze. "I look forward to it."

Francesca waved a hand toward her door. "Then go, and bring me the wolf."

CHAPTER TWENTY-TWO

R oger said they spent half the day in pelt again," Sylvan said as
Drake returned their young to the collective sleeping pile.

"I know, Marta told me when I stopped by earlier." Drake settled
Kendra next to Kira on the blanket with the other young. The twins
curled up together, arms and legs and fingers touching, and went back to
sleep. She straightened and met Sylvan's eyes. "Maybe this is because
of me. Whatever made me heal the way I did has affected them too.
Allowed their wolves to ascend sooner."

Sylvan shrugged, her heart aching at the uncertainty and worry in
Drake's eyes. She held out her hand. "Whatever the cause, it's natural
for them. Don't worry. They're the healthiest young I've ever seen."

"If you say so."

"I do." Sylvan tugged Drake into her arms. When Drake looped
both arms around her waist and settled her head on her shoulder,
Sylvan just held her, watching their young sleep peacefully. So simple,
life at this moment. Her mate, her young, and the quiet safety of the
Compound. The tranquility was marred by the knowledge she could
lose it all with one misjudgment, one wrong decision, one failure in
battle.

Drake kissed her bare chest. "You won't fail."

"Why are you always so sure?" Sylvan rubbed her chin against
Drake's cheek. Drake smelled of oak and autumn leaves and home.

"A million reasons. The first being that you're wise and don't
make bad calls. Second, you were taught by a supreme Alpha to be
masterful in a fight."

"My mother was a very great warrior." Sylvan chuckled, relaxing a little. "And my mate is very good at flattery."

"So not true." Drake nipped her neck. "But most importantly, you lead from the heart as well as the head. We all trust you."

"That means everything to me."

"Then trust your wolf, follow your heart, and know that we are all with you."

Sylvan took her hand and led her from the nursery. When they reached the main hall, Niki was waiting.

"The warriors are assembled, Alpha," Niki said formally, touching her fist sharply to her heart.

"Good. We'll take the Rovers as far as the border. Then we'll go in pelt."

Niki's brows rose almost imperceptibly. "Without arms?"

Sylvan's wolf shone bright and clear from her eyes. "We will face Bernardo as wolves, and I will kill him as one."

"Yes." Niki's smile curled into a snarl as she fell in beside Sylvan and Drake.

Outside in the Compound, twenty warriors waited in front of the idling Rovers: all of the *centuri*, Callan and his lieutenants, and a cadre of soldiers.

Drake's grip on Sylvan's hand tightened. "Fight well. Come home safely."

"We will."

Gray broke from the group of soldiers and loped over to them. She bowed her head as she stood before Sylvan. "Alpha, Katya is not here."

"Where is she?"

"I don't know. She left a few hours ago. She should be back by now."

"We cannot wait." Sylvan glanced at Drake, knowing Drake could feel what she felt. Katya, wherever she was, was disconnected from her Pack link. Only a few things could cause that, none of them good.

"We'll find her," Drake said. "Do what you must and leave this to me."

"Be careful." Sylvan kissed Drake again and leapt down from the porch. She raised an arm in a silent signal to her wolves, and they all piled into the Rovers. She climbed into the first vehicle and Niki took the wheel.

"We should reach the border at just about midnight," Niki said.

"If Bernardo has any brains at all, he'll have increased his perimeter guards," Sylvan said. "Stop a mile before we reach his territory and secure the vehicles."

Niki shifted into gear, and the Rovers filed out onto the single track into the dense forest. "I wouldn't give Bernardo credit for much of anything, which makes him a dangerous enemy. Unpredictable."

"Yes, and I'm still not sure why he perpetrated this lie. What does he gain by sending his wolves into my territory? He must know we will come after him."

"It's a trap of some kind."

Sylvan couldn't disagree. She stretched out her legs, dropping into the calm before the battle. There had not been a major war between neighboring wolves since her mother put down the uprising led by Bernardo's predecessor. Perhaps every generation they would need to do this, or else expand their territories and put more distance between the Packs. Once, that might've worked, but now, unclaimed and undeveloped territory was growing scarcer. And with the world aware of their presence, she was even more pressed to protect her Pack land, not just from encroaching Weres, but from human agencies bent on regulating them. Bernardo's Pack was smaller than hers, but his territory was almost as vast. If he was wise, he would spend his energy securing what he had, but Bernardo, like so many others, lusted for power. But he'd made a mistake when he'd sent his wolves into her territory, bent on destruction.

"Are you looking forward to this as much as I am?" Sylvan asked quietly.

Niki's canines gleamed in the moonlight. "More."

They traveled northeast swiftly and reached the borderlands well before midnight. Niki pulled the Rover into a secluded clearing abutting a steep rock face, and Callan parked the second vehicle behind her. The warriors disembarked and gathered a distance from Sylvan. She faced them, her strongest warriors, even though some were yet young and inexperienced, and her heart swelled with pride—along with something else she couldn't show them. Their faith in her was humbling, but she would never say so. She ruled because she claimed the right to rule and held her place through strength and dominance, but in her heart she knew she ruled because they let her. They gave her their trust and their lives.

"This land is ours," Sylvan said, her words carrying across the small clearing easily although she had not raised her voice. "We have fought for it, claimed it, and will hold it against all comers, now and forever. This is our destiny and our legacy. Bernardo has issued a challenge, and tonight, we will answer. Are you ready?"

Every voice rose with a resounding *Yes, Alpha.*

Sylvan's wolf ascended, calling her warriors to pelt, and within a minute her wolves surrounded her. Turning, she raced into the forest, Niki at her right shoulder, the *centuri* on either side of them, and the soldiers fanning out to protect their rear. Minutes passed as they arrowed into Bernardo's territory, and still they proceeded unchallenged. Where were the guards?

They passed a deserted outpost and then, miles farther inside the perimeter, another empty bunker. The scents left by the Blackpaw *sentries* were a day or two old. Why had Bernardo pulled back his border guards when he should have been reinforcing them?

Niki bumped Sylvan's shoulder. *Something is not right. Maybe they are waiting in force until we are too far inside their territory to retreat.*

We'll know soon.

If this was an ambush and they ran into all of Bernardo's army with no clear line of retreat, Sylvan could be leading her wolves to their deaths. But she knew Bernardo. He was impatient, reckless, and overestimated his own strength. His ego clouded his judgment. If he was lying in wait for her out here in the wilds, he would have to face her, Alpha to Alpha. No. He would want to weaken her forces by making her fight her way to him. Then, even if she defeated his advance fighters, her ranks would be depleted by the time she reached him. He would not stop at sacrificing his own soldiers in the process, holding back his *centuri* and lieutenants until she was outnumbered and at a disadvantage. A coward's fight, but pure Bernardo.

We're only a few miles from his main camp. Instruct the soldiers to close ranks and expect attacks on their flanks.

Yes, Alpha.

Niki barked commands and the warriors moved into tight formation, a phalanx of muscle and might knifing through the night like a giant blade.

Drop back with the centuri.

You'll be a target!

Sylvan snarled and snapped at Niki's ruff. *Do as I say.*

Niki fell back a few paces, allowing Sylvan to outdistance her. The *centuri* closed in around Niki, and the soldiers drew in behind them. Sylvan raced on alone, a great silver beast leaping over fallen logs and rocks with the lethal grace of a speeding missile. She was Alpha, and she would bring the fight to Bernardo so all would know who to fear.

The red glow of campfires grew brighter through the trees. Sylvan sped toward Bernardo's stronghold, her wolf howling a challenge. Two wolves launched themselves out of the dark on either side of her, jaws snapping and snarling. Sylvan slowed and swung her head from side to side, growling a warning. They were half her size and young. The black male on her left and the red female on her right shuddered as her power washed over them. Both dropped their gaze but held their ground, quivering with indecision. She signaled Niki, who guarded her rear.

Take the female.

Gladly.

Sylvan and her *imperator* both struck at the same time. In one powerful lunge, Sylvan dragged the male to the ground, her jaws clamped on his throat. Behind her, she heard Niki's growl and a cry of pain as the female fell beneath Niki's assault. The wolf beneath her instantly turned on his back and showed his belly. He whined and his cock discharged against her thigh, his submission complete. She held him down, her canines buried in the muscles of his throat, and she squeezed until he quivered. When she released him, he whined again and rubbed his muzzle beneath her chin, acknowledging her dominance.

Niki?

She submitted with no fight at all.

Sylvan growled at the young male, and he flattened to the ground.

Where is your Alpha?

Gone.

Sylvan signaled to Callan. *Have your soldiers guard these two. They will not fight.*

She shook herself and trotted over to Niki, who crouched over the cowering female. *These are weak young dominants. Not soldiers.*

I know. Niki's lip curled in disgust. *Where are his lieutenants?*

Let's find out.

Shoulder to shoulder, Sylvan and Niki advanced into Bernardo's camp. A few wolves tried to challenge but submitted quickly as Sylvan and Niki overpowered them. Within minutes, her wolves had corralled all of Bernardo's in the center of his camp. No one fought back.

Sylvan shed pelt as did her soldiers, and the Blackpaws followed, congregating in an uneasy group near the central fire pit. Rough log barracks ringed the half-acre clearing. No perimeter stockade. No guards. No protection. Sylvan seethed at Bernardo's disregard for the safety of those entrusted to him. "Who is in charge here?"

A dark-haired male stumbled forward, his eyes downcast. "I am, Alpha."

He reeked of fear. He was no soldier. The others with him were maternals and nondominants or weak, untrained dominants. No lieutenants, no *centuri*, and no Bernardo.

"How long has your Alpha been gone?"

"Two days, Alpha."

"Where?"

He was silent.

Sylvan grasped his neck and dragged him close. "Where?"

He shook in her grasp. "Please don't kill me. I don't know."

She released him. "What is your name?"

"Nathaniel."

"What of the rest of the Pack? Where are they?"

"Those of us who live here are just…waiting. Many live off Pack land, and we have heard nothing from them."

Sylvan glanced at Niki. Bernardo's Pack was without a leader. Without someone to maintain order, even nondominant Weres would begin fighting among themselves, searching for someone to establish order. Niki's eyes glowed green-gold, her wolf raging.

"Where are the young?" Sylvan asked.

His shoulders rose, and for an instant, Sylvan glimpsed a wolf of worth.

"We have none."

"If you lie to me or mine," Sylvan said softly, "I will tear your throat out. Where are they? Your borders are open and some of the Catamounts will not care who they kill. Your young need protection."

"In a cave not far from here. We have only a few. There are only maternals with them, but they will fight."

"Good," Sylvan said, "but they will not have to tonight." She called to Jace. "Take a squad and secure the young and their caretakers. Make sure no one is injured."

"Yes, Alpha." Jace disappeared into the inky forest with her soldiers.

"Jonathan, Gray. Come here."

The two jumped to her side.

"Stay here and organize these wolves. See that they are fed. No one leaves." She fixed on Nathaniel. "You will see that everyone follows my warriors' orders. Understood?"

Nathaniel swallowed and nodded briskly. "Yes, Alpha."

"They will lead you on a hunt so your wolves will have food. If you disobey, they have my leave to kill you."

"Yes, Alpha."

Sylvan looked over Bernardo's wolves clustered in the clearing. Some continued to cower, watching her timorously from beneath lowered lids. They expected her to hurt them. "As of this night, you are mine. I and my warriors will protect you with our lives. Do you give me your allegiance?"

"Yes, Alpha," every new Timberwolf responded.

Sylvan turned to Callan. "Have your soldiers spread out between here and the border. That land is now ours. Secure it."

Callan grinned. "Yes, Alpha."

"Niki," Sylvan said, wrapping an arm around Niki's shoulders, "let's go find Bernardo."

❖

After Katya left her, Michel headed upstairs to the club to avoid Francesca, who would instantly know she had fed, and fed deeply. As soon as she reached the club, she perceived something amiss. The club was overrun with Weres, dominant Weres who were not regulars, and more than she had seen congregated in one place in centuries. None of them were hosting. She didn't sense hostility yet, but she alerted all the Vampire enforcers to report upstairs immediately.

Come join me, my darling.

Michel smiled wryly. So, the summons she had been expecting had finally come. Francesca had accepted her absence from her bed for far longer than Michel had anticipated. Now she had run out of time.

She quickly completed her circuit of the main floor and paused. She couldn't be sure how long she could keep her shields in place if Francesca decided to roll her mind and rape her thoughts, and she needed to be sure Katya was beyond danger. When she reached out for her, all she came upon was a wall of darkness. She should have been able to reach a blood-bonded cohort over a far longer distance than Katya could have traveled by now. Dread, something she hadn't experienced since her turning, churned within. Something was blocking their connection. Ruthlessly, she buried her apprehension. Francesca could not know.

I grow impatient.

Forgive me, Regent. I am on my way.

She worked her way through the crowd of Vampires, humans, and Weres, past the security doors, and down the winding stone staircase into Francesca's lair. When she knocked at the door to Francesca's sitting room, the sultry voice called, "Come in, darling. Come in."

Michel feigned nonchalance as she entered and took in the gathering.

Francesca lounged on her blue velvet sofa in one of her gossamer dressing gowns that revealed everything while reminding the observer they must have permission to touch. Her nipples blushed a deep rose, her full breasts gleamed with creamy splendor, and the dark triangle between her thighs beckoned with the promise of untold pleasure. Francesca had fed already and her unleashed sexual thrall choked the room. Charles, in full court regalia, stood at her left side and Bernardo, bare chested in leather pants, at her right. Both men displayed prodigious erections. Francesca had obviously not allowed them the privilege of answering her sexual invitation.

Michel bowed her head but kept her gaze fixed on Francesca's amused face. "Regent."

Francesca's smile widened. "You remember Bernardo."

"Yes," Michel said, not looking at the Were.

"You've been…so busy lately, I haven't had a chance to tell you of some of my new plans."

"My apologies, Regent."

Francesca waved a hand as if it were no matter. "Well, I've always enjoyed history." Her incisors glistened as she laughed lightly. "Especially having lived it all." She reached up and stroked Bernardo's flank, letting her fingertips graze over the fullness along his thigh. "And I think it's time we had our own army again, don't you?"

If I might speak with you in private, Regent, Michel said silently.

You disapprove?

If we raise our own army, Sylvan will see it as a challenge. So will every other Vampire seethe in your Dominion.

Yes, I expect they will. But I prefer an alliance with a wolf I can control, and we cannot survive in this new order of things without expendable fighters.

Even if it means a war we might lose?

Our alliance with the humans may prove useful in adding to our strength. And we're not without leverage against Sylvan.

Leverage?

"Oh, I grow careless." Francesca glided to Michel and slipped her arm through Michel's. Her fragrance enveloped Michel in a seductive cloud that fired her hunger. "Come, let me show you what I mean."

CHAPTER TWENTY-THREE

I have a meeting," Drake told Tomas, the senior soldier in charge in Callan's absence, when she arrived at headquarters. "If you need me, I'll be in Sylvan's office."

"Yes, Prima."

Staying behind, waiting while Sylvan fought, was a thousand times harder than being in battle herself. Even if all went well, Sylvan wouldn't be able to call her until after all was secured. Once Sylvan was near, their mate bond would let her know if she was seriously injured, but she was too far away still. If Sylvan was wounded in battle, Niki would call, and if both fell, one of the *centuri* or Callan would inform her. And thinking about it was not going to change what happened. Other work needed to be done, and other battles would need to be fought. As Drake strode into the great hall, Sophia and her father both jumped to their feet.

"Prima," Leo said, bowing his head for an instant.

"Leo." Drake clasped his shoulders. "Thank you for coming at such short notice."

"Of course." He smiled, but his eyes were filled with questions. Although he looked only a few years older than his daughter, trim and strong, with thick blond hair and brilliant blue eyes, faint strain lines creased the corners of his eyes. He glanced at Sophia, love and worry in his gaze.

Drake knew now, in a way she never had before, that a parent's love for their child never ended, even when their young were far beyond the point where they could be shielded from danger. The desire to protect never ended. She sympathized with him, knowing more than anyone else what his worries might be. That's why she'd called him here. They shared some of the same fears, and time was not on their side.

"Let's talk upstairs." She led them to Sylvan's office and waited while they took seats in the chairs across from Sylvan's desk. She didn't sit behind it—that was Sylvan's province—but stood with her hand on the back of Sylvan's chair. The heat of her mate's body seemed to linger there, and she pressed her palm closer.

"The days ahead will likely be challenging and some things can't wait," Drake said. "We can't pretend what is happening in the world outside our borders will not eventually affect us." She met Sophia's anxious gaze. "It already has."

Leo nodded. "Those who criticized the Exodus were wrong in thinking we would be safe if we continued to hide. If we cut ourselves off from those who seek to destroy us, they will only gain in power, and we will not recognize the enemy when we face it. Our visibility must become our strength."

"Only you and your mates can know of what we discuss today," Drake said.

"Yes, Prima," Sophia and Leo replied.

"I believe the genetic transformation that allowed us"—Drake came around the desk and took Sophia's hand—"to become Were is substantially different than the mutant viruses that produce Were fever in nature. We need to know what those differences are and how they may be expressed in us."

Sophia drew a shaky breath. "Until now, I let myself believe that whatever I am—"

"*You* are a Were," her father growled. When protecting their young, every wolf was an Alpha. "And you are strong and healthy."

"Let me finish this," Sophia whispered, grasping her father's arm. "I never wanted to know because I was afraid of what you might find. I was afraid that what was inside me was dangerous, and if I only stayed far enough away from everyone, I could never hurt them. I let myself believe there was no reason to care. But now, there is." She looked at Drake. "You have a mate, and the most beautiful young any of us have ever seen. I want that. I want Niki to have that."

Drake crouched in front of Sophia and rested both hands on her thighs. Her wolf crept closer, touching Sophia's where she watched uneasily from the shadows. "Do you trust the Alpha?"

"Completely," Sophia said.

"So do I. She says she would know if you or I were in danger of causing anyone harm." Drake stood. "But we must know what our enemies are trying to do so we can protect our children and their children to come—and some of those answers are inside us."

"Some of the genetic changes may not show up for generations," Leo said, his tone reluctant.

"We can't know if the changes will be positive or not without further study," Drake said, thinking about her own recent injuries and the way she had recovered. "It's possible some of these alterations may enhance our abilities. Not just for Sophia and me, but perhaps for all of us."

"We need new samples from both of you." Leo hesitated. "And your young."

Drake smiled and held out two small vials with white labels. "Neither of them cried, although Kira did show her teeth."

Sophia laughed. "An Alpha born."

"Yes," Drake said. "Take our blood samples, sequence the mitochondrial DNA. Map any similarities or dissimilarities to control specimens from born Weres. Start there, let me know what you find."

Leo took the specimens and placed them in his pocket. "We'll start immediately."

"Thank you," Drake said.

Sophia rose with her father and kissed his cheek. "I'll meet you in the infirmary in a minute and you can get my sample."

Leo stroked her face. "Good."

Sophia watched her father leave, her hands clenched tightly at her sides. For her to outwardly demonstrate her uneasiness was unusual, and could only be from worry over Niki.

Drake slipped an arm around her waist. "I haven't heard from them yet, but they'll be fine."

Sophia nodded, a flush coloring her pale cheeks. "I know, I'm sorry. I shouldn't worry—"

Drake pulled her close. "You love her. Worrying is natural. But you trust her also, don't you?"

Sophia nodded. "Always."

Drake smiled. "Good. Because she will need your faith and trust every time she goes into battle. You are her strength."

"I'm afraid of what my father might find." Sophia trembled. "But Niki shouldn't have to fight on every side every day. Without the mate bond, she is vulnerable to the call of others, even if she doesn't want it. And I...I want her to belong to me in every way."

Drake held her shoulders and looked directly into her eyes. "Everything will be fine. No matter what he finds, I promise you, we will deal with it. We are Pack."

"Thank you."

"How's Misha?"

"Healing quickly."

"Good. And Tamara?"

"She's malnourished, but strong by nature. We're feeding her," Sophia said with a soft smile. "And she is healing too."

"Good. Despite what she's done, I don't believe she's an enemy."

"No, I think she and the others were misled, and any wolf would have done what they did."

"Still," Drake said, "she needs to be guarded until we know where her loyalties lie."

"I understand."

"Be careful." Drake walked her to the door. "Niki would be most upset if you were endangered."

"Niki is easy to upset," Sophia said, her eyes shining with love.

"Niki is a strong and able general. And her temper is the fire we need in one such as her. We all have our roles to play."

"I'm so glad you are here."

"So am I." As Sophia left for the infirmary, Drake signaled for Philip, a *sentrie* lieutenant, to report. He loped across the yard and jumped up to join her. "Have the trackers found anything?"

"No, Prima, nothing reliable." He rubbed the fine dusting of auburn beard along his jaw. "Katya was in and out of the Compound frequently all day. We can pick up her scent on several trails, but they cross and recross her own and those of other wolves until we lose the scent. I'm sorry."

Drake gripped his arm. "You've done your best. Call back your soldiers. Make sure they're fed and keep them close. I may have need of them soon."

He saluted, still looking unhappy. "Yes, Prima."

Drake reached out again for Sylvan and felt a tug in their

connection, but she could not judge where Sylvan was or how soon she might return. She hadn't planned to take action without discussing it with Sylvan, but uneasiness roiled in her depths. Katya would have known a fight was coming, and she would have returned, if she'd been able. Waiting would gain nothing and might cost more than any of them were willing to pay.

Decision made, she vaulted across the Compound into the infirmary and down the hall. She rapped quickly on Misha's door and walked inside. Torren sat by Misha's bed, one hand combing through Misha's hair, the other hand entwined with Misha's.

"Prima!" Misha started to rise and Drake held up her hand.

"No, stay. How are you feeling?"

"Fine, Prima."

Misha's eyes burned with a hint of fever, and if Sophia hadn't just told Drake that Misha was healing, she'd have been more worried. Still, she found a stethoscope on the side counter. "Let me check you over."

Drake did a quick exam and stepped back. "You're doing well."

"She is better," Torren said quietly, "but she is not yet completely healed."

"You were there," Drake said, studying Torren curiously, "with my wolf in the forest. When I was healing."

"Yes." Torren smiled softly. "I did not mean to intrude."

"You didn't. My wolf welcomed you, but I don't know why that is."

"I don't think you would understand if I tried to explain how—"

"You don't need to." Drake laughed quietly. "If I were concerned about all the things I couldn't understand, I would spend all day worrying. My mate and my wolf trust you. That's enough for me."

"What is it you need?" Torren asked.

"One of my wolves is missing."

Misha jerked. "Who?"

"Katya. She went out for a run hours ago and told Gray she'd be back soon. She knew the Alpha was calling the warriors. She would not have missed it if she was able to be here."

"And you can't track her?" Torren asked.

"Our best trackers are with Sylvan. The ones who remain are good, but they can't pick up her trail. Can you?"

Torren stood, her hand still in Misha's. "I can track anyone, across any world."

Her tone was completely devoid of arrogance, and Drake didn't need to know any more than what Sylvan had already said. Torren was the Fae Master of the Hunt. She could cross dimensions, time, and barriers of which Drake could not even begin to conceive. "This is not the kind of hunt you're used to. You will not be collecting any souls at the end."

Torren smiled. "Perhaps. Perhaps not. When do we begin?"

"Now."

Misha sat up. "I'm going with you."

"No," Torren said.

"She is not yours to command," Drake said quietly.

"No, she isn't," Torren said, undeterred by the steel in Drake's tone, "but she is mine to care for. And she is not yet ready for battle."

"Misha?" Drake asked.

Misha shuddered and fleetingly looked away. "I am not totally better, but I can run. And if I have to, I can fight."

"You will stay here, rest, and finish healing." Drake read the disappointment in her eyes and squeezed her bare shoulder. "This will not be our last battle."

"Yes, Prima." Misha looked at Torren and the fire in her eyes clouded with uncertainty. "Will you return?"

"You heard your Prima. I am not collecting souls this night. Besides, the Gates of Faerie are closed to me—to everyone."

"Do you know why that is?" Drake asked.

"No," Torren said, "but it would not be the first time. Centuries ago when the humans came into power and the Vampires and the Weres went to war, the Fae withdrew to Faerie. Our Queen closed our Gates to all who might attack us. If Cecilia suspects chaos here in this realm, she may very well have done the same."

"And leave her Master of the Hunt stranded?"

Torren shrugged, unconcerned. "Queen Cecilia worries little about the fate of an individual, and this would not be the first time I have been earthbound. Although this time"—she stroked Misha's arm—"the experience is not unwelcome."

"Well, you're welcome here for as long as you like. Are you ready?"

Torren leaned over and kissed Misha. "I'm always ready for the Hunt."

❖

Katya woke in blackness with a throbbing pain in the back of her neck and no idea of where she was. She lay perfectly still, listening, scenting.

Silence.

Cold, damp.

Death everywhere.

Her heart leapt and her chest convulsed. She knew this place. Prison. Captivity. Pain. Torture.

Run!

She jerked upright on the bare platform. Metal bolted to the wall. No shackles on her wrists. No collar on her neck. The wall behind her back was stone. Her skin did not burn. Not silver. Not like the last prison.

She touched her neck, felt teeth marks and blood on her nape. A recent attack. Still healing. The attack. Running through the forest, home on her mind, Michel in her heart. A heavy weight falling onto her from above, strong jaws, razor-sharp teeth. Thrashing, fighting, no air. She growled, the attacker's scent in her nose still. Cat Were. Ambush.

She jumped up. Raging. Paced the small dark cell. Walls of stone. Steel bars on the door. She gripped the metal. Cold, not burning. Iron, not silver. She breathed deeply. Her wolf growled softly, wary and watchful. Strong. Her fear melted. Imprisoned, but not poisoned. She gripped the bars again, shook the door.

"You won't be able to escape, precious," a low lyrical voice crooned. "Not even the mighty Sylvan could bend these bars."

Two forms emerged from the shadows, their pale faces illuminated by the light of a pair of torches. Francesca and Michel. In the firelight, Michel's face was as beautiful and blank as a statue. Her gaze slid over Katya without the slightest pause. As if Katya was not worth her notice.

Metal scraped on metal and the cell door swung open.

Katya jumped back, making space to fight.

"See, darling? I told you I had something Sylvan would want,"

Francesca said with delight. She appeared at Katya's side and stroked her face. "One of her chosen."

"You think Sylvan will risk a war for one wolf who isn't even grown yet?" Michel said coolly.

"Sylvan has the Fae, and that is worth *my* going to war. Sylvan won't want to risk being blamed for that. A trade will let her save face—and you know how much her honor means to her."

A ripple passed through the muscles along Michel's jaw. "And if she won't trade?"

"Well, we'll find a use for this one, won't we?" Francesca's voice was ripe with seduction. Delicately, she tilted Katya's chin up and kissed her. "I do love the young ones, don't you? So strong, and their blood is so sweet."

Katya jerked back, canines exposed. "Touch me again, and I will kill you."

"Oh my, I do hope you try." Francesca glided behind Katya, her grip on Katya's throat tightening. Katya struggled but Francesca was far older and far stronger. She pressed her incisors into Katya's throat until a thin stream of scarlet trickled down her neck. With a flick of her tongue, she licked it away. Katya jerked, her chest heaving.

"If you feed from her against her will," Michel said quietly, "Sylvan will never negotiate. She won't stop until one of you is defeated."

Francesca regarded Michel over Katya's shoulder. "I almost think you don't want her to be touched."

Michel regarded Katya flatly. "I don't care what becomes of her, but I would prefer not to die at Sylvan's hand for something that matters so little. I can bring you a dozen just like her right now if you wish."

"Sylvan won't know, will she, if we avail ourselves of her young wolf." Francesca cast her thrall and Katya shuddered, her back arching with the sexual allure. "After all, she won't remember."

CHAPTER TWENTY-FOUR

The wolves ran full-out through the forest on trails no wider than the deer that had made them to keep pace with the Hound, Drake in the lead, her two lieutenants following. The great beast moved with the lightness and grace of a bird on the wing, flowing between trees and over the rocky ground as if gliding on air. Drake's sides heaved, her lungs tingling with the cold night air, her pelt rippling in the breeze. She never felt as alive or as free as when she ran in pelt, and nothing could have been better except having Sylvan running by her side. She missed Sylvan like an ache in her bones, so deep nothing could lessen it short of the sight and scent of her mate. The Hound slowed, lifted its broad muzzle to sniff the air, and padded around a small break in the trees where the trail forked. Drake, Anya, and Philip slowed, and Torren rose where the beast had been. Drake and the others shed pelt to join her.

"Here…" Torren indicated the break in the dense woods with a sweep of her arm. "Your wolf fought a cat here."

Drake stared at the ground and saw nothing but hard-packed earth and scattered leaves in the moonlight. She drew a deep breath, searching for traces of Katya, and caught a fleeting tinge of Were blood. She growled softly. "She fought here, but there'd be more blood if she had lost. If she'd won and had been too injured to reach the Compound, we would have found her or her trail."

"The cat came from up there." Torren pointed to a wide overhanging branch twenty feet above their heads. "From that distance, your wolf would've been stunned by the weight of the attacker dropping on her back. She probably was easy to subdue."

"An ambush?" Drake asked.

"Cats routinely stalk prey from the trees," Torren said, "but if the cat was hunting, where is the kill?"

"And where did they go?" Drake fought down her fury. She could not change what had been done. She could only set it right. "Katya, even unconscious, wouldn't have been easy for a single attacker to transport. There must have been a vehicle somewhere nearby."

"I can follow their trail until she's placed in a vehicle." Torren lifted a thin elegant shoulder. "I'll still be able to track her, but it will take more time."

Anya, a communications specialist with skill at tracking, said, "They likely went north if the cats took her. We might be able to catch them while they're still in our territory." Her grin was lethal. "We will have the advantage—and the right to kill them all."

Torren shook her head. "They didn't go north. They went south."

"Why?" Anya muttered, staring into the black forest as if answers might appear out of the shadows. "There's no cat stronghold to the south."

"No," Drake said, "but we know there are still laboratories somewhere, and those kind of facilities are easier to hide in the cities than the mountains. The cat Weres are notorious mercenaries, so possibly she was taken as a test subject."

"Again?" Philip asked, his lean face elongating as his wolf fought for primacy. "Are they targeting her specifically?"

"I can't think of a reason Katya would be singled out," Drake said, although trying to assign rationality to the motivations of madmen was futile. "Both Katya and Gray are young dominant females, but so are half a dozen other young females, and not all of them are trained fighters. Others would have been easier to capture."

"Maybe the cats didn't take her for the labs," Anya said. "Maybe the cat is working for someone else."

"Someone whose stronghold is to the south," Drake murmured. "Someone whose loyalties are always changing."

"The Vampires," Torren said. "That's possible. And if it's true, freeing her will not be easy."

"Can you follow her alone for now?" Drake asked. "No matter where she's being held, we're going to need more forces to free her. I'll return with a strike force as soon as I can."

"It might be wiser to wait until you know *why* she was taken." Torren paused. "They went to some trouble to take her alive and uninjured. She is a pawn, capital in some game we do not yet understand. If you wait, whoever has her will have to make the next move."

"No," Drake said. "We do not allow our wolves to be held captive for any reason. If her captors think to have a game, they will be disappointed. We will not be playing when we strike."

"I'll track her, then," Torren said, "and contact you as soon as I find her."

"We'll be ready with our warriors." A ball of anger coalesced in Drake's chest. "If it's the Vampires, sunrise will be the best time to breach their stronghold. Except for Francesca's guards and human servants, all of the Risen will have left Nocturne."

"True," Torren said, "but those who remain in the lair will be the strongest of Francesca's Vampires."

"Yes, but even they will not be at full strength during the daylight hours."

Torren nodded. "The human servants on guard at the gates to the lair will be no match for Weres, and even the oldest Vampires have some diminution of strength during daylight hours. You will also have the element of surprise."

"Whoever Francesca has inside her lair," Drake said with a slow, ominous snarl, "does not matter. We will free our wolf."

❖

Michel swallowed the rage turning her vision scarlet. The taste of Katya's fear and the desire triggered by Francesca's thrall was a madness tearing at the fabric of her being. Katya had never been simple prey, but now she was no one's to touch. No one but hers. Katya's blood flowed in her, and hers in Katya. The blood bond evolved as a physical link to protect the Vampire's existence by ensuring they would always have a source of life from which to feed, but Katya was far more than a promise of eternity. She was what made eternity worth having. The clouds of purposelessness shrouding Michel's existence had been banished with the light Katya shed on Michel's endless night. Katya was the sun that no longer touched her skin or dazzled her eyes with brilliant color at the break of dawn. She was every lost chance and broken dream, every promise Michel had ever made and long forgotten. Katya was all that mattered.

Michel shuddered. The need to attack anyone who dared feed from her bonded consort was a fever inside her. If she challenged the Viceregal, Francesca would kill her, but death, true death, was preferable to watching Katya be violated and broken. If she struck now, while Francesca was alone, Katya would have a chance to escape. Michel took a step forward, her incisors lengthening, and Francesca's eyes gleamed in anticipation. Francesca pressed her mouth to Katya's neck, poised to take her, her thrall so potent Michel's sex throbbed in time to the beat of Francesca's heart. And then another beat rose, overshadowing Francesca's, capturing hers. Katya's heart. Strong, resilient, brave.

Michel's gaze slid to Katya's for an instant, and Katya's amber eyes bored into hers, clear and steady. Katya would not be so easily broken. Michel took another step and slowly, with her hand cradling Katya's jaw, leaned past her to kiss Francesca. Their lips met a breath away from Katya's ear. "I will join you in the feeding, then. Perhaps Sylvan won't take Katya's lack of memory to mean anything. If Sylvan doesn't suspect what we've done, she might still be willing to negotiate."

"Sylvan," Francesca sighed. "If she were only Bernardo, my life would be so much easier." She kissed Michel, a long lingering kiss meant to inflame her.

Michel felt nothing, only the heat of Katya's flesh against her palm.

Francesca drew back from Katya's throat. "I suppose until we hear Sylvan's answer, we should leave this one alone."

"Whatever you decide, Regent." Michel slid her hand down Katya's neck, over her bare chest, and rested it for an instant over her heart. Francesca was too powerful not to hear a silent communication, but she ached for Katya to know that she would die eternally before she would let Francesca have her.

"It's almost sunrise." Francesca released her hold on Katya. "Time for us to take our pleasures, darling. Our hosts will be waiting."

Katya slumped backward onto the platform and gripped the hard edges to keep herself upright. Her chest heaved, and her skin shimmered with sex-sheen and fury. Her jaws lengthened and sun-kissed pelt streaked down her torso.

"Oh dear," Francesca said, slipping an arm around Michel's waist, "I'm afraid our guest is going to be quite uncomfortable. We seem to have excited her."

"Nothing unusual for a Were," Michel said, closing her trembling hands into fists. "They're so easy to seduce."

"Such a pity to leave her. They do taste so good when the fever is on." Francesca studied Michel intently. "Are you sure you wouldn't like a small taste?"

"I've a bit of the fever myself," Michel whispered, easing her hand up Francesca's side to cradle her breast. Francesca's nipple hardened instantly and her body surged against Michel with a wave of lust that vibrated throughout the small cell. "But not for a Were too unseasoned to be interesting."

"Come then, darling," Francesca said with a lilting tone of victory. "Come feed with me where you belong."

CHAPTER TWENTY-FIVE

Drake stood before the open window in Sylvan's office, waiting for the first glimpse of Sylvan and her warriors. Downstairs, Anya organized the lines of communication and oversaw the transfer of equipment and armaments to the Rovers. Outside in the Compound, Tomas prepared the soldiers, reviewing security protocols with those who would stay behind and appointing squad leaders to head the field forces. In the infirmary, Sophia and Elena readied field packs to be used on the wounded until they could be transported back to the Compound. Drake mentally reassessed all that must be done on the eve of battle and put aside the things for which she could never prepare.

They would have injured, and probably deaths. A year ago, in a different life, she would not have conceived of facing an enemy in the flesh to exact justice. She would have called on others to represent her and might even have still believed that the law and justice were one and the same. Now she knew better. She was no longer the human physician who waited beyond the fray to heal the warriors and victims alike. She was the warrior now and stood for others, and some of those she loved would be among the wounded. But no one she loved or had sworn to protect would ever be among the victims.

She and Sylvan would protect their own. The imperative to preserve the lives of their Pack and secure the future for their children and their children's children was bred into Sylvan's genes, into her blood, into her deepest self. Sylvan could do nothing less and Drake was her mate—when they bound their bodies and their hearts, they also bound their destinies. Human laws did not recognize or support or seek to represent those whose lives, whose existence, followed a different order. The Weres—all the Praeterns—existed as singular nations side by side with humans, but without the same rights and protections. Until the governing powers expanded to encompass the realities of a coalition society, the human justice system was irrelevant.

So she would fight.

Stars glittered brightly in the inky sky, and in the distance, other lights winked on. Both her heartbeat and the tension in her belly ratcheted up a notch. Headlights. The Rovers were returning. She braced an arm against the window where Sylvan often stood looking out over their territory, the weight of leadership heavy on her shoulders. Tonight, Drake appreciated the burden of that weight in a way she never had before. The whole time she focused on the many decisions required when mobilizing forces, she'd had to fight her instinctual urge to simply shift and storm into the lair of whoever held Katya and tear them apart. Her wolf cared nothing for strategy and battle plans. She was Were, and deep in her brain, the instinct to protect flamed brighter than any other. That drive burned even hotter in Sylvan.

Every hour of every day, Sylvan balanced her primal urges against her reasoning mind in order to guide her Pack through a modern world. The struggle never ceased and the cost was great, but she bore the mantle of responsibility with honor. Drake knew Sylvan's duty would never end, and hers was to share the burden in any way she could. Tonight she had willingly taken up the banner of leadership, but she was very glad the Alpha had returned.

The Rovers were still a few miles away when she caught Sylvan's scent. An instant later the silver wolf bounded high over the stockade and landed in the center of the Compound. Every Were turned as one to greet her with joyous leaps and barks. Sylvan howled a greeting, never slowing, and sailed through the window into the center of her office. By the time Drake reached her, she had shed her pelt.

"Tell me you are well," Drake said, sliding her arms around Sylvan's naked waist.

"I'm fine." Sylvan pushed both hands into Drake's hair, kissed her, and dragged her across the room to the huge leather sofa against one wall.

Drake went willingly and pulled Sylvan down on top of her, opening her arms and legs to enfold Sylvan. Her mate's skin was hot and slick with the aftermath of battle frenzy. She was full and insistent between Drake's thighs, already pushing into her, her teeth already at Drake's throat.

"I'm here," Drake whispered. She set her claws into Sylvan's ass and gripped her tightly with her legs clasped around the back of Sylvan's thighs. She pressed her mouth to the bite on Sylvan's chest, forcing Sylvan to thrust hard and lock them together. Sylvan growled and her nipples hardened against Drake's. They would not be parted now until they had both finished.

"I'm yours." Drake threw her head back, rocking in time to Sylvan's thrusts.

Sylvan growled again, her hips an avalanche between Drake's thighs, pumping power and *victus* deep inside her. Drake came, the flood of hormones swamping them both. Sylvan bit her, her clitoris pulsing hard against Drake's, and emptied with a tremendous shudder. Drake readied over and over, her need endless. Sylvan didn't soften right away but kept thrusting harder and harder until she spent completely. Until she had nothing left.

Panting in great unsteady gasps against Drake's throat, Sylvan slowly relaxed. She kissed the bite where she had just seconds before buried her canines. "Hello, mate."

Drake laughed softly and stroked Sylvan's sweat-soaked hair. She ran her fingers up and down the muscles along Sylvan's spine and clasped her ass. "Welcome home, Alpha."

Sylvan nuzzled Drake's throat. "How are you?"

"Fine, now that you're here. Tell me about Bernardo."

"I will, but first tell me what's happened. The soldiers are organizing for battle."

Drake sighed. Their private moment was over. She held Sylvan a second longer, absorbing the touch and the scent of her. When she relaxed her hold, Sylvan leaned up on an elbow and regarded her through the eyes of her wolf, watchful and waiting.

"We've tracked Katya to a point south of here where she was attacked by a cat Were," Drake said. "We think the Vampires might be behind it."

Sylvan remained completely still, a predator in the final second before it strikes. "Tell me."

Drake relayed her decision to enlist Torren's help in tracking

Katya, what they'd found, and what they'd surmised. "Torren will continue to track Katya until she finds her. Once we have confirmation that she's been captured, my plan was to go get her."

"Your plan is right." Needing to ground her wolf in Drake's essence, Sylvan sat up, drew Drake onto her lap, and wrapped one arm around her waist. She cradled Drake's breast and kissed her throat. Even though the battle at Bernardo's had been an easy one, she'd been away for hours and her wolf had been constantly on edge—first poised to fight, then repelling the young Blackpaws, and finally furious at the state of Bernardo's Pack. By the time she was ready to return home, her need for Drake overshadowed everything else. She'd run ahead of the Rovers, pounding through the dark forest with the only thing on her mind reaching her mate and joining. Now, her duties had returned. "If you're right and Francesca is behind this, she'll have surrounded herself with her most experienced guards."

"Can we defeat them?"

Sylvan's lips drew back and her canines flashed. "Of course. We were once their army for a reason. We are born to fight and their numbers are small."

"If we attack, we'll be declaring war against all the Vampires." Drake paused. "And their allies—the humans most likely, and possibly the Fae. Queen Cecilia allowed Torren to remain imprisoned, after all. Maybe she supports Francesca."

"But Torren aided you," Sylvan said.

Drake smiled. "Torren appears to have little regard for convention. She does as she will."

"Enviable," Sylvan muttered.

"But lonely."

Sylvan smiled and kissed Drake. "Yes. And not a life I would want."

"I know."

"As to those who might be loyal to Francesca?" Sylvan lifted her shoulder. "Vampire politics are labyrinthine. Who knows if she can command the other seethes to join her. And even if she does, she has no army. Vampires have grown complacent over the centuries, guarding their territory through terror and intimidation. They have not had to protect their borders because we have had a truce."

"We have to warn Jody," Drake said. "We are allies, and she must be given the choice to join us, or at the very least alert her father to prepare to defend their Dominion."

"Yes," Sylvan said. "I'll advise her—"

A knock sounded at the door, and Niki called, "Permission to speak to the Alpha."

Sylvan said, "Enter."

Niki strode in, dressed in regulation black BDUs. Power radiated from her in waves and the glitter in her eyes said she too had already found her mate. She bowed her head sharply. "Alpha. Prima. Forgive the intrusion. Torren is downstairs and wishes to see you."

"Send her up," Sylvan said.

"One minute, if I might," Niki said, her gaze shifting to Drake.

"Go ahead," Sylvan said.

"Sophia told me about the blood tests."

"I asked her father to look at our blood," Drake said to Sylvan and Niki both. "It's necessary for the good of us all, and we've delayed long enough."

"I understand." Niki straightened, her chin lifting. "Sophia explained that to me and I agree. This is about the results. I don't care what they show. But if there's something wrong—"

"Sophia deserves to know," Drake said.

Niki snarled. "I won't have her hurt."

Sylvan rumbled a warning at Niki's challenging tone, but Drake slid her hand behind Sylvan's neck and stroked her softly. "Niki, Sophia is ours to protect as well as yours. And I believe what we find will allow her to live fully, as she should."

"No matter what it shows, we will be mated," Niki said, her tone a notch less challenging.

"As you should be," Drake said.

"Trust Drake." Sylvan slid Drake from her lap, rose, and took clothes from an armoire next to the door. She pulled on black fatigue pants and a T-shirt. "Send Torren up."

"Yes, Alpha." Niki saluted.

"Then see to the soldiers. We're not yet done this night."

Niki smiled. "Yes, Alpha."

Torren entered as Niki left. She wore the same black BDUs as

Niki, but Niki was a blade, honed and gleaming. Torren was as elegant as an arrow, impossible to follow and just as deadly.

"Have you found her?" Sylvan asked.

"Yes. As I suspected, the cat who attacked her carried her a few miles and waited for transport. She's at Nocturne."

"Then we will free her." Sylvan's growl reverberated through headquarters and stretched out into the Compound and beyond.

The call to battle was a fire in the blood of every wolf, and the air filled with answering howls.

❖

Francesca rode Michel with their legs intertwined and raked her nails across Michel's chest, scoring her breasts with razor-thin slashes of flame. The two Weres in bed with them were barely conscious. Francesca had fed repeatedly from both throughout the last hour to keep her sexual potency at its peak. The wolf lay splayed out on his back, his penis curled limply against his thigh, rivulets of blood drying on his chest and belly where he had not yet healed from Francesca's teeth. Dru, still awake, panted fitfully by Francesca's side, her thighs and belly slick with her repeated emissions as Francesca fed from her neck and groin.

Michel was caught in the web of Francesca's sexual thrall, but what had once brought pleasure now delivered only pain. Her clitoris was tense and aching, but she had not fed or climaxed and could not pretend otherwise. Francesca came for the fourth time and fell on Michel with a cry, her mouth hot against Michel's throat. She ground her swollen, demanding sex against Michel and ordered, "I want you to fuck me, and I want you to come when you do it."

An image of Katya being held naked in a cell filled Michel with fury as raging as the need burning through her. Francesca would never let Michel go until she had what she demanded—Michel's submission, and until Michel was free, she could not help Katya.

"Whatever my mistress desires." Michel rolled onto Francesca, held her down with a hand pressed between her breasts, and filled her with a single hard thrust. She straddled Francesca's thigh, the pressure against her tense, throbbing flesh an unbearable ache. While she stroked

Francesca's clitoris with each deep plunge, Francesca's blazing blue eyes transformed into burning pools of deepest crimson.

When Francesca's clitoris turned to stone beneath her fingers, Michel struck the male's throat swiftly, drinking deeply of his rich blood. The taste was ash against her tongue. Francesca glowed with power, and a pulse of sexual thrall struck Michel with such force her sex exploded. The orgasm was more pain than pleasure, and she doubled over with a hoarse cry. As she moaned, she heard Francesca laugh.

When Francesca finally reached for the champagne from the bucket beside the bed, Michel sat up, took the bottle from her, and poured them each a glass. She tapped her flute to Francesca's.

"To your continued success."

"Oh, darling," Francesca murmured, watching Michel as she sipped, "to our victory."

"Yes." Michel set the flute aside and stood. "And if we are to remain victorious, I should see to our friends upstairs."

"Mmm, yes." Francesca stroked Dru's abdomen, drawing her nails through the thick pelt. "Don't be long."

"I'll hurry." Michel turned back at the door long enough to see Francesca slip between Dru's muscular thighs and slide her incisors into the femoral vein. The image of Francesca's hips undulating as she climaxed with every swallow followed her into the dark hallway.

CHAPTER TWENTY-SIX

Katya crouched on the narrow platform bolted to the rock wall of her cell, her back against the cold, rough stone. Icy droplets of water seeped from the deep underground foundation and trickled down her bare back. Judging the distance to the iron bars that made up one side of her cage, she leaned forward and gripped the edge of the shelf. She coiled her legs beneath her, poised to spring. She was fast, and she was certain she could cover the ten feet before whoever came through that door next had a chance to reach her. Faster even than the Vampire bitch who had tormented her with images of unbearable pleasure until her glands had filled and her sex had pulsed on the brink of erupting.

Her lip curled, thinking of Francesca's delight in exciting her. She wasn't nearly as incapacitated by sex frenzy as the Vampire believed. She'd experienced the same torture many times over when her previous captors had tormented her with need so fierce she would have begged for release if they hadn't stimulated her until she ejaculated for them. This time she knew her tormentor, and she wasn't drugged. This time when the thrall consumed her and her body craved the ultimate release, she knew she was being forced. She had not welcomed the pleasure, had fought against it, and she would not forget who had compelled her. Francesca. Somehow, she would kill her or die trying.

She would not be a prisoner again. She would have only one chance, and she might die before she could make a killing strike, but just knowing she would try kept her wolf from going completely mad. The dungeon was meant to contain Vampires, and the cell had no windows. She didn't know how long she'd been unconscious before awakening in the dark. Didn't know if it was day or night. She wasn't even sure if she was alone. Once, she thought she heard a low moan, of pain or pleasure she wasn't certain, but the sound disappeared so quickly, as if choked off in midgroan, she couldn't place the direction. The iron bars held no silver, but the Vampire Regent had been right—even with all her strength, she could not budge them. Francesca was wrong about Sylvan, though. The Alpha would be able to breach them. Except the Alpha did not know where she was. The Alpha was in battle somewhere to the north and might not know for many days she was missing, and even then would not know where to look for her. If Sylvan knew, she would come. Katya had waited during her first imprisonment, believing then as she did now that eventually the Alpha would come for her. *If* she knew. If the war did not escalate. If the Alpha was not wounded in battle, or worse.

This time she could not wait. Her wolf was frenzied at being caged and Katya could not hold back the need to shift for long. Once freed, her wolf would fight. She knew no other way, but if she lost, as surely she would, at least she would die with honor.

The shadows moved and a shape appeared before the bars of her cage. Her thighs tensed and her vision honed. She let her wolf rise. Her only hope was to strike the throat and incapacitate the Vampire long enough to reach the hall. Then she might find a way to freedom. A growl reverberated soundlessly in her chest, and her pelt erupted down the center of her naked body.

"Do you trust me so little?" Michel murmured as she stepped close to the bars.

"It's not you I distrust." Katya trembled, her canines elongated, her fingers claw-tipped. So close now. So close to freedom. "The one with you."

"I am alone, and it is not yet time to release your wolf."

Katya shivered, struggling not to shift. She stared across the divide between them, searching for the part of herself that knew this voice, this flesh, this heartbeat that pulsed in time with her own. With a shuddering breath, she leapt down and across the stone floor worn smooth by the bodies that had lain on it over the centuries. She stood opposite Michel, only the thickness of iron separating them. "Why am I here?"

Michel reached through the bars and cupped Katya's face. "Francesca is bored and has decided to play games. She wants the escaped Fae returned and thinks your Alpha will want you back badly enough to exchange the Fae for you."

Michel's hand was warm. She'd fed, and with feeding came sex. "What did she do to you?"

"Nothing she hasn't done thousands of times before. Nothing that matters." Michel stroked Katya's neck along her pulse line. "I would free you now, but you would not get far, even with me by your side. We must wait until after dawn when Francesca's forces are fewer and otherwise occupied. Will you trust me?"

"Why are you doing this?" Katya kissed Michel's palm and pressed it to her face. "Francesca will kill you if you defy her. If she tries to negotiate with the Alpha, the Alpha will come for me. But if Francesca knows you tried to help me, she will destroy you no matter what happens."

"She will destroy me sooner or later anyhow." Michel smiled fleetingly. "You would not be here if she did not know what you mean to me. She could have taken any wolf, but she chose you. I have dared take my affections elsewhere, and she cannot allow that from one in my position."

"I'm sorry," Katya whispered. "I would never have endangered you—"

"You did not ask me to come to you in the labs." Michel's hand gentled on Katya's throat, her fingers as light as a kiss. "You did not ask me to drink of you. And when I hungered for you, you did not bid me come to you. I came because you are more to me than life."

Katya reached through the bars and gripped Michel's arm. "Then do what must be done to stay alive."

"Are you so sure your Alpha will come once she knows you are here?"

"Yes," Katya said instantly. "She will."

"And me? Do you have such faith in me?"

"You're here now."

"I love you."

A wave of power struck Katya so hard she trembled on the verge of shifting. She leaned against the bars and took a deep breath. "I love you. I don't want you to risk yourself for me, but I will not give her the chance to touch me if she comes in here again."

"I will not let her touch you," Michel said. "No one will touch you again except me."

"Feed from whomever you must. Fuck that Vampire bitch if you must." Katya caressed Michel's face. "But no one will touch you the way it matters except me. Promise."

Michel kissed Katya's fingers. Her eyes flared red for an instant as hunger and desire roared through her. "I will do what I must, but I will take no others. When your Alpha comes, I will find you. If she does not come, I will free you. Once you are free, in time you will be strong enough that I will need no others, even for sustenance."

Katya's wolf slowed her frantic pace and sighed deeply. Katya traced a line of red down the center of Michel's throat, a reminder to her Vampire of where she belonged. "Then stay alive, *Senechal*, and I will do the same."

"Your trust will be my shield."

"Promise me," Katya said, "if fighting breaks out you will find a way to free me. I will not die in this cage."

"I promise." Michel's smile was grim. "And I do not think you'll have long to wait. Francesca hungers for blood."

❖

"I'd still feel better if you at least carried a rifle," Drake said, tucking her black T-shirt into her trousers.

Sylvan regarded her with a raised eyebrow as she tied the knife sheath to her thigh. "You doubt my skill, Prima?"

"Never." Drake checked the magazine on the rifle Niki had delivered to her a few moments before and stood it next to the door. "But I am armed, and Niki and the *centuri* all have handguns."

"I am the Alpha. I lead with tooth and claw and blade." Sylvan smiled, a cold arrogant twist of her beautiful mouth. "Every wolf who follows me has faith that I will destroy all in my path. And anyone who stands in my way will have a second's uncertainty when they see me coming. That is my advantage."

"I would prefer you have more than a second's advantage." Drake gripped Sylvan's shoulders and jerked her close. Once they walked outside they would have no chance for private words. Even now she could not voice all she felt—all she feared. Sylvan already knew of her love, words she need not speak now, and she could not burden her with fears that must remain unspoken. Sylvan was powerful, but she needed more than physical might when she went into battle. She needed to believe she could not fail. She needed the trust of every wolf she led to battle, but most of all, she needed her mate's faith. "*Two* seconds would be better."

Sylvan cupped Drake's jaw. "I am faster than any Were and as fast as most Vampires. I can clear a path between armed opponents with my blade before anyone else could shoot them."

"As long as you can kill them before they can shoot at *you*." Drake kissed her. She'd meant it to be only a swift reminder of all Sylvan was to her, and she to Sylvan, but the taste and scent of her mate stirred a need so great she deepened the kiss until enemies and treachery and the war to come faded away. "I love you."

"I will not fall today," Sylvan murmured against Drake's mouth. "I have young to teach and new wolves in New Hampshire to safeguard. And a mate to satisfy when the fighting is done."

"I'll hold you to that promise," Drake said.

"Promise me instead that you will stay back with Sophia to tend the wounded. We need medics as much as fighters today."

Drake knew what Sylvan was asking. That she let Sylvan fight while she remained safe. Every instinct cried out in protest.

"Drake?"

Once given, she could not break her word. "If you are injured, I will come. Then and only then will I leave the rear."

"Agreed."

"If gunfire breaks out and fighting spills into the street, we'll have human police involved."

"If we're lucky," Sylvan said, "we'll be able to immobilize Francesca's guards quickly and contain the fight inside."

"Do you think she will have fortified the club?"

"She has one of my wolves." Sylvan pressed her palm between Drake's shoulder blades as they walked outside together. "She will expect retaliation, so we must expect to be met with force."

Four Rovers idled in the Compound, surrounded by squads of warriors. Niki waited at the first, Callan at the second, Max at the third, and Dasha and Sophia at the last. Torren and Misha strode across the yard from the opposite direction and stopped next to Niki. Dawn was less than an hour away.

Sylvan signaled her warriors to gather around. "We'll reach Nocturne just after dawn. If we meet resistance, you may unleash your wolves, and you may strike to kill."

"Yes, Alpha," everyone replied.

Sylvan met each soldier's gaze and the yard shimmered with power. "You will follow me, and I will lead you to victory. Today we fight to free one of our own, and we will leave no one behind."

"Yes, Alpha!"

Sylvan swung up onto the running board of the Rover, her shadow streaking across the fire-lit Compound and seeming to climb into the forest beyond. "Then let us go and free our Packmate."

The Compound filled with howls, and the warriors piled into the Rovers.

Sylvan sat in the front. Niki got behind the wheel, and Drake, Misha, and Torren crowded into the rear seat while other soldiers climbed into the back compartment. Niki swung the Rover out along the same track they had taken earlier, and the others fell in behind her.

"Take the quickest route south to the river," Sylvan said.

"How far will we go by vehicle?" Niki asked.

"All the way to the doors of Nocturne."

Niki grinned. "Yes, Alpha."

"If we strike just after dawn," Sylvan said, "the club will be clear of the Risen and Francesca's guards will be feeding. She makes them wait all night. They'll be distracted, possibly even lost in bloodlust. We'll have a chance to immobilize them, but we still have to get into the lair."

"And your plan for that?" Drake asked.

"We'll have to take at least one guard alive and force them to open the security locks."

"I can help you there," Torren said.

"How?" Sylvan asked.

Torren smiled. "The guard will open it for one of Francesca's inner circle."

"Even if we're fortunate enough to capture one, we can't be sure they'll cooperate. They might be willing to sacrifice themselves to protect Francesca's lair."

"We won't need to capture or coerce one," Torren said. "I was imprisoned for a long time. I'm familiar with her royal guards and her human servants. At one time or another, they've all touched me."

Misha snarled and Torren slipped one arm around her shoulders.

"Ah," Drake said, wishing she had more time to ask for details. "Transmogrification?"

"Shape-shifting, yes. I know their imprint."

"Is that why someone with your power accepted imprisonment?" Drake asked. "So you could...familiarize yourself with Francesca's inner circle?"

"Let us say my Queen took advantage of an unfortunate situation. I agreed...for a time."

"The Fae are long-range planners," Sylvan said wryly.

Torren laughed. "We have aeons in which to play out the game."

"Then let this night be the beginning," Sylvan said. "And we will make the first move."

CHAPTER TWENTY-SEVEN

S top here," Sylvan said a few minutes before sunup. They'd kept to the river on the drive south, avoiding the highways by following barge paths and utility roads that were little used at night.

Niki slowed at the edge of Nocturne's vast concrete parking lot. The other Rovers pulled up alongside and cut their headlights. In the awakening predawn light, the long, low building looked as lifeless as the souls of those who occupied it. The Risen who frequented the club for sex and blood had left already, hastening to their lairs before sunrise. Francesca's inner circle—Vampire guards, her blood servants and slaves, and whatever hosts had been chosen for the last feeding before daytime slumbers—would be sequestered in the chambers below.

A few scattered cars and trucks dotted the concourse, and as Sylvan and the others watched, humans straggled out of the club, some appearing to stagger uncertainly in a daze before climbing into vehicles and driving away. After they departed, the lot should have been deserted, but the first glint of sunshine reflected off a gleaming chrome handlebar. A row of motorcycles stood along the near side of the building.

"I count twenty bikes," Niki said. "What are they still doing here?"

"Looks like Francesca has daytime visitors," Sylvan murmured.

Drake leaned forward from the backseat and peered out the windshield. "Not Vampires. They wouldn't have come on bikes in case they needed to leave during the day. Too risky."

"No. Humans, possibly." Sylvan grumbled. "But I've never known

Francesca to keep that many humans around. They're too weak to host all day. Those most likely belong to Weres."

Niki gripped the steering wheel, her claws glinting in the silvery morning light. "Bernardo's crew are bikers."

"Yes, and that would explain where he's gotten to." Sylvan opened her door, stepped outside, and, raising her face to sky, drew in a deep breath. Her growl reverberated through the blood of every Were in her company. "Wolf Weres, at least thirty."

Niki and the others climbed out to join her. Behind her, the warriors silently slipped from the vehicles.

"Many of them will be hosting now," Drake said.

"Yes," Sylvan said. "And since the Vampires like to share their food, they're all probably still on the main floor where they can gang feed."

Torren said, "The Were presence is unexpected, but that might work to our advantage. The Vampires and Weres will be occupied for a time while they feed and fornicate."

"It makes things simpler," Sylvan said. "They'll all be in one place and distracted. But not for long." She signaled for the warriors to gather around. "We'll go in the front door. We'll have a few seconds' advantage before everyone inside realizes they're under attack." She pointed to the squad leaders. "Spread out around the perimeter, one squad to a side. Drive anyone you see into the center of the room— incapacitate those you can, kill those you must."

The lieutenants saluted.

"Some of the Weres and Vampires are innocent in all of this," Sylvan said, "but if they fight, they will have declared their allegiance to Francesca, and by doing so, they make themselves our enemies."

"What about Katya?" Niki asked.

"Torren and I will make our way into Francesca's lair and find Katya."

"I know the way to the cells," Torren said, "and I can open the dungeon door."

Drake said, "Take Niki to guard your backs."

Sylvan nodded. "Agreed. We don't know how many Vampires Francesca has with her in her lair, but they will all be powerful. Strike the heart or the neck."

Niki's canines gleamed. "Understood."

"The Prima and Sophia will see to the wounded." Sylvan gripped the back of Drake's neck. "Prima?"

"Lieutenants, assign someone to get your injured back here," Drake said. "Sophia and I will treat them and load them into the Rovers. Once a vehicle is filled, we'll designate drivers to transport them to the Compound."

Sylvan said, "If any of you are separated from your squads and surrounded by enemy, make your escape and regroup at the Rovers. Once you have reformed a squad, resume the attack. We will not leave here until Nocturne is ours and Katya is free." She looked over her warriors and saw resolve and eager determination. She saw no fear, and her heart swelled with pride. "Are you ready?"

Every warrior snapped to attention. "Yes, Alpha."

Sylvan kissed Drake. "I'll see you soon."

"Yes, Alpha," Drake said softly. "Fight well."

Sylvan loped across the expanse of open lot toward the black door, her wolves a lethal phalanx at her back.

❖

Katya waited in the near dark, listening for the scrape of metal on stone, the hiss of a breath. She wouldn't hear a Vampire coming, but she would scent a human servant or the cat Were who had attacked her, and she would be ready. She tried to reach out for some connection to the Pack but got lost in a tangle of strange scents and the overwhelming tang of blood wafting through the air. Too many Vampires. Too many hosts. Too much blood.

Francesca would contact the Alpha soon, and then the Alpha or the Prima or the *imperator* or one of the *centuri* would come for her. Whoever led would come. Let it be soon. Before Francesca returned, before Michel tried to stop her. Before they both died. She wasn't afraid to die in battle, protecting the Pack, but she did not want to die under a Vampire, helpless and controlled. And she did not want to live if Michel died eternally. They were bonded now—body and heart.

She would know soon if she would see the sun again before she died.

❖

Michel made her way down the deserted stone hallway to Francesca's private quarters. Upstairs in the club, the guards were feeding on the wolf Weres. Bernardo was collecting payment for his allegiance—sexual pleasures for him and his wolves. He would be blood addicted soon enough, and Francesca would have her puppet. Unless Sylvan Mir learned of Bernardo's pact with the Shadow Lords and their plans to assassinate her—then Bernardo wouldn't live long enough to become a blood slave. Knowledge of the Shadow Lords was a card Michel still had to play, and she would need every edge she could find if she was to break free of Francesca. For now, she needed to keep Francesca away from Katya. She knocked on Francesca's boudoir.

"Regent?"

"Come in, darling," Francesca called.

Michel stepped inside and bowed her head. "Our guests are being tended to."

"Good. And how is our prisoner?"

Michel smiled. Of course Francesca would know she had gone to see Katya. She had half expected Francesca to appear while she was in the dungeon. "Angry."

Francesca rose naked from the bed and casually riffled through her armoire before drawing out a red satin robe. She belted it around her waist, leaving the top open wide to frame her creamy breasts with shimmering crimson. She shook back her hair in the careless way of those who knew they were beautiful, her eyes alight with power and amusement. "The Weres are so short on control. I'm surprised you find that attractive."

Michel said nothing.

"Although the young have their own special appeal, don't they?" Francesca pressed close until her hardened nipples brushed across the front of Michel's silk shirt. She ran a nail along the edge of Michel's jaw, a caress that drew blood. "Is that what it is? Youth? I can't believe it's the sex."

"You've said it yourself," Michel said steadily, ignoring the pulse of sexual allure that hardened her clitoris. "Were blood is more potent than human."

"And as you said, Weres are easy to come by." Laughing, Francesca gestured to the monitors behind her. "We have dozens upstairs right now. You could have any of them. What is it about this one that seduced you from my bed?"

"Was I not just in your bed, Mistress?" Michel caressed Francesca's breast. "Am I not here now, at your bidding?"

"Yes, you are here now."

Francesca kissed her, her power a burning claw that raked Michel's soul. Her hips jerked with a burst of arousal.

"You may think you want something else," Francesca murmured, "but you always return here, don't you?"

"You know me well." Michel readied to strike. The cat Were slept on Francesca's bed. The other host was gone. She might never have a better chance to take Francesca. But if she failed, Katya would be alone. If she waited until Sylvan had been notified, she might have allies. Sylvan would never negotiate and, in the mad impulsive way of the Weres, would attempt to free Katya by force. In the chaos of an attack, she might have an opportunity to free Katya. All she had to do was keep Francesca occupied with something other than torturing Katya. She rubbed her thumb over Francesca's nipple. "There's no one to compare to you."

"You would do well to remember that." Francesca opened the buttons on Michel's trousers, lowered the zipper, and slipped her hand inside. She gripped Michel and squeezed.

Michel groaned, her thighs weakening.

"I would taste her blood in you," Francesca whispered, her mouth at Michel's throat.

Francesca took pleasure where none was desired, forcing need none could resist. This time, this time the need would become Michel's weapon. Over Francesca's shoulder, the monitors flickered, and Michel saw the front door of the club burst open and a tide of wolf Weres flood Nocturne.

She lifted her chin and offered her throat. "Take what you will. I am yours."

The pain was blinding, the pleasure crippling, but stronger than either was something she hadn't experienced in centuries. Hope.

CHAPTER TWENTY-EIGHT

Sylvan gave over to her wolf, and her mind was as clear and calm as a still summer morning. Her wolf never struggled between two paths, never hesitated out of fear or uncertainty. The law was clear—she was Alpha and duty bound to defend her Pack. She was born for this moment. There could be only one outcome when her rule was challenged—victory or death. She kicked open the door and bounded into Nocturne.

The hisses and moans and growls of dozens of Vampires and Weres in feeding-sex frenzy muted the crack of splintering wood. She had a fraction of a second to survey the terrain. The windowless expanse was a kaleidoscopic landscape of shifting shadows. Pheromones thickened the air and coated her tongue. Blood and sex. Predators and prey writhed in tangles of bare bodies on the bar, benches, oversized sofas, and floor. Weres in sex frenzy snarled and lashed out with claws and canines at each other, and at those who bled them. Vampires knelt over throats and breasts and cocks, their incisors glinting like myriad feral eyes in a primeval forest. Sylvan, with Torren and Niki at her side, arrowed straight into the heart of the chaos while the rest of her wolves streamed to the left and right, encircling the Vampires and Weres. Sylvan's wolf pressed to attack, but she contained her battle frenzy long enough to offer one chance at amnesty. She rose into half-form, her torso expanding with a covering of silver, her arms and legs thickening, her jaws elongating.

"I am Alpha to every Were in this room," she roared, the force of her call freezing the Weres in place. Some Vampires paused in midstrike. "Swear your allegiance to me now and you will live." She drew her blade and carved a shining arc in the air. "Any Vampire who stands in my path will die. What is your answer?"

The Vampires rose from where they'd been feeding like shimmering wisps of fog from a fetid marsh and launched themselves at Sylvan and her warriors. The weaker Weres, dazed and lost in thrall, remained sprawled around the room. A few turned their backs on their Packmates and joined Sylvan's warriors, but at least two dozen dominants, Bernardo's lieutenants, snarled in challenge and engaged the Timberwolves in battle. In close quarters, handguns and rifles were useless, and Weres and Vampires alike fought with tooth and claw and blade.

Sylvan stood her ground and swept aside attackers with slashing blade and claws, sending streamers of blood into the air. Again she roared, "Where is the wolf who claims leadership here? Challenge or submit!"

Bernardo, shirtless in black leather pants and boots, jumped up onto the bar. Tangled hair framed a heavy, unshaven face, and blood streamed down his broad chest from multiple punctures in his neck. His dark eyes glowed with madness. "This is my territory, and you have no claim here." He smiled and waved toward the shattered door with a mock bow. "Take your wolves and leave now, and I will show you mercy."

"Submit to me now and your wolves will live," Sylvan said. "Do not sacrifice them in a fight you cannot win."

"I will line my bed with your pelt," Bernardo said, "and fuck your mate on it aft—"

"I will show *you* mercy and kill you quickly." Sylvan leapt onto the bar.

Bernardo, without the power to hold a half-form, shifted to pelt and sailed down into the thrashing melee. A female Blackpaw lieutenant jumped up from where she'd been crouching behind Bernardo on the bar and pointed a Glock at the center of Sylvan's chest. Sylvan caught her gaze. The same madness burned in her eyes as in Bernardo's. Sylvan threw her blade into the female's chest. The lieutenant's finger twitched on the trigger as she fell, and a bullet sailed past Sylvan's face. Another Blackpaw took aim, and Niki's red wolf streaked through the air and took his throat out before he could fire.

Sylvan bounded after Bernardo, keeping her towering half-form. Most of Bernardo's Pack fought in pelt, but his black wolf was larger than any other in his Pack, and she saw him behind a wedge of Blackpaws. Hiding behind those he was sworn to protect. Coward. Not fit to lead. She howled and stormed toward him. Two wolves jumped at her throat, and she plucked them from the air by their ruffs and tossed them over her shoulders into the swarm behind her.

Her wolf had waited long enough. She shifted to pelt and leapt at Bernardo. Their wolves were matched in size, but he was no Alpha. When she struck, the force carried them both to the floor in the center of the room. She bit through the sleek pelt into his throat. The smoky taste of Vampire feeding hormones lingered in his blood. His back claws raked her hindquarters. Flame shot down her leg. She clamped her jaws tighter and shook her massive shoulders to snap his neck and kill him quickly. His neck was thickly muscled, and his desperation gave him strength. He kicked and thrashed and they rolled together, a mass of fury, knocking over bar stools, crashing into chairs, upending tables. His claws churned beneath her, ripping at her belly. His jaws snapped on her foreleg, and the bone cracked. The pain blinded her but her hold never loosened. Her wolf was incapable of surrender or retreat. She would fight until he submitted, or until she killed him, or until she bled out from her wounds. Her canines closed on his windpipe.

Bernardo was weakening—his claws gouged less deeply, his canines bit less forcefully. Sylvan slashed his belly open. A gush of warm blood soaked her chest. A whine of submission erupted from Bernardo's chest, and he went limp.

Sylvan returned to half-form so all might see the power of the Alpha unleashed. Rearing up to her full height, she dragged Bernardo up by the throat and telegraphed a message to every Were in the room.

Bernardo violated my territory. He challenged me, and he has lost.

The massive black wolf dangled from her jaws. With a roar, she shook him until his neck snapped, then dropped him into the center of the room. She howled in triumph. The agony in her left arm faded with the rush of victory. "I am Alpha. Challenge me or submit."

Most of the Blackpaws had already stopped fighting. They all dropped to their knees and were quickly surrounded by her warriors.

As if knowing only one enemy really mattered, Francesca's Vampire guards left off fighting her wolves and converged on Sylvan from all corners. She bounded over to the dead lieutenant splayed out on the bar, pulled the blade from her chest, and waited for their attack.

❖

Francesca raised her head, blood trickling from the corners of her mouth, fingers still clamped onto Michel's clitoris, and swiveled toward the monitors. "I see that Sylvan has paid us a visit."

Michel shuddered in her grip, the orgasm forced by Francesca's thrall a molten river of agony in her blood. She struggled to surface through the pain and registered the silent warnings of Francesca's guards hammering at her mind.

We are under attack. What will you have us do?

She focused on the images of the fight upstairs. Sylvan dropped Bernardo's lifeless body, and a dozen monitors reflected the gleam of victory in her glowing gold eyes. Throughout the club, Bernardo's soldiers faltered, stopped fighting, and submitted to Sylvan's warriors.

"Well, Bernardo didn't last long, did he?" Francesca said irritably. She kissed Michel absently and released her from her thrall.

"He was no match for Sylvan under the best of circumstances. He had no chance against a surprise attack." Michel's mind cleared, and she calculated how quickly she could get to Katya without arousing Francesca's suspicions.

Francesca drew a snowy lace handkerchief from the pocket of her gown and daintily wiped the blood from her lips. "I must admit, Sylvan has surprised me. Our guards should be able to hold her back."

"Our numbers are evenly matched," Michel said, "which should give us the advantage, but we will lose some in the fighting. Our ranks of seasoned fighters are thin and we can't afford to lose many."

As they both watched, a beast Michel had never seen ripped and tore at the Vampires closing in around Sylvan. Arms and legs and heads littered its path.

"Is that…"

"Not Were," Michel said, "Fae."

Francesca's power flared and her face transformed for an instant into a furious mask. "That was no ordinary tracker we were holding in our dungeon. Cecilia has been keeping secrets."

"Whatever it is," Michel said, doubting that twice as many

Vampires as they had would be able to defeat Sylvan and her forces with that beast on Sylvan's side, "stopping it will not be easy. I'm going up to organize our guards. You need to call for your personal guards and leave for a safe house with your servants and slaves now. I'll contact you when we—"

"Now, darling. I can't afford to lose you, can I?" Francesca gave her a long look and stroked her face. "I think we have what we need to deal with Sylvan." She linked her arm through Michel's. "After all, blood is so much better shed for pleasure."

❖

Sylvan searched the circling Vampires for the leader. Take out the strongest and the others will falter. Niki's wolf soared into the center of the Vampires and pressed close to Sylvan's left flank. The Hound shimmered into form on her other side.

"Been collecting souls?" Sylvan said to the Master of the Hunt.

The Hound, standing nearly as tall as Sylvan's shoulder, rumbled. Its dark eyes, fathomless burning pits, tracked the Vampires who streamed into the room from the hallway behind the bar.

We can wait for them to pick us apart, Sylvan subvocalized, *or we can take the fight to them. What say you both?*

Niki's wolf howled a challenge.

The Hound roared, its ears flattening to its great skull and its jaws opening to expose its dagger-like teeth.

Sylvan smiled. *Good hunting.*

Sylvan rushed the nearest Vampire and buried her blade beneath his breastbone. As he dropped, she pulled her blade from his chest and decapitated him in one swift swing of her blade. Niki's wolf sailed by her and struck another Vampire in the neck, dragging it down. She ripped out its throat and cracked its spine. It might not die, but it would not rise to fight again this night. The Hound tore off the head of another, and a fountain of blood shot across the floor.

A Vampire jumped on Sylvan's back and bit her neck. A wave of pain shot through her chest, her vision blurred, and she went to her knees. She twisted away, her broken left arm useless. The Vampire crouched, a sword gripped in both hands. Sylvan was outdistanced by the longer blade, and possibly slower than her opponent. She circled, knife in hand, staying out of range of the slashing blade, and waited for an opening.

"Sylvan," Francesca's silky voice cut through the sound of battle. "Let's be civilized about this. There's no need for us to be at each other's throats."

Sylvan, half-mad with pain and battle frenzy, swung toward the sound of Francesca's laughter. Francesca, nearly naked and her face alight with insane power, stood at the far side of the room. Michel, her face a blank, was at her left side. A huge mountain lion crouched on her right. Francesca held Katya against her body with one arm wrapped around her waist, as if in an embrace. In her left hand she held a long silver dagger to Katya's throat. Her glowing eyes met Sylvan's and her power pulsed against Sylvan's mind. "After all, we each have something the other wants. A simple trade will save us all a great deal of trouble."

CHAPTER TWENTY-NINE

The Vampires surrounding Sylvan backed away, their hungry expressions vacillating between Francesca and Sylvan as they waited for the signal to attack again. Sylvan ignored them—the only threat in the room that mattered now was Francesca. Sylvan's choice was clear, and she studied the Vampire through wolf's eyes, assessing her as she did any prey, preparing for the kill. She would never bargain for the life of one of her own, nor would she betray an ally. Torren had risked her life for Misha, tracked Katya to this place, and fought by Sylvan's side. Sylvan was in her debt, and more—Torren was a friend to the Pack.

"You have violated Pack law by attacking one of mine," Sylvan said. "Our alliance is dissolved. Release my wolf."

"Attacked?" Francesca's brows rose. "You'll find no marks on her. Why, I wouldn't even let Michel feed from her, and you know how fond my enforcer is of young Were females."

Michel remained as immobile as a statue, but Sylvan sensed her fury and wondered why Francesca didn't. Sylvan reached out to Katya's wolf and found only murky confusion. Katya hung motionless in Francesca's grip, eyes glazed. Enthralled. Helpless to help herself, walled inside her own mind by the force of Francesca's will. Empowered by the Pack's collective consciousness, Sylvan intensified her link to Katya and found a flicker of recognition and determination. Not completely enthralled. Sylvan discovered something else too, something new. A bond not of her making—not of wolf. Of Vampire.

"Release her, or I will take her." Sylvan spoke to Francesca but stared into the opaque blue surface of Michel's eyes. Michel—a willing or unwilling connection to Katya? "Anyone who stands in my way will die."

"Our energies can be put to much more pleasant uses," Francesca said. With her reasonable tone and pleasant smile, she might have been remarking on the weather, as casually as if the floor of Nocturne did not run red with the blood of dozens. "Give me the Fae, and we can put all this nastiness behind us."

"The Fae does not belong to me," Sylvan said.

"The Fae fights for you. You gave it sanctuary." Francesca lifted a creamy white shoulder. "That makes it yours. Your responsibility at the very least."

Beside her, the Hound growled faintly, a menacing sound that despite its softness carried throughout the room and beat against the eardrums like thunder. The Hound's thick lips skinned back, its deadly mouth painted with blood. The impenetrable darkness in its eyes seemed to come to life and swirl into the room like decaying fog, cloaking Francesca and her Vampires in midnight mist. The Vampires—all save Francesca and Michel—stumbled back, clawing at their own throats.

Francesca laughed. "Oh, Cecilia, Cecilia. What have you sent me? Fae magic to choke on?" She threw back her head and laughed, the eerie cry of thousands of lost souls screaming. Her eyes glowed blood red as she stared at the Hound. The black mist pulsed as if alive, electricity sparked in the air, and the fog drifted away like harmless smoke.

Pressure intensified inside Sylvan's head, as if giant hands held her in their grip and squeezed. A trickle, wet and warm, ran from her nose. Blood coated her lips. Her own blood. "Release my wolf and I will allow your Vampires to leave. You and I will settle this, wolf to Vampire."

"I've always loved your arrogance," Francesca said, her lips thinning. "But today, I grow tired of it. I will give you your wolf, but the Fae is mine."

"No," Sylvan said.

From behind Sylvan a smooth, cultured voice said, "The Vampires have no fight with the wolves. Clan Night Hunter stands with Sylvan, Alpha of the Timberwolves."

Sylvan smiled as Jody Gates, Lara, and a mountain lion half again the size of the one by Francesca's side stepped up beside her. "Good to see you."

Jody, in an impeccably pressed white shirt, creased black trousers, and shiny black boots, said, "Sorry we're late. It took Lara and Raina a little longer to get here than we expected."

"You didn't miss much."

"I noticed." Jody flicked dark hair out of her eyes with long elegant fingers, a diamond cufflink glinting at her wrist. "Clan Night Hunter claims Dominion over this territory and declares Francesca relieved of any sovereign rights. Any Vampire who joins me now is welcome."

"I hold Dominion here," Francesca screamed, all humor gone from her face. Her power cut the air like a lash.

A wound opened on Jody's cheek and blood ran down her face, staining her white shirt. A crushing weight encircled Sylvan's chest, and blinding pain filled her head. From the shadows, Vampires rushed toward them on all sides. Lara quickly pressed back to back with Sylvan, and Jody and Raina pivoted behind Niki and Torren. Six against dozens.

Raina's cat screamed a challenge, the Hound roared, and Niki howled a battle cry. Jody brought a dozen guards to their knees, enthralled and dazed.

Sylvan shifted to pelt and sent her call to every wolf warrior to join her in the hunt. The room filled with howls, and Katya, trapped in Francesca's arms, shifted along with the rest of the Pack.

Free yourself, Sylvan called to her and leapt at Francesca. Sailing through the air, she saw Katya's wolf claw her way out of Francesca's arms. A glint of silver slid into Michel's hand, and the Vampire plunged a long, thin blade into Francesca's chest.

CHAPTER THIRTY

Sylvan landed with her legs planted on either side of Michel's torso. Michel still held a blade, streaked in crimson, in her right hand. Sylvan growled, her canines millimeters from the Vampire's throat.

A cat screamed nearby.

All around her, wolves howled.

Sylvan's wolf met Michel's unblinking stare. *Friend or foe?*

The Vampire bared her teeth, her incisors unsheathed and challenging.

Sylvan lunged for her throat and Michel froze.

A white-and-black wolf lowered her head in front of Sylvan's and snarled in her face. *She is mine.*

Sylvan searched Katya's wild eyes, hunting for her wolf. The wolf who stared back at her in defiance was hers, but *not* hers. Not all hers. Part of this wolf belonged to another. To the Vampire. Sylvan growled. *She must submit.*

She will never submit. Katya's eyes shone with pride and strength. *You can trust her.*

On your life?

With my life.

Sylvan lowered her weight onto Michel's chest, pinning her to the floor, and closed her jaws around Michel's throat. *Hear me, Vampire. I will have your loyalty or I will have your life.*

"I will pledge alliance, but the Vampires and Katya will always come first. My loyalty is to them above all others."

As it should be. Sylvan slowly closed her jaws another fraction of an inch, reminding this once-enemy now-friend she was Alpha, and released her grip. *I declare you a friend of the Pack. Betray me or my wolves on penalty of death.*

Michel smiled. "A threat I take seriously now." Her gaze flicked to Katya's wolf, who nuzzled her face. "I declare blood rights with this Were."

Katya?

Yes. I take her as my mate.

So be it. Sylvan let Michel go and swung her head around to survey the room.

Francesca was gone. At least half the Vampires had disappeared. Those who remained congregated in an uneasy circle between Michel and Jody. Raina padded back in from the shadows at the far end of the room, shaking her head and rumbling unhappily. The Hound prowled through the ever-darkening recesses around the perimeter of the room, finishing her Hunt.

The battle was over.

Sylvan shed pelt and rose. Throughout the room, Weres did the same. She studied Michel, who stood with an arm around Katya. "Is Francesca dead?"

"Unless I see her severed head, I would not swear to it."

"Don't you...have a connection to her?"

Katya growled and Michel smiled, the arrogant self-satisfied smile of one whose mate has claimed blood rights. "No one touches Francesca's mind unless she allows it. If she lives, she is well-shielded."

"Do you know where she would go?"

"Possibly."

"Later you will tell me." Sylvan signaled to Niki. "Take the *centuri* and a cadre of warriors and sweep the lair. Offer amnesty to any Vampire or servant you find. If they resist, execute them. If Francesca remains, she is mine."

Niki saluted and disappeared.

Sylvan cupped Katya's jaw. "Are you hurt?"

Katya's chin came up. "I'm fine, Alpha."

"Good. You did well." Sylvan turned to Jody and Raina. "What about the cat with Francesca? The one who took Katya."

"Gone." Raina's lip curled. "I can go after her, but in the city I can't give chase in pelt. Tracking her will be slow."

"No, there is no need. She is either with Francesca or has disappeared back into the mountains. Another time."

"I promise you," Raina said, "I will find her and exact retribution for her part in this."

Sylvan nodded and met Jody's gaze. "Well?"

Jody gave a predatory smile. "The Vampire clans need a supreme leader. Otherwise we will have civil war."

"Vampire business." Sylvan shrugged. "Are you claiming Francesca's rule?"

Jody turned to Michel. "You are Francesca's second-in-command. Do you claim Dominion?"

"I have never been interested in rule. Politics are not to my taste." Michel stroked Katya's hair lazily. "But some things are. I want Nocturne."

"It's yours, as are any of Francesca's Vampires who wish to stay under your sovereign command. As to the rest..." Jody faced the Vampires. "I hereby claim Dominion over the Eastern Territory and all who dwell within for Clan *Chasseur de Nuit*, in the name of Viceregal Zachary Gates. Do you swear allegiance?"

Each took a knee, including Michel. "We do."

"Michel le Clare is named Liege, and Nocturne and all its holdings are now under her sovereign rule. Those of you who wish to serve her may stay. The rest will return with me to clan home."

Sylvan felt Drake approach before the light touch on her shoulder signaled her presence. She turned and kissed her. "Hello, Prima. How are my wolves?"

Drake pressed a hand to her back. "None lost, but some need more than I can do here. We've moved the Rovers to the front of the building and the wounded are being loaded now."

"Thank you." Sylvan caressed the back of Drake's neck. "Take all the Rovers but one and get the injured back to the Compound."

"You need to be among them. Your arm needs attention and you're bleeding on the floor."

Sylvan grinned. "It's nothing a few hours in pelt won't cure. As soon as we've secured this place, I'll be back."

"Then I'm staying."

"As you wish, Prima."

CHAPTER THIRTY-ONE

Sylvan woke to the sensation of two small bodies clambering over her. Laughing, she pushed up in bed and gathered the pups into her arms. They licked her face and yipped ecstatically. Kira bit her ear, and Sylvan grabbed her by the scruff and shook her lightly. Kira bristled in a tiny show of defiance and then lowered her gaze. Laughing, Sylvan rubbed her cheek against the silky soft muzzle and looked at her mate. "Is it time?"

"They seem to think so." Drake sat beside Sylvan, rested a hand on her stomach, and kissed her. "I think they've doubled in size overnight."

"Certainly feels like it."

"How is your arm?"

Sylvan released the pups, who tumbled onto the bed and immediately began growling and play fighting. She slid the arm Bernardo had broken around Drake's waist. "Perfectly fine. I told you I only needed to spend some time in pelt, and it would heal."

"And of course you were right." Drake tugged on Sylvan's lip and Sylvan's growl deepened. Drake laughed softly. "More of that would be good too. Later."

"How are the others?"

"I've just come from the infirmary. Elena and Sophia report they should all be released sometime in the next day or so."

Sylvan sighed. "We were fortunate we did not lose anyone."

"I know. When the wounded started emerging, I was afraid…" Drake rested her forehead against Sylvan's for a moment. "Not being with you, waiting, was the hardest thing I've ever done."

"Thank you for trusting me."

"Always." Drake curled against her and watched the pups tussle with innocent abandon. "It's just that I want to be by your side. I need to be with you."

"You are. Always." Sylvan ran her fingers through Drake's hair and kissed her. "No matter where I am, no matter what I'm doing."

"It's not over yet, is it?"

"No. Not all the Vampires will be happy about Gates assuming power—and we are Jody's ally. If she fights, we may also. Our priority must be to find the remaining labs and destroy them." She raised a shoulder. "As to the Fae…who knows what the Fae are doing? Torren promised to return after she carried those she gathered across to Faerie and reported to Cecilia."

"Do you think she'll come back?"

"Yes."

"Because of Misha?"

Sylvan grimaced. "Partly, yes. But she is a royal Fae, and their motives are never simple."

Drake stroked Kendra's ear. "I never saw Francesca leave, and Sophia and I were watching the exits."

"That means nothing." Sylvan's eyes flashed. "She might be dead."

"Why don't I believe it?" Drake said darkly. "If it were so easy to kill her, someone certainly would have, hundreds of years ago."

"If she returns, she will have to face Jody and Michel's forces as well as our own." Sylvan sat up on the side of the bed and collected the pups, handing one to Drake and holding the other against her chest. "Right now we have more pressing business. We need to teach these two to hunt."

"Yes, enough of war." Drake smiled and kissed her. "Let's run."

Light-headed with exhilaration, Veronica Standish leaned over the incubator in the isolation lab. The specimens were perfect. She set the stethoscope into her ears and checked the heart rates again. One hundred and fifty. Normal. Neurologic systems seemed normal. Both of them—perfect. At last her true work could begin!

The intercom beeped and she punched the *on* button with a gloved finger.

"What is it?" she asked shortly. "I gave strict instructions not to be disturbed."

"I'm sorry, Dr. Standish," said a voice she recognized as that of the security guard stationed at the entrance to the high-security wing. "I have an urgent message for you."

"What then?"

"Er...the Vam—ah, Luce insists on giving it to you personally."

"All right. I'll be out in a moment." Veronica rubbed her face, settling herself. She wasn't normally so short-tempered, and her focus was usually much better. Of course, the pressure of moving her lab, losing all of her previous work, and the weight of everything that depended on these new experiments explained her lack of control. Nothing to be concerned about. What was it she needed to do? Luce. Luce wanted to speak to her. She smiled. Luce was here. Luce must be as hungry as she. Just thinking about the piercing pleasure of Luce's bite, the flood of ecstasy that followed, made her clitoris tighten. She dashed off a few notes in the recorder she carried in her pocket and hurried toward the decontamination area. She pulled off her mask, gloves, and gown, hurriedly washed up, and keyed the combination to the airlock door. When she pushed through, Luce waited on the other side.

Veronica took Luce's arm, pressed her breast against Luce's side, and whispered, "I'm so glad you're here. I need you too."

"I'm sorry, you might have to wait."

Veronica frowned. "What are you talking about?"

"Come with me."

"I don't understand—"

"I took the liberty of using your office," Luce said, hurrying Veronica through the halls.

"My office?" Veronica shook her head, finding it difficult to concentrate again. Whenever she was around Luce, she seemed to lose her train of thought so easily. Reason surrendered to sensation. Urgency, hunger, need. Such incredible need. "Yes, yes. Whatever you say."

Luce grasped the handle on Veronica's door and pushed it wide. Veronica stumbled into her office in a haze of sexual need.

"First we must see to your guest," Luce said, and locked the door.

About the Author

Radclyffe has written over forty romance and romantic intrigue novels, dozens of short stories, and, writing as L.L. Raand, has authored a paranormal romance series, The Midnight Hunters.

She is an eight-time Lambda Literary Award finalist in romance, mystery, and erotica—winning in both romance (*Distant Shores, Silent Thunder*) and erotica (*Erotic Interludes 2: Stolen Moments* edited with Stacia Seaman and *In Deep Waters 2: Cruising the Strip* written with Karin Kallmaker). A member of the Saints and Sinners Literary Hall of Fame, she is also a RWA Prism, Lories, Beanpot, Aspen Gold, and Laurel Wreath winner in multiple mainstream romance categories. She is also the President of Bold Strokes Books, an independent LGBTQ publisher.

Find her at facebook.com/Radclyffe.BSB, follow her on Twitter @RadclyffeBSB, and visit her website at Radfic.com.

Books Available From Bold Strokes Books

The Heat of Angels by Lisa Girolami. Fires burn in more than one place in Los Angeles. (978-1-62639-042-3)

Season of the Wolf by Robin Summers. Two women running from their pasts are thrust together by an unimaginable evil. Can they overcome the horrors that haunt them in time to save each other? (978-1-62639-043-0)

Desperate Measures by P. J. Trebelhorn. Homicide detective Kay Griffith and contractor Brenda Jansen meet amidst turmoil neither of them is aware of until murder suspect Tommy Rayne makes his move to exact revenge on Kay. (978-1-62639-044-7)

The Magic Hunt by L.L. Raand. With her Pack being hunted by human extremists and beset by enemies masquerading as friends, can Sylvan protect them and her mate, or will she succumb to the feral rage that threatens to turn her rogue, destroying them all? A Midnight Hunters novel. (978-1-62639-045-4)

Wingspan by Karis Walsh. Wildlife biologist Bailey Chase is content to live at the wild bird sanctuary she has created on Washington's Olympic Peninsula until she is lured beyond the safety of isolation by architect Kendall Pearson. (978-1-60282-983-1)

Night Bound by Winter Pennington. Kass struggles to keep her head, her heart, and her relationships in order. She's still having a difficult time accepting being an Alpha female—but her wolf is certain of what she wants and she's intent on securing her power. (978-1-60282-984-8)

The Blush Factor by Gun Brooke. Ice-cold business tycoon Eleanor Ashcroft only cares about the three Ps—Power, Profit, and Prosperity—until young Addison Garr makes her doubt both that and the state of her frostbitten heart. (978-1-60282-985-5)

Slash and Burn by Valerie Bronwen. The murder of a roundly despised author at an LGBT writers' conference in New Orleans turns Winter Lovelace's relaxing weekend hobnobbing with her peers into a nightmare of suspense—especially when her ex turns up. (978-1-60282-986-2)

The Quickening: A Sisters of Spirits novel by Yvonne Heidt. Ghosts, visions, and demons are all in a day's work for Tiffany. But when Kat asks for help on a serial killer case, life takes on another dimension altogether. (978-1-60282-975-6)

Windigo Thrall by Cate Culpepper. Six women trapped in a mountain cabin by a blizzard, stalked by an ancient cannibal demon bent on stealing their sanity—and their lives. (978-1-60282-950-3)

Smoke and Fire by Julie Cannon. Oil and water, passion and desire, a combustible combination. Can two women fight the fire that draws them together and threatens to keep them apart? (978-1-60282-977-0)

Love and Devotion by Jove Belle. KC Hall trips her way through life, stumbling into an affair with a married bombshell twice her age. Thankfully, her best friend, Emma Reynolds, is there to show her the true meaning of Love and Devotion. (978-1-60282-965-7)

The Shoal of Time by J.M. Redmann. It sounded too easy. Micky Knight is reluctant to take the case because the easy ones often turn into the hard ones, and the hard ones turn into the dangerous ones. In this one, easy turns hard without warning. (978-1-60282-967-1)

In Between by Jane Hoppen. At the age of fourteen, Sophie Schmidt discovers that she was born an intersexual baby and sets off on a journey to find her place in a world that denies her true existence. (978-1-60282-968-8)

Under Her Spell by Maggie Morton. The magic of love brought Terra and Athene together, but now a magical quest stands between them— a quest for Athene's hand in marriage. Will their passion keep them together, or will stronger magic tear them apart? (978-1-60282-973-2)

Rush by Carsen Taite. Murder, secrets, and romance combine to create the ultimate rush. (978-1-60282-966-4)

Scars by Amy Dunne. While fleeing from her abuser, Nicola Jackson bumps into Jenny O'Connor, and their unlikely friendship quickly develops into a blossoming romance—but when it comes down to a matter of life or death, are they both willing to face their fears? (978-1-60282-970-1)

Homestead by Radclyffe. R. Clayton Sutter figures getting NorthAm Fuel's newest refinery operational on a rolling tract of land in upstate New York should take a month or two, but then, she hadn't counted on local resistance in the form of vandalism, petitions, and one furious farmer named Tess Rogers. (978-1-60282-956-5)

Battle of Forces: Sera Toujours by Ali Vali. Kendal and Piper return to New Orleans to start the rest of eternity together, but the return of an old enemy makes their peaceful reunion short-lived, especially when they join forces with the new queen of the vampires. (978-1-60282-957-2)

How Sweet It Is by Melissa Brayden. Some things are better than chocolate. Molly O'Brien enjoys her quiet life running the bakeshop in a small town. When the beautiful Jordan Tuscana returns home, Molly can't deny the attraction—or the stirrings of something more. (978-1-60282-958-9)

The Missing Juliet: A Fisher Key Adventure by Sam Cameron. A teenage detective and her friends search for a kidnapped Hollywood star in the Florida Keys. (978-1-60282-959-6)

Amor and More: Love Everafter, edited by Radclyffe and Stacia Seaman. Rediscover favorite couples as Bold Strokes Books authors reveal glimpses of life and love beyond the honeymoon in short stories featuring main characters from favorite BSB novels. (978-1-60282-963-3)

First Love by CJ Harte. Finding true love is hard enough, but for Jordan Thompson, daughter of a conservative president, it's challenging, especially when that love is a female rodeo cowgirl. (978-1-60282-949-7)

Pale Wings Protecting by Lesley Davis. Posing as a couple to investigate the abduction of infants, Special Agent Blythe Kent and Detective Daryl Chandler find themselves drawn into a battle over the innocents, with demons on one side and the unlikeliest of protectors on the other. (978-1-60282-964-0)